ENTERTAINING WELSEY SHAW

Entertaining Welsey Shaw

John Grabowski

Millennium
San Francisco U.S.A.

This book is a work of pure fiction. References to real people, events, establishments, organizations, or locales are intended only to provide a sense of authenticity, and are used fictitiously. All other characters, and all incidents and dialogue, are drawn exclusively from the author's imagination, and are not to be construed as real.

Millennium Publishers
Oakland, CA

Manufactured in the United States of America

172507-IS-002

ISBN 978-0-9984645-1-0

www.entertainingwelseyshaw.com

Printed in the U.S.A.

First Printing
December 2016

For Dana

Who has been more patient than I ever could have asked…

ENTERTAINING WELSEY SHAW

1

Her famous blonde locks are tangled and wet. That's the first thing I notice. That and she appears tired. And perhaps still a touch angry. Her eyes are puffy and a bit bloodshot. The face is flushed, but maybe that's because she just came out of the cold. The most shocking thing about Welsey Shaw as she talks to me right now—quietly, to avoid being noticed—is how different she looks from when she's on the screen. An intricate scarf covers her face, a face that without makeup is actually small-featured and maybe even plain. This is a far cry from how I imagine her, not that I imagine her much. I'm not a fan, nor a reader of the tabloids, where she is often seen walking, running, head down, eyes shielded. On one occasion, or maybe ten, a finger has been extended to the cameras. Once or twice, fists—those of hired bodyguards, reportedly—have bruised the faces of paparazzi.

I have to admit that even now there is something about her, something luminous, something effortless. A born star. Or should that be with a question mark? I'm not sure. This time she has actually removed her sunglasses, and I can see the eyes are a little small. Or am I just used to them appearing bigger—maybe a foot across on the screen? For someone who has achieved stardom through her "richly-nuanced performances," they remain oddly expressionless. And there are her lips, tight, seemingly slightly amused at something. Being a writer I despise clichés, but Mona Lisa smile describes it best. So shoot me. At least she doesn't have Bette Davis eyes.

I am inhabiting a slightly surreal world, even though I'm inside an everyday Starbucks in the middle of Manhattan on a rainy Wednesday. It's one of those days where a cup of coffee seems like the best idea in the world to everybody right now. There are people here on the move and people who sit all day, nursing their French Roast. Before me is someone who does everything in her power to avoid unscripted, unarranged contacts, because, well, it's almost impossible for a celebrity, especially this celebrity, to have a normal conversation with regular people. True she has one foot and her right hip positioned toward the door...

But her sunglasses are off. And she is apologizing. To *me*.

Welsey Shaw is not as tall as you would think. Five-seven, five-eight maybe. Thin, but hippy. Porcelain-perfect skin that seems lit from within. Okay, maybe she is beautiful, but not the way she is on screen. She has an interesting walk, energetic, not elegant, a little jerky but she makes it work.

I'm sitting by myself, leafing through a picture book bought after a long meeting and a longer lunch. If anyone were to look up, they might notice that Welsey Shaw is standing here. True, she's in faded jeans, scuffed brown flat boots, purple scarf and green sweater. Someone at a table behind her gets up and shoves his chair right into her buttock. He excuses himself without really looking at her face. He and his companion, a matronly Asian woman with short, spiky hair that belongs on her daughter, leave their cups and teabags on the table. She folds up a laptop much newer and sleeker than mine, sticks it into a fancy blue bag, and they are off.

I blink, and Welsey Shaw is still there.

"I want to apologize for what happened earlier today," she says, voice light, almost musical. "I was rude, and I'm sorry."

"It's okay. I should apologize," I hear myself saying, though I don't know why.

"How's your hand?" The "musical" goes out of her voice now.

"It's fine."

"You're sure." —More of a statement than a question.

"Don't worry, I'm not going to sue you," I say for some reason. She's being too nice and it just comes out. For the second time today I'm an ass.

I came into town dreading my meeting today. I always dread meetings with Brooke, my editor, twenty-nine, round faced, whip smart, neurotic, and gorgeous. An auburn bob, plump lips, and killer legs in a plaid above-the-knee skirt.

That is not why I dread seeing her.

I dread seeing her—and hate getting her emails and phone calls late at night with UTMOST IMPORTANCE attached—because Brooke has been in her current job exactly three months tomorrow. Thus her emails are of UTMOST IMPORTANCE because they come from her. She recently moved up the ladder, and like all first-timers—especially all young first timers—she is terrified about holding on. They were taking a chance on her, they said. That always does it. Their reward was someone who promised to give up her personal life for significantly less than Harvey Swanson, my previous editor, who, at 50, had three college-bound kids and a house in Chappaqua. At least he did until last year.

I am lucky not to have such worries. I enjoy the fact that I can generally work without leaving my home or my bathrobe. Brooke's office is two hours from my one-story ranch house back in Sullivan County, which is just far enough to be inconvenient. So meetings are infrequent. I hate meetings.

This morning I rose at 8:30 and caught the train that dropped me at Penn Station. A brisk walk through frigid November air down 33rd and then up Park Avenue got me to Brooke's offices early. Nearby: warm yellow lighting on the bottom floor of an office tower, the sight of many people hunched over steamy paper cups of coffee, almost as if in prayer. No advertising could persuade better. I understand that the mermaid originally had breasts and a navel. When they decided to go corporate, these were eliminated, which confuses me. Isn't sex supposed to sell more product? The Starbucks at 48th and Park is larger and perhaps fancier than most, with seating along two walls and the counter against the far wall. On this day the line is out the door and onto the patio. The building itself takes up the entire block on the west side of Park, 1.2 million square feet filled with Deutsche Bank, General Electric, Credit Suisse, and other prestigious names of commerce. Around its perimeter huddle the smokers, looking miserable. The patio is set above and away from the street by about 20 feet and six cement steps. Never in my years coming here have I seen a line this long, but it moves fast, and with hands in pockets I wait. My meeting is mere blocks away, with Brooke and a 25 year old woman named Absinthe. Just Absinthe. I will be writing a book for her, putting words in her mouth and on paper that the world will be told are hers but which are really mine.

And here's something else I've never seen before: the blonde, the *uber*-blonde, hair between platinum and honey, almost lighting up the day. The blonde dressed in clothes that expensively have been made to look inexpensive, huge shoulder bag, large wrap around sunglasses, and a small dog. The woman is suddenly behind me and on the phone, her small, nervous animal turning spirals at my leg, jumping on me to paw my crotch. I take a step forward. I feel the nip again. "*Sorry*," the woman says, not really sounding it.

The dog is on a long leash, and the blonde is not doing a good job keeping him reined in or reining in her conversation. I hate hearing halves of phone calls, because I start trying to figure out the other half. I'm doing it right now, so the blonde turns away from me and her pet.

I'm about to turn back when something stabs at the corner of my brain. I look at her again. She's in a hot argument with whoever's on the other end of the phone.

And I remember where I've seen her.

Celebrities don't interest me much. I know them primarily from TV and glancing at tabloid headlines as I stand in line at the supermarket. Celebrities are shallow, self-centered, and spoiled. Pretty, that's about it. And I'm not a big movie-goer, preferring a five-day rental long after the hype has faded. I don't keep track of each new "it" girl, and I could put a name to the face less than 50 percent of the time on a good day.

But I know who's standing behind me. And I have to admit to a little excitement, if only because she'd be the last person I would expect to find with me in a long line on a miserable day.

But right now Welsey Shaw seems a lot less glamorous than usual, even with her designer dog. The animal is running loose, or as loose as he can get. And soon he's entangled himself around my legs. I try to dislodge myself, as well as push him away (I say "him" even though I haven't peeked between the legs), but he leaps at me, sinking his teeth into the skin between my thumb and forefinger. It feels like a knife wound, and I pull away with a shout. He retreats, too, but then advances boldly again (as boldly as a hairy little dog with a diamond-encrusted powder blue collar can) and barks. That gets other people's attention.

I say, "Hey, your dog bit me." Even I'm surprised how loud it comes out. But the starlet is oblivious. There's another part of me that wants to say, "And you're Welsey Shaw," even though at the moment I can't remember if I've seen any of her movies aside from the big one, the one everybody's seen, *Mystery at Alessandro Creek*. The others...oh, there are lots of others. Dumb comedies and smart ones. I may have seen some of them, I really don't remember. For a second I reflect on the fact that, if you're going to have legs in her business, you've got to be willing to take on everything. Welsey Shaw has been in pictures that have ranged all over the map, yet has this aura of Serious Artist, equipped to tackle The Biggest Projects, someone who can be counted on to bring gold home every few years, someone with depth. Mostly I just think that if people like her are going to take their pets into a public place they have an obligation to keep them under control. They can no doubt afford the best trainers. Why is that dog being allowed to run loose like a bratty child?

I've read the same stuff everyone else has: the young and fast rise to fame, the temper, the reclusiveness, the lightning marriage at 19, the divorce at 20, the fact that she refuses to talk about it, to anyone. Reporters must sign an agreement before interviewing her, and have to submit their questions in advance. Her private life was a forbidden topic; mother was a particularly sensitive spot, and could never be mentioned. It was as if she'd been a virgin birth, as some comedian once put it. Welsey Shaw is rarely seen alone, even here in New York; she supposedly has a big phobia about it, about crowded places, about vulnerability, about people. Yet there she is, casually standing next to me.

I look at my hand. No blood, though it feels like there should be. When I raise my head, the movie starlet is off the phone and motioning with a nod that the line has moved, and I should, too.

"Your dog bit me," I repeat. She may have looked at my hand through the sunglasses—I can't say because she is still expressionless. The Sphinx, with yellow-blonde waves. She asks in a monotone, "Do you want to see a doctor?"

It takes me a little off guard. I don't know what to say, so I say nothing, and she gestures again that the line has advanced into the store. I am struck by how she stopped me cold with her question, leap-frogging past any acknowledgment, apology, discussion, or argument. She probably effortlessly handles difficult people every day. Yet she can't control her dog, who's called Chevron I remember, which is dumb even for a celebrity dog name, and who's back to pawing my pants and trying to sniff me. I now decide to get more familiar, slapping him away, striking him lightly on the nose. I don't know how to handle it gracefully and furthermore don't want to. I look at my hand again, expecting to see some blood by now. Nothing. But it throbs. I shake it. Theatrically. (Later I realize how stupid I was to be theatrical in front of an Oscar-winning actress.)

Welsey Shaw steps out of line, grabs some napkins from a counter, moistens them with a pitcher of ice water next to the creams and sugars, and hands them to me just as her phone rings.

I take her offering and blot my palm; she turns sideways to resume her phone conversation. Her words are muffled, but her tone and body language say it is not a happy call. We're almost to the front of the line by the time it's over, and she throws the phone back in her bag. "I'm sorry," she says, seeming to truly notice me for the first time. "Are you hurt bad?"

How quickly her attention changes things. I now feel embarrassment for making a fuss. Are you hurt bad seems to me a line reserved for the victim of a tragedy, a real tragedy, not an errant dog nip. "No," I say to her question, wondering if I should have said yes. It did hurt, for 60 seconds. Now it's just warm. She picks up the dog. "Let me see." I show her my hand and she muzzles Chevron. "Seriously, go inside the bathroom and wash it with warm soap and water. I'll hold your place."

Reluctantly I do, and return to a spot that's advanced to the register. I expect squawks as I get in front but no one says a thing, except for Welsey Shaw.

"Good. Now keep your hands off my dog, please," she says.

"Can I help you?" The man at the register looks at me. I've

forgotten what I'd planned to order. A simple coffee would be the quickest. But I hate plain coffee unless it's full of cream and sugar. As I scan the menu I notice my hand is now bleeding. Two pinpoints of blood, rapidly expanding, from dots to beads, now running down my palm.

"There's an emergency room near here," she says, wrapping the leash around her wrist as if to go.

Welsey's barista, a round faced Asian female decked to the nines in a way that seems to say she belongs somewhere more important than here, turns to mine, a tall, balding guy with sideburns halfway to his jawbone, and says, "Gold really backs up this time of day."

"There's also the walk-in clinic," mine replies.

"Just as bad. You could go to Presbyterian, but that's a hike, and their check-in is gonzo," the woman says to me. I wonder how she knows so much about emergency rooms.

"Forget it," I say.

"I'd like a venti peppermint mocha," the famous actress now says to the girl, whose nametag reads YUKIKO.

"Sorry, the dog isn't allowed," says Todd, the tall guy at my register.

"He's a service animal."

I snort a laugh. It just happens, and I don't mean it like it sounds. But people look. Why am I being such an asshole?

"The hand isn't even bleeding," she hollers, turning, but when she looks at it it is. Red runs down my fingers and all over my palm. "Oh wow." She goes to the counter again and returns with lots of wet napkins. "We've got to get you to an emergency room," and her tone is serious and attentive this time. She is about to reach for me but hesitates and just hands me the wet towels. We've both sideways-stepped out of line now, and I blot away the blood. The actual wound is very small, and after a minute of patting I'm clean again. I've never been to an emergency room, and today's not going to be my first time. "Come on," she motions, taking out her phone again and speed-dialing a number.

"No. I am a busy man," I say, wondering who's talking. "I have a meeting to go to in ten minutes. But I would like a record of his shots," I impossibly add.

That does it. Welsey Shaw's temper ignites. "*He's a nine-thousand dollar purebred Pomeranian. He's had his shots.*" She grabs her drink, which I never even saw her order, and goes over to the bar downline and off to the side, adding more cream and sugar to her already diabetic concoction. "You're out of half-and-half!" she announces.

"I just filled it," Todd says. "You've got the lid on wrong."

"Sometimes you have to shake it," Yukiko adds, speaking more to herself because raising her head seems like it would be work.

"I'm shaking it," Welsey Shaw says sarcastically, making an exaggerated waving gesture with the container. The top comes off and lands with a thud at her feet. A white ribbon of milk fat rains down on her hair. And I laugh.

The rest of the line is divided between laughter and pity. Those who are paying attention, that is, which is surprisingly few. I regain composure and reach for some napkins for her, which is only fair since she did likewise for me. The dog is licking the floor as fast as he can.

Welsey Shaw ignores my offering and leaves with the dog. Someone quips, "You overpaid," and I realize he's talking about the dog. Feeling a little guilty about everything, I throw napkins all over the floor and wipe the spill up.

Absinthe is a Goth, although Brooke says she hates that word. She wears a racy, lacy black fishnet bodystocking, her black bra clearly visible underneath; the sleeves reveal sexy forearms, slender and talcum-powder white. I find myself staring at her arms as if they were breasts, trying to avert my eyes. Form-fitting black vinyl pants worn with platform knee-high boots—featuring buckles and straps that look like the kind they use to fasten the condemned to electric chairs—complete the outfit. She doesn't get an A for originality but definitely wins points for presentation. Especially those elbows. Her black hair is done up in one of those Cleopatra-type bang haircuts. Lots of makeup, also dark, of course. Surprisingly, no piercings—visible ones, at least. She sits near a wall to the right of Brooke, back straight, legs crossed, and hands clasping knee, looking like a Transylvanian schoolgirl. She smiles and offers a confident handshake as Brooke introduces us. And then she goes, "Wow!"

Absinthe looks at my hand, fascinated. "A vampire bite," she declares in a very serious voice, looking at me as if awaiting confirmation. I glance at Brooke for some indication how to respond; her face is the blank smile of a game show hostess. Fortunately, small talk follows, and we forget about my hand.

Then Absinthe fills me in on her background. Her Dad—her *idol*, she emphasizes—a Lebanese businessman who describes himself as a "serial entrepreneur," founded and still runs a company that makes custom fittings of all shapes, sizes, and price ranges for theme restaurants. The papier-mâché volcano that erupts every hour in San Diego's famous theme restaurant, El Castillo Encantado? He did that.

More recently he started a software company that's done CGI effects for commercials and even a few Hollywood films. He's been seen with his arm around big-name creative people, including a couple of writers, which is why I know something about him. My agent, Carla Vanderhoof, loves to visit the Encantado when she goes home to see family; in fact, she says she enjoys it more than seeing her family. I can relate, and that might have influenced me to meet Absinthe, too.

My editor couldn't be more different from the black and white apparition seated next to her. Brooke Parker defied New York by wearing color, lots of it, from her nails to her scarves to her stockings to her shoes. Perfect skin, a tiny mole on her right cheek just below the auburn bob, toned body, voice bright and enthusiastic, a touch conspiratorial, a suggestion she just might reveal a different side of herself after work and a few tequilas. But she never has so far.

Absinthe says how much she loved *Heaven's People*. That's always a good way to start. The natural pessimist in me believes that people only flatter to gain something, and I accuse everyone of this, unfortunately, with or without justification. But somehow this woman is chipping away my defenses, without seeming to try.

And then Absinthe—that is, she says, her birth name—launches into the story of her novel, crossing her legs with a synthetic squeak, distracting me completely. I can see the overhead ceiling lights reflected in the Goth's pants. I miss her first few sentences, which embarrasses me and forces my eyes away from the pants and back to Absinthe's face. The working title of her opus, she says, flipping up her thin laptop and launching an elaborate flowchart demo, is *Apocalyticus: Dawn of Flames*, the first of what will be a series of thick bricks of novels set on a fixer-upper earth of the far future, where humanity is divided into two sets of people, which basically amounts to those who are moral and empathetic and those who are not. Our hero, a young man named Trax, starts out as the latter but gradually starts to change once meeting, and becoming unlikely friends and allies with Leev, who's older, wiser, with dark, dramatic hair and dark, dramatic clothes—basically Absinthe with bigger breasts and buttocks. Trax and Leev meet via a brutal S&M-spiced rape scene that makes me squirm as she describes it; Brooke sits as if she were checking email. I like the moral angle, despite the level of violence. (I remember when parents only had to worry about too much sugar in their kids' cereal.) Absinthe further entices me by saying she wants a lot of inner-dialogue and what she calls "philosophy," about what's right, what's expedient, and how hard it is to see the world one way when you've spent your life looking at it in another. I agree that is hard. I tell her I think it will be a very challenging yet rewarding project and that I am very eager to begin working on it.

Okay, it's crap. Beggars can't be choosers.

Originally *Apocalyticus* was a multi-player video game that Absinthe claims to have coded herself before it became a massively-popular graphic novel. Now she wants a novel novel, with nuance and detail, the broad brushstrokes to be filled in by me while she develops other aspects of her property. We will be in near constant contact—but only through emails, messages, "chats." Absinthe only meets physically with her employees once, and I guess I'm now an employee. Too bad, because I would enjoy walking into La Grenouille with a woman in form-fitting shiny latex pants, black nails, and blood-red lips, and asking the maître d' for a table.

And now I'm back in Starbucks, procrastinating my return home, flipping through a beautiful picture book just bought from Barnes & Noble, when a shadow makes me look up.

"I hope you haven't been sitting here all this time."

For her second appearance she's returned in different clothes—a nicer sweater, nicer pants, same boots. Not surprisingly, she's washed her hair as well, and it's still damp. Instead of Chevron's leash she holds her sunglasses.

After a stunned moment I inhale and manage a smile. "No," I say. "I had an appointment up the street."

"Ah yes . Busy man." Then her tone changes and she sounds like a healthcare worker. "Let's see your hand."

I hold it out. It actually looks pretty good now, and she says so. Then she apologizes for her bad behavior. She takes a breath and holds it, or seems to. "I had one of those days. From the moment I went out the door."

I tell her I can't imagine her having "one of those days," and she smiles—genuinely, I think. I'm beginning to feel a bit drawn into her spell, and I do not like it: movie star becomes regular person, but calculated, so that she can leave with a clear conscience. Still, it's hard to reconcile the figure in front of me with Welsey Shaw. This Welsey Shaw must come from a parallel universe.

She keeps her head down and leans closer to my table to let other people pass—people who bump her as they press by without noticing who it is—and glances at my book. "Edward Hopper!" Her voice is a mixture of surprise and delight. "Can I see?" She catches me completely off guard, and I turn it to face her.

With the care of a museum curator she starts turning the pages. All this time I'm amazed that no one recognizes her, even though she keeps her head down, and she's buried in thick clothes. "I love this one," she says, mostly to herself.

"How did you come to like Edward Hopper?" I ask, wondering if that is a stupid question.

It must have been, for she says in a monotone, "What do you mean?"

"What is it you like," I rephrase, "about Edward Hopper?"

At first I thought she was ignoring my question. She takes about 20 seconds—a long time—to answer. "To explain it I would need words, and that would mean he didn't do his job because there was something left over for me to say. I don't know if that makes any sense."

"It does, actually. It makes perfect sense."

We look at Edward Hopper's haunting pictures for another three or four minutes. This is a tremendous amount of time to spend alone with any movie star, let alone this one. But I can't deny we are both paging through the paintings in reverent silence, which seems the appropriate way to look at them.

She lifts her head. "So, are we square?" She's all business again. I affirm that we are, and she puts the glasses back on. I actually want her to stay longer. I want her to sit down, look at the book more and talk about Edward Hopper.

But possibly someone is outside—a driver, waiting to take her somewhere. Maybe she has appointments to keep. Maybe she's just shopping, and I am an interruption to her day, one of so many. So I say I'm fine, slide the book back to myself, and smile. She gives a small shrug, thanks me for letting her look at the pictures, and departs.

That was my first encounter with Welsey Shaw.

2

That was yesterday. This morning my computer said it was already 9:35. I had no reason to doubt it, even though the drapes behind me, the side window that looks out on my neighbor's house, and the window in the adjacent kitchen, look pretty much the same any time of day. My battleship gray Toshiba laptop, which looks like it's seen a few battles itself, is my only link to the outside except for the TV above my head and the mail which arrives every day somewhere between nine A.M. and five P.M.—God bless the U.S. Postal Service.

I sit down at this spot every morning in my faded brown bathrobe, try to wake up, eat a half-assed breakfast that's usually cold, because I don't trust myself with fire so early in the day. I can barely manage coffee. Then I start to write, much the way a cold car accelerates when you hit the gas the first time.

Nobody ever plans on becoming a ghostwriter. At least that's my take. Others will disagree. They'll say they do it because they love it. I do it because I haven't had anything of mine published under my own name since November 2003, which feels like the Neolithic Period by now. I did have something published last month under the name of an up-and-coming pastry chef who bakes brilliantly but can't write to save her life. Netted me fifteen grand and an amazing assortment of cupcakes. This chef smiles sweetly on the cover of her new tome titled *Bake On!* and writes the wittiest foreword, as well as heart-warming comments in each chapter, sandwiched between recipes, as warm as her brown eyes and sweet country looks. And it's all me, sitting in my underwear typing on a computer in this living room.

There are three aspects of my job that are hard. In no particular order: 1) keeping interest in a project through its many permutations and contradictions, 2) justifying that it is in any way important to the betterment of the world, and 3) selling to my friends and family that this is the life I wanted. These are people, after all, who are doctors, engineers, and lawyers. They drive cars that talk to them, and sport power fold-in mirrors. When they get together they discuss retirement plans and the new hot tubs and barbecue pits in their backyards. I live in a split-level ranch house, with weeds for a backyard.

I've written a seven thousand-word article about a man struck by lightning four times. He survived three. I penned a salacious piece about what goes on in the cockpit during the boring middle part of a flight. (Hint: not much—I had to stretch the truth, but the job paid well.) I followed a truck driver for three days and four nights through the Alleghenies and reported on what it was like: he slept on a piece of foam that smelled like stale laundry, smoked four packs of L&Ms and listened to talk radio and college football. He hit on waitresses at every diner and said he had a son somewhere in West Virginia.

I wrote about a local news anchor's tumultuous relationship with his father while growing up. He managed to make peace just before landing the top job at a number-one ranked TV station, only to have the very first story he covered be his dad's death in a pileup on I-76. There are some stories you wish you hadn't written no matter how well they pay.

I wrote one of those "What is the government hiding?" pieces after some people in eastern Ohio said bright green lights appeared in their skies one March. A farmer's dog ran off to investigate and never came back. No trace of the dog was ever found, but witnesses say they did encounter holes in the ground that could only have been caused by something weighing hundreds of tons. I later got an email from someone who said the dog *had* come back that night, and the holes were probably caused "by Jimmy Weaver's pickup truck that got stuck in the mud." Jimmy was embarrassed so he made the rest up.

I rarely reject work, which probably means I'm kidding myself about my motivations. Looking around my house, you would not find it difficult to understand why. There are cracks in the walls. The ceiling is still stained from last winter's water leak. The pipes bang like Buddy Rich until you let the air out by running the water.

My mind wandered to what Absinthe's pad, wherever it was (and I'd heard she had many, scattered about), looked like. Brooke had said she reportedly kept crows for pets and also had a thing for snakes. But maybe that was just hooey. Hooey is prime currency in this business.

We had watched her depart after the meeting. An ivory colored sedan with rear window shades sporting a cursive "A" double-parked in front of the building. The driver, complete with black hat and uniform, set out orange cones along its periphery. He then led his charge from an overhang to the rear seat, all the while holding an umbrella over her to ensure that half a dozen raindrops would not touch her head.

"It's how she rolls," Brooke said simply. Afterward we broke for a ritual lunch at one of her favorite expense account restaurants.

Few things make Brooke smile more than the menu at Aquavit.

"Soft porn" she calls it. Keep in mind that five-seven women with 24-inch waists can do this with impunity. I also have to admit that when Brooke reads the entrees—and she always reads them aloud, even if the other person isn't listening—she makes them sound lurid. Just the words *Chantilly cream* seem raunchy when they come out of her round little mouth. And I've heard them many times.

I wanted to sit in the less stuffy bistro area, but my boss insisted on the dining room, despite my not having the proper jacket. Scandinavian cuisine isn't among my favorites, and despite living near the Delaware, where some people catch their own dinner, or perhaps because of it, I do not have a taste for fish. Brooke, however, devoured the chanterelle velouté and bouillabaisse. I picked at my plate while contemplating a ham and cheese sandwich from a deli on my way home.

The waiter arrived with the dessert tray. Brooke pointed to what she wanted, as if somehow not saying it aloud shaved off some of the calories. I spoke. "Cheesecake."

"Tell me, Daniel, is it unreasonable to be exercising at two o'clock?"

"In the—"

"Ay-*yem*. My downstairs neighbors are complaining to the building owner. But what can I do? It's the only time I have."

"What you need," I said, "is a father who keeps you liquid in papier-mâché volcano lava."

"Not Daddy's. Since she turned eighteen he doesn't give her a cent."

"Bad blood?"

"Not at all. She says he always felt children had to make their own way, just the way he did. And she agrees."

"How'd she get so rich so fast then?"

"Stripper."

I raised my eyebrows. Brooke smiled that conspiratorial smile.

"You can't make that much money stripping," I said.

"In Bahrain you can."

"Shitting me?"

"She did the palaces. Princes with some serious kinks—hardcore S&M, cutting, drawing blood. She had a blast."

I absorbed that while Brooke spooned her dessert.

"Did you see her leave in the car?" I asked.

"Saw her arrive too."

"Wasn't that a Rolls?"

"Bentley. I hear she likes to be known as the only Goth in New York who rides in a Bentley. Only I happen to know another one," Brooke said as our desserts arrived. "And I don't have the heart to tell her."

She put the spoon in her mouth and swallowed slowly with her eyes closed.

"Why do you think humans love sugar so?" she asked.

I shrugged.

"They say," she went on, "that people who constantly crave sweets are unhappy." She looked at me to let that sink in. "But I'm not unhappy. I can't say if I'm happy—that's a different thing—but I'm not *un*happy. That's the important thing. I live in New York. I work in New York. My father called the other day and asked if I wanted to come back home. I laughed. I think I hurt his feelings."

"Studies have found that sugar intake releases dopamine."

"What's dopamine?"

"Substance in the brain. Controls our pleasures. People behave differently on dopamine. Sort of like cocaine for the rest of us."

She smiled. "For the rest of us. I'm not going back to Long Island. I feel bad about mom and all, but..."

I took the first bite of my cheesecake. I'd forgotten to tell the waiter to hold the strawberry topping, which always turns it into an eight-year-old girl's dessert to me.

"Okay, here's the news for you," she said after a minute. "I'm throwing you over to Debra Austen. She's my new assistant, just out of college. Nothing else, other than she emails less often than I do and her caps button isn't superglued down like mine. Yes, your comment got back to me."

"I'm in trouble, aren't I?"

"Big time."

"And where are you going?"

"I don't know. I mean, I'm still here, but, well, they've got plans for me. That's what I'm hearing anyway. I'm a star..." She made a wanking gesture.

"Speaking of stars," I jumped in. "Can you believe I saw Welsey Shaw earlier today? Ran into her. Had *words* with her."

"Where?"

"In the Deutsche Bank Starbucks. Can you believe it? With her dog."

Brooke winced. "She used to go to my gym. For like two weeks. Then she complained she couldn't get any privacy and demanded a room all to herself, which they couldn't do, of course. Then she asked if they could close the club just when she came. They said no. Someone told me later she just bought all the equipment and put it in her home."

"Did she ever talk to you?"

"Once I passed her near the showers. Our eyes met and I guess she could see that I recognized her because I sort of smiled. This look flashed across her face like I *dare* you to speak to me."

"What'd you do?"

"It was strange. I'm not the kind to get intimidated. But my throat closed up and I had to look the other way."

And now I am sitting at my desk in my house on Callicoon's fabulous River Road. A quick email check reveals nothing new in the last two minutes. A look at headlines. I scan the side links: "10

Things Waiters Hate about Customers." I read it and turn out to be a pretty good customer, all things considered, although I do sometimes ask for too much bread, it claims. For five seconds I feel guilty, then figure screw it, that's what bread's for. For some reason, I then check my house on Google satellite view to reassure myself it's still there.

Just east of where the top of Pennsylvania stops being straight, you'll see Callicoon, a tiny hamlet of Sullivan County, New York, about 100 miles northwest of Manhattan. It was settled nearly 400 years ago, but very little of the place today goes back before 1888, when a fire gutted nearly everything.

There's Main Street, divided into Upper and Lower and separated by railroad tracks. Some businesses have been around for generations. Others aren't around anymore, but their buildings still are. There are the restaurants: The 1906 and Matthew's on Main ("Food, Bar, Happiness") and Peppino's. There's one hotel, the Western, and you can get a room anytime except the weekend of the annual tractor parade, because that's when the town comes alive. Rooms can't be begged, borrowed, or stolen. The tractor parade is a big day in Callicoon.

Originally the town was called *Kollikoonkill*, "cackling hen"; once upon a time the hills were alive with wild turkeys and the hunters who shot them. Some families grew up here. Others, like mine, were quasi-hippies who came from the Florida Keys, of all places, and bought land for cheap. And I mean *cheap. Buy land*, the man said. *They ain't makin' more.*

There are the farmers' markets every Sunday in the summer and fall. They're near the stone monument, REMEMBERING VETERANS OF ALL ARMED SERVICES IN ALL WARS. You can listen to WJFF Radio Catskill, the world's only hydro-powered radio station, in next-door Jeffersonville. In fact it frequently keeps me company while I'm writing. I've even filled in on some shifts, playing Copland's *Rodeo*, Holst's, *The Planets* and Mozart's *Jupiter*

Symphony.

Like just about everyone else here, I shop at Peck's and know almost everyone there by name. I've given the guy who cuts my meats rides home when his car wouldn't start. He's thanked me with endless cassette tapes of his favorite bluegrass songs, which I erase and reuse. Silly projects like that can keep me busy all day when I'm supposed to be working. I've read that all good writers are always at least a little bit behind. I'm an extraordinary writer.

I expect big things from you, Daniel. Mr. Reynolds, my 12th grade English teacher, *haunted* me with that line from the day he wrote it in my high school yearbook. There was no doubt: I was the one. Graduated at the top of my class. I was going to make the school, the town, proud, everyone except my parents had decided, without my input. At graduation Mr. Reynolds made a point of singling me out to the crowd. It was unscripted, not in the ceremony. He just did it. I still hate him.

Regardless of praise, it all came down to money. And because of a colossal lack of planning or, possibly, interest, on my parents' part, there hadn't been a lot set aside for college. Cars, yes. College, not so much. SUNY Albany fit my budget, if not my aspirations and SAT scores.

In high school I'd challenged my teachers on all sorts of things without shame. Most of them enjoyed it. Maybe they felt they had to, as part of their job. College was a different animal. I learned to answer questions the way I knew professors wanted. I also made sure to ask what they were expecting. I could tell when I'd succeeded. The professors would always stand away from the lectern and look a little bit taller. Their voice would go up when answering. (When I had the bad form to ask a question they didn't like, I noticed there'd usually be a throat-clear first.) I went on to learn how to regurgitate exactly what they wanted in a test, yet make it seem like my own. I thought this was brilliant, until I discovered my classmates were doing the same thing, without thinking they were so clever, or even realizing that wasn't the purpose of their being there.

I found my first post-college job in a realtor's office. I learned about creative writing. The business featured lots of properties near elite locales. The word *near* was what we called a taffy word. "There's no really clear definition of 'near,'" I was told on my first day. *Quaint, rustic, extraordinary, unique, charming, intimate*, and *spacious* were other taffy words. I also tried my hand at cold calling, but no salesman ever had to worry I'd snatch his job. I could never come up with a response to the tiniest objection from the other end of the line; on one occasion I received the ire of my bosses because I had no snappy response when the woman I was cold-calling told me she'd just returned from the hospital with a terminal diagnosis. I was to have told her those tests are sometimes wrong.

But my time at Moffat Realty was not a total waste. For one thing I created many pages of lovely brochure copy they still use today (now it's on their website). For another, writing those elastic descriptions reconnected me with my first love, fiction. So two months after my manager called me into his tiny office and asked for my key card, telling me he'd be willing to write me a glowing recommendation, and a day after the last phone calls failed to produce any new job leads with or without his glowing recommendation, I sat down in a cold sweat and started on my first novel, *Heaven's People*, from an idea floating around in my head since my junior year at SUNY. I told no one. I lied and said I had interviews. I wouldn't tell anybody I was sitting in my undershirt every day, while others got into their cars and drove off to real jobs.

"What do you do?"—I got asked that a lot. Awkward pause. There's a reason writers are anti-social, unless they're the authors of splashy bestsellers, in which case they show up at parties reeking of fame and good cheer.

My idea was not material for a splashy bestseller. But I knew that I had secrets. Do you know how hard it is to have secrets? Our modern world makes it impossible. And *I've* fucking got them! That's what justifies staying home in my undershirt, which has now regressed into bathrobe, and why bother shaving? I'm smarter than you. And you. And you. I may not have been adding to the GDP, but I was going to dazzle 'em with my insights, produce something that people would close with a sigh and maybe even a "Wow," patting the cover and telling friends, "You should read this. Guy's brilliant. Just brilliant."

My parents—now really, I usually think of them as Mom and Dad, or perhaps Mom & Dad, with an ampersand, because that's what they were, two people who cohabitated and shared meals and chores and a tax return and a bed. But they were never on the same page most of the time. They took separate vacations, had separate hobbies, and basically lived like two trains passing on opposite tracks in the night.

Anyway, my parents, practical as always, had thoughts of renting out our house after they retired and moved away, but *I* was living in it now. I had to pay rent and upkeep, while Dad charged what he'd have charged any tenant and raised it every year until I bought the house outright, or bought the small amount still owed on it. Still felt like it was his, though.

"When are you going to get a job?" they'd say whenever they called, which was often in that first post-college year.

"Dad/Mom," I would say, "I *have* a job."

"What is it?"

"Writing."

"Oh," I would hear, the receiver sounding a little farther from the mouth. That was from Mom. From Dad it was usually, "When you want to get a real job let me know. I still know people out there." He let it hang in the air.

Other family members were patronizing in their own way. I was never certain if they were mocking me when they made comments like, "I'm sure it will be a best-seller," as if I'd really believe that, as if the act of getting *published* weren't heroic enough. "I'll bet you'll be on *Charlie Rose*," said an uncle I wanted to punch in the mouth. "I always knew we'd have a famous writer in the family," was the worst. Didn't they appreciate that I *knew* how hard this was? Treating me like I was still seven, when I said I wanted to be an astronaut and fly to the moon, made me dread every family social, every holiday get-together. I no longer talk to any of them.

Sometimes I'd try to make my father see things my way. "Dad, didn't you say you admire—" And I would rattle off a list of writers whose mass market paperbacks I'd seen him devour, back when he read a lot. They weren't authors who would win any sort of prize but he did like them, and even once expressed envy for the life they led, pumping out page-turners while sitting at home on their sofas, their biggest concern where to buy new typewriter ribbons.

"Yeah," he'd agree. "But *they're* famous. When you're famous you can say you're a writer."

Then the phone was turned over to Mom. "Did you hear about Ben Saffire?" Ben Saffire was a just-out-of-college writer-producer for a rising shock jock, whose political talk show was about to go national.

"Ben Saffire was at a party at the Renfoes," Mom would say, "and he had this brand new Lexus convertible. I'll bet that job pays the *beaucoup bucks*."

But it wasn't all bad, not by a long shot. I should have experienced countless rejections of my finished novel, because that's the path, right? Anger and frustration with a generous helping of self-doubt, and maybe some self-mutilation. But it didn't happen that way. It was all very surreal just how easy getting an agent was, and after that, a publisher. Maybe I had something after all. At any rate, I might know how a father holding his newborn feels. I lovingly cradled those first copies of my first novel, a year and three-quarters later. The book seemed to be a living, breathing thing; I almost wanted to name it. Steve. It was a Steve. Or Stephen, with a "ph," because it was, after all, literary fiction.

What a kick to be in stores and see the cover atop a high stack on a table, my name—Daniel Ferreira, Daniel Ferreira, Daniel Ferreira—on display over and over. Locals asked me for my autograph; sex didn't feel this good. I was the person most people brought up when they talked about the area—not just the town, but the area, as in "Did you know Daniel Ferreira the author lives here?" or "Did you know Daniel Ferreira the author lives in the Catskills?"—not strictly true, but that was fine. Only they'd run it all together, saying, "Did you know Danielferreiratheauthor lives here?" That's who I was for a time—*Danielferreiratheauthor*.

Everyone would look up when I walked into The 1906 or Peck's. Clerks would stop me between the horseradish and the aluminum foil to tell me how much they loved my novel, how they'd read it two and three times, how it was their favorite. Was it really? Often I doubted it—what townie is going to go up to you and say "It sucked," especially when I knew where they lived? But my head swelled anyway. I never got a surly cashier or waitress anywhere. They laughed at my unfunny jokes. I got my drinks comped—I'm not that much of a drinker but I enjoyed them nonetheless. Waitresses let me stare, and smiled (mostly). The local papers, and even a couple of non-local ones, interviewed me. I was mentioned in the town's modest tourist brochure: *Daniel Ferreira, author of the acclaimed novel* Heaven's People, *lives in Callicoon.* (The next year they changed it to *bestselling*!)

Brimming with confidence, I started on a second novel. This one went easily, everything clicking into place. When *No Room for Coincidences* made its debut two stressful years later, I learned why Amish shun those they wish to punish. In the painful months that followed I would often open copies of both books and study them page by page, reading a chapter of each, or just examining the dialogue. Several times I thought I had hit upon the secret: *Heaven's People* had more energy. Or more likeable characters. A freer style. More humor. Less humor. Funnier humor. But then after another pass, I would think *Coincidence* was the better read.

For a while I freelanced magazine articles on subjects I cared little about, all the while frantically scribbling a new novel to reverse my fortunes and shore up my ego. *Screw* literary pretensions; this one was commercial! With cliffhangers on every page and a great part for Thora Birch. I believe I still have a copy of it on a Sony floppy disk.

At that point I gave up and accepted a fact that I'd been avoiding since graduating: I was or-din-ary. Mom was right: lucky once. A trip to Vegas. I so resented Mr. Reynolds, resented his vandalizing my yearbook, getting my hopes up. Once I pretended I didn't see him: He was going into a Foot Locker with his daughter. I tried to key his car. Damn, paint on cars today is tough.

I became a ghostwriter.

Hardly anyone realizes how many books are not written by the names and faces on the covers. Monets were painted by Monet. Hitchcock films were directed by Hitchcock. But a shockingly large number of the books you see, particularly the most popular ones, are written by us, the ghosts, who must let others' passions become ours, at least for a time, and keep secret about our work. Far from being the man behind the curtain, however, we're closer to the actor inside the tin-man suit. How many people know what Jack Haley looked like?

So I've been sitting at my desk, staring into my laptop, for an hour. I should begin working. I call Ann instead. "What's new with you?" I say. "Nothing," she replies in her soft, slightly flat voice. "We never get customers this early." "So why on earth does your dealership open at eight-thirty?"

She sat down next to me one night at one of the town's weekly pot-lucks. Ann Louise Geyer was strolling through her mid-thirties. During the evening it had felt like I'd always known her, and we just hadn't officially met until now. She listened to everything I said—and seemed interested. She listened to everything everyone else said—and seemed interested in them, too. Ann had the gift of being able to circulate through a room and make everybody feel they'd gotten her exclusive attention. When she tired of talking to one person, she'd introduce them to someone else instead of just leaving them lonely, and damn if that didn't work perfectly.

Zaftig. Warm and pleasant rather than drop-dead beautiful. Centered and comforting. There was something about Ann—her carefully modulated voice, her quiet laugh, her gentle face and blue-gray eyes, that made me drop my usual guardedness, my aloofness, whatever you want to call it. She got people to open up without seeming to do anything. And for some reason, one night in late July, she'd zeroed in on me. We were the first to arrive and, it turned out, the last to leave. The next day she invited me over for stuffed eggplant and Scrabble, though over the phone I thought she'd said "scrapple," a regional food whose description she listened to with mounting horror when I told her what it contained.

Ann worried constantly about what I ate, how I felt, the exercise I (never) got, the brand of body scrub I used. When I told her I didn't use any body scrub, she was stunned, and said something about me probably not exfoliating properly. I said I was sure I didn't. Then we talked about natural vs. unnatural pillows.

She swallowed green health drinks that smelled like the underside of my Dad's lawnmower. She wanted me to try them. Perhaps she was on to something. Ann never got sick and looked ten years younger than she was.

The first time I was invited over I marveled at the antiques she used as everyday objects. She kept her clothes in a cedar chest that was supposedly pre-Revolutionary War, and said to have been used to hide important Colonial papers from the British. It also might have smuggled someone over enemy lines, she wasn't sure. Her cat liked to sleep on the chest, and his claws decreased its value every time he jumped on it. Ann didn't care; it was a cedar chest, she said, meant to hold clothes. A lot of those clothes were handmade, and Ann knew the people who made them. She owned the only one-slice toaster I've ever seen. "I'm just one person, I always eat one piece of toast. Why heat the other slot every time?" There are some things you just can't argue with.

Since graduating college with an accounting degree Ann had been in the finance department—*was* the finance department—for Callicoon's one and only Ford dealership. Ever since meeting me, her mission had been to get me into a brand new Focus filled with all sorts of airbags, which my car, an ancient Volvo with fading paint, lacked.

"The Focus is so much safer," she'd say. "The new models are in. You should come see them. Wayne could get you a deal."

Ann worried about my diet. I snuck cheeseburgers when she wasn't around. The incriminating wrappers were tossed in a neighbor's trash. But over time I grew fond of her vegetarian lasagna, her Brussels sprouts, her gingered carrots with dates. She made me love string beans. One night she came over and thoughtfully cooked an amazing dinner while I watched and, at her insistence, took notes so that I could make it better on my own. Then we went to a movie—not a first-run movie, because you can't actually do that in Callicoon. This one had been all the rage six months ago, and we had the theater almost to ourselves. Ann said I was an exception, that she usually didn't open up quickly or easily, that after her divorce three years ago she'd only dated once.

Soon she had her own house key, and came and went freely. Sometimes she'd just sit in the living room and knit, or read, or do crossword puzzles out of dog-eared books with broken spines, while I wrote or parsed Absinthe's thoughts. We started shopping together, and she got me to read ingredient labels. Since I worked alone all day she rarely called, which annoyed me because I like to be interrupted. When she did call she would tell me in great detail about her day and ask all about mine. After a couple of weeks, however, I began noticing that she couldn't separate the interesting from the mundane. She was like an unedited manuscript, a sprawling first draft.

Ann liked everything; she was passionately undiscriminating. Her favorite books, movies, and songs were a menagerie of the great and the small. She confessed she anthropomorphized madly; she felt that everything had feelings, and if she rejected something, even a paperback book or a knick-knack, its feelings would be hurt.

So today we had our morning conversation, which had been our ritual for months now. Most conversations aren't actually necessary. We talk about the same things over and over, the things we talked about last time, restating them to assert their importance, and also finding some comfort in the repetition. My chats with Ann have taken on a certain sameness, even after just a few months. Not all the time, of course. But I'd estimate a conversation is only about 30 percent new, often a test of mood more than anything. Yet without them life loses a lot, not so much because of subjects that are not discussed, but because of the absence of the act of conversing.

I didn't mention the encounter with Welsey Shaw; it already felt far away. I already doubted some of my memory about it. And how do you bring up something like that between morning small talk and dinner plans?

After hanging up I sat for a while doing nothing and then, still not wanting to work, started reading everything I could find about Welsey Shaw. Which largely turned out to be colossally unenlightening. My eyes blurred, and I felt thoroughly unsure in the end about exactly who I'd met yesterday.

Welsey Anne Shaw is one of a kind, literally. There are no other Welseys; you can look it up. She was named after her maternal great-grandmother—originally spelled *Wellesey*, Irish. Except there are said to be no other Welleseys, either.

She is one of those stars who seems to have always been with us, fully formed. Wikipedia says she was born on July 25, 1984 in New Rochelle, New York. Her parents divorced when she was young because Lynne wanted her daughter in show business and Bryan did not. After years of chasing agents, auditioning, and crashing parties, mother managed to get her only child into show business, and from then on lived her life through her daughter: No one enjoyed the success of Welsey more than Lynne Shaw.

Welsey had perfect manners—*curtsied* after her first appearance on *The Tonight Show*—and always seemed to have the right thing to say, her mother just out of frame, one eye on the script.

At 19, it all unraveled. Welsey, apparently no longer able to play the puppet, declared independence and eloped with a stunningly handsome actor sixteen years her senior. This new life lasted one year, and neither party will talk about what happened. Rumors were of an ugly codependent relationship, but even the mention of his name ended any interview with her. More recently she has dated a string of men—mostly actors, mostly for a short time. Sometimes at night there are so many flashes when she appears in the outside world with anyone that I am at a loss to understand how she can find her way to wherever it is she's going.

On movie sets her behavior is legendary. There are stories of people fired for practically anything, real or imagined. She refuses autographs and reportedly tells fans she'll pose for a photo if they'd pay her as much as she got for her last role (said to be $15 million). But no matter how many times tabloid writers have put her in or close to rehab, she claims she spends much of her time in her jammies, watching TV, mostly alone. "I am," said one online article, quoting her, "a homebody. I enjoy scrubbing the kitchen and keeping house. I hate parties. I'm really a simple girl."

At 21 she became the youngest person (by just 29 days) to win a Best Actress statuette for art-house Oscar-bait *Mystery at Alessandro Creek*. I'd seen it and liked it, though typically for me forgot about it by the next day. But I was home the night she won her prize and happened to be watching as she stood on stage and gave a perfectly composed speech in which she omitted only one person, making it clear to the world her mother had been excommunicated from her life.

She was still big. Her name was huge on movie posters. Photographers still made her life hell. But some were saying her star had dimmed, or was dimming, or would soon dim. Great parts were harder to come by, and *Alessandro* just might have been her peak. Peaking in your early 20s can be rough, even devastating.

I know something about that.

3

There aren't many places where you can find people from all walks of life anymore. Sports events, rock concerts, airports, office Christmas parties—these all come with social boundaries, even though we may not like to think so. There are sky boxes, guest suites, roped-off spaces, gated communities, tiered services, and exclusive perks for high-fliers. At airports, VIPs bypass lines, and sit in special lounges not marked on any concourse map. They order off menu in restaurants and have access to special rooms in hotels, so that regular clientele, the "raggedy-assed masses," don't even know they're there.

Coffee shops are one of the few exceptions. They may be as close as we'll ever come to, if not a classless society, then one where the classes mix smoothly. Young and old. Famous and plain. The hip, the painfully hip and the painfully unhip, standing in line together. There's something about walking into a small, cozy hideaway and smelling the aroma of crushed beans that humanizes people again.

Romances start at the tiny round tables—or end there. Businesspeople hire and fire here. Startups are hatched, companies dissolved and liquidated. For many it's a nicer atmosphere than a fluorescent-lit Manhattan office. You actually could do much worse than the comfy chairs and muted lighting of the 280 Park Avenue Starbucks, located between 48th and 49th Streets, with its artsy yet homey décor and furnishings.

Once upon a time I used to think I didn't like coffee. Now I realize I don't like coffee *people*: all this talk of delicately complex and cautiously ripe flavors—the bold earthiness in the unwashed beans, the finely balanced, subtle acidity, with hints of chocolate, rosemary, blueberries, and citrus offset by the delicate, reluctant endnotes of butterscotch, cinnamon and licorice—five dollars, please!

But maybe that's just progress. Something has happened in recent times to coffeehouses; it's similar to what's happened to rock 'n' roll, blue jeans, and Harley-Davidsons. What used to be delinquent has now been tamed by dual forces: familiarity and capitalism. (Maybe they're part of the same force, like electromagnetism.) Former bourgeois parlors have become hives for busy entrepreneurs. Some even come with their own extension cords, USB hubs and three-way adapters, grabbing spare chairs near outlets and setting up all-day offices for the price of one cup of decaf.

I'm somewhat guilty of this too, but I will gladly close my computer for a good conversation. I don't bring my own extension cords and I don't charge my cell phone in public because I don't have a cell phone. I keep waiting for *Smithsonian* or *National Geographic* to do a cover story about me, "The Last Man without a Cell Phone"; I'd be like one of those tribes anthropologists discover that's never seen a slow cooker.

Standing in line today, an appointment with Brooke's new assistant editor in my future, I'm the only customer without some electronic device claiming my attention. The staff stares blankly, probably as instructed, even when someone won't put their gizmo away long enough to order. Just such a person was testing their patience right now. She took her time on her BlackBerry and then asked all manner of questions about what the drinks contained and how they were prepared, before settling on one served in a clear plastic cup topped with way too much whipped cream. Manhattan is filled with striking blondes sporting sunglasses and I-don't-give-a-damn manners. Still...

"Next?"

I have an odd habit of noting—and remembering—dates and times. That made me a whiz in AP History. The first moon landing, the sinking of the Titanic, Abraham Lincoln's last laugh—I can tell you when they all happened. I don't know why, or what purpose this odd talent serves, but there it is. And I can tell you that exactly one week ago at this very moment, Welsey Shaw stood here next to me, blotting my hand with a napkin.

"Can I *help* you?" said Yukiko, now with a look that indicated she'd probably never read *The Green Apron*, the handbook for new employees that tells them to "smile, connect, discover, and respond." I noticed for the first time that her nails were gunmetal gray, which suited her. "A large Ethiopian," I said. "*Venti*," she helpfully corrected, without smiling or connecting. Meanwhile I kept glancing to my left. Of faces my memory is less certain than times or dates. And once again sunglasses—different ones, pink metallics—hid the eyes.

I caught myself staring at her sideways, and must have looked silly. I didn't care. She didn't seem to notice me. Indeed she didn't seem to be noticing anybody, head straight ahead, sunglasses appearing where hair left off. She could have been a mannequin. She barely even moved.

Then the same purple scarf came out of the jacket, and was flung about the neck. It was her. I couldn't decide if the second time was less or more believable than the first.

"Hi!" She stiffened, just a little. "How are you?" I asked.

Confession time: On the train down I'd been having a conversation in my head with Welsey Shaw. What we'd talk about if we'd ever meet again. It had been easy. It had been smooth. The right subjects just fell into place and we'd had a great time. Now that I stood two feet from her the void between us swallowed me up. I had seconds to smile, connect, discover and respond. I felt like a kid called to the front of the class who hadn't read the assignment.

After a moment that felt like an hour she answered "Fine." But it was more a question, and it was followed by a cautious stare. "Aren't you glad the weather's warming up again?" I soldiered on.

"Yes," she said in an evasive way, as though my simple question were a trap. She stepped back a little. "We met at Larry Gagosian's party, right?"

"No," I said, feeling my face turning red. "It was a week ago. Here." I tried a smile. I knew it looked forced without having to see it.

"I don't think so."

"Yes, remember? You—" I didn't want to say the one thing that would remind her.

"I didn't 'anything.'"

She walked away with the dog, who was behaving perfectly. I sugared and creamed my coffee and approached her table, not really sure if we were through talking.

"How's your little dog?" I offered.

She bristled. "Excuse me, who are you?"

I heard a funny rattle in the back of my throat.

I didn't know if it was a good idea, but I held out my hand, the one on which two canine marks had now healed. Last week I'd been threatening her with all sorts of retribution and now I was smiling as if showing my vacation snaps.

"Oh," she said. "*Oh*! Oh…"

"I'm sorry," I said. "I thought you'd have remembered something—"

She looked up. "Did I say you could sit with me?"

I actually hadn't thought about it one way or the other. I looked around. "Would you *mind* sharing a table? There's no place else."

"Well, sorry about that, but I'm not sitting with anyone today." She kept her gaze fixed on me. Something about her stare *pushed* me out of the chair. She didn't seem to be doing anything, but it was terrifying.

"I was just wondering how you were doing. Since last week. That's all." I knew that sounded insincere before it came out of my mouth, but out it came anyway. She looked around the room vaguely and pointed to a man alone in a corner. "Do you wonder how he's doing?" She smiled. "Or how about—" and her eyes drifted again, "Her? How about her? Bursting with curiosity are we? Or him, or them, or the guy with the long beard on the computer?"

"Sorry," I said. "I thought we'd just talk."

I felt almost an obligation. After all, there is positively no way I am ever going to meet Welsey Shaw *again*, right? Would I want to tell people I bumped into her a second time...and *said nothing?*

When I looked back at her she was donning white earbuds and opening a spiral notebook, one with many doodles on the cover. As if on cue a table opened up on the opposite side of the room and I took it.

After more procrastinating I creaked open my laptop. When I glanced up she was looking right at me, cup pressed to her lips, hiding her mouth. The sunglasses hid her eyes. She had achieved total blankness. She wrote something and spent the next twenty minutes with her head down.

I worked for the next half hour, and when I looked up again she was still taking notes, scribbling rapidly, playing with her phone, taking bites from an almond cookie. At one point I got up to get something from the counter ("something" being whatever I thought of when I got there) and passed her within inches. She studiously ignored me, making sure her already hidden eyes looked straight down at her notebook when I passed.

About the notebook: I tried, when I came back with a few unneeded napkins, to see what she was writing. The pages were filled with tight print, no margins, in a scrawl that looked like barbed wire. The book looked like it had been hastily commandeered, grabbed out of a back closet, appropriated randomly. I tried to read some words but it was impossible in the brief time I had. And she knew I was watching her.

Welsey Shaw didn't seem particularly comfortable. Her chair was away from the table and her left leg stuck into the aisle, like an animal prepared for flight. But she was absorbed, too, bent over her notes with complete dedication. My watch beeped. I looked at my screen and realized I hadn't written anything in the last 15 minutes. Glancing back as I left, I saw an incognito movie star watching me, closely. The cup went up to the mouth again.

That was my second encounter with Welsey Shaw.

Ann was talking about a play. It was off-Broadway, way off. "I've never actually gone to a play before. Well, that's not true, really. In high school they took us to see *The Glass Menagerie*. I was depressed for months and I still think some part of that play spooked me. What an awful experience for school kids! My mother wrote the teacher a note about it."

"That's understandable," I said, looking at her in the doorway from my spot on the bed.

"How about you? How many plays have you seen in your life?" she asked, disappearing into the hallway. "I bet it's a lot."

"Not really, no," I confessed, suddenly feeling inadequate in some way.

It was odd, as well as terrible of me to say the writings of most other authors don't interest me much, a few heroes excepted. I had my own universe, others had theirs. Nothing wrong with that. I don't see how they can make me see my universe more clearly. So why bother?

And there was a part of me that didn't feel terribly excited about seeing a young writer's work produced on stage—or published in a beautiful hardback book with cream paper and deckled edges, type set in Garamond, my favorite. Every time I saw a new hit novel in the stores I immediately flipped to the back flap to determine if the writer was older or younger than I was. I admit it. I'm a vain, insecure, jealous human.

Ann entered holding a pair of colorful martini glasses.

"What are you thinking about?"

As I took my margarita thoughts drifted back to *Apocalyticus* and the eight urgent emails to cross my computer in the last hour. "Mm, the end of mankind, basically."

She raised one eyebrow and set down the glasses. "Wow, that's heavy stuff. Drink this..."

I took a sip as she kicked off her shoes and stretched out on the chair next to me, shaking her hair as if sloughing off the entire day. "Well, I'm intrigued. Roz got tickets because of some organization she did lots of work for, tons of work, and they have no money. But somehow they have these tickets. Five of them."

Rosalyn Sommers. She was Callicoon's other original *wunderkind*, a pianist and jazz musician, but then, not really. Describing her was impossible; nature had made only one. Once, at a friend's party, she played brilliant, knotty jazz variations on Happy Birthday, seeming to dig as much out of that silly melody as Beethoven did from Diabelli's waltz. She could coax music from her instrument in the most unconventional ways, hammering, caressing, slapping.

She taught. Students trekked to her house from far away. The farthest away was Belgium, and he roomed with her for four months, paying her by doing yard work and gardening. That summer she had the most beautiful backyard in Sullivan County.

Other pilgrims came on weekends to jam, or just to be with her, feeling they might improve just through osmosis. Maybe they did.

Rosalyn Sommers did not look like a jazz musician. She didn't dress in black, talk like a woman trying to talk like a man, by saying, for example, "man," or "cat," or "gig." Yet despite a wide and deep classical training, that's what she basically was—tiny, lithe, unassuming and still, until she sat down at a keyboard and reordered the universe with two hands. (It sounded like more than two hands; I often found myself peeking to see if she didn't have another one hidden under her sweater.) Her sound was ageless, borrowing from nothing and everything.

Speaking of age, I could not estimate hers. She was older than me, though by how much I couldn't say. Her snow white, shoulder length hair (once honey blonde), baby-smooth skin and small green eyes looked forever young. Her voice had a perpetually musical lilt. I've never known anyone who sounded happier than Rosalyn Sommers.

"So who are the two other people? You said she has five tickets."

"I don't know them. A double adventure."

"When is this?"

Ann pulled a pocket calendar out of her bag and pointed to a date circled in purple. "Let's do dinner. You pick a place. Big and splurgy, but not too far from the theater in case service sucks. And you have to take my special dietary hang-ups into account."

Ann maintained rigid eye contact as she unbuttoned the conservative clothing she wore for work, revealing something lacier.

For some reason a woman who stares you right in the eye while undressing is unbearably sexy.

She took her time with the buttons. So often in movies you see the man help. But I just watched, as though I were auditioning her, which got me rock solid. Ann wasn't a stunner, but she'd get the part, because she was the best performer. She had the softest touch, the surest hands, which she guided to the perfect spots at the perfect moment with the perfect rhythm. And that shirt was still on. Unbuttoned, but still on and now all crinkly, which made it sexier somehow. She hiked the sleeves up as far as they'd go. Ann liked to take off clothes slowly, making an issue of each item as she removed it. Buttons were fussed over. Shirttails were wiggled slowly out of skirts. And when she got down to the bra, well, let's just say I hadn't realized how sexy a woman could be by keeping a bra on for so long.

Next her hands were on my own shirt, which she rubbed against my nipples as she pulled it off. I felt warm fingers on my belt buckle, thumbs brush against penis, and when I opened my eyes again my pants were below my knees. Ann started stroking, and I responded, closing my eyes once more as I cupped her breasts and parted them, unsnapping the bra and letting it hang, sliding down under her and taking her nipples into my—

I looked up: Ann was gone. "Where are you?" After a confused moment I heard the refrigerator door open and close, footsteps in the hall. She reappeared. "Forgot to put the ice cream away. That would have been a mess."

We continued. She sadistically brought me to the edge and then relaxed; I tried the same on her, but she was so much better. I always envied women not just for their multiple orgasms (the *effortless* multiple orgasms) but because my one had to be perfect. Ann needn't worry about such things, and so I was convinced she had more fun, and for longer, too.

"I like it on," she said, grabbing my arm as I reached for the light. She watched while we did it. I didn't have anything like a ceiling mirror, though I think Ann would have been pleased if I did. When we finished, a good 25 minutes later, she shook her hair some more, turned the light off, and asked if anything interesting had happened today.

I opened my mouth, thought, shut it again.

"Not really," I said.

Welsey Shaw once decked a paparazzo. I thought about that in my bathrobe as I watched two eggs come to a boil. It had happened a few years ago. The battered photographer quickly and mysteriously dropped the charges.

She'd made all the critics' lists. Best dressed (on the red carpet). Most annoying celebrity. ("*Welsey Shaw hates her fans but loves her fame.*") Most hypocritical. ("*Highest paid actress says Americans are too materialistic.*") Most egotistical. ("'*I'm fucking good at what I do, and I make no apologies for it.*'") Most difficult to work with. ("'*I don't like the way certain actors smell.*'") Rumor had it that on the set of several pictures she had a 25-foot perimeter wherever she went. Both her main dwellings, the "small" one in L.A. and her spectacular New York penthouse, had to have, according to *Architectural Digest*, their climate controls set to a perfect 72.5 degrees. *No one* working for her at either locale was allowed to change this, even when she wasn't there.

But she was popular, too. Always good for a story, with a quick wit for quotes. Sympathy because of the Mom, who was good for a lot of the copy herself. And Welsey Shaw was always *there*, because she made at least one top-tier movie a year, sometimes more. Most of all, she just didn't give a damn. They loved that. A screaming match outside her apartment at two in the morning. Walking off the set of a movie because the director forgot to send her flowers on her birthday. She'd show up at a restaurant with her entourage minutes before closing, demand a table, and stay till three. For everyone's trouble she would leave tips that doubled the bill. Or five bucks. Or no tip at all. Or maybe an autographed photo. Depended on who you asked.

Once, so the story goes, she was in a restaurant in Michigan and the food was too cold. So all of it went back—even the salads, even the bread—and after a few minutes it returned, only to be found too hot. So new food was prepared while she complained about how long it all took, and this effort was the right temperature, but she had since changed her mind and wanted sushi. The problem was she and her entourage were in an Italian restaurant. At which point she supposedly raised such a stink that they slipped someone out the back door to pick up six orders of salmon, fatty tuna, unagi, and herring roe with kelp, which they then regifted for the fabulous thespian.

Some versions of the story are even better, and say she left a thousand dollar tip.

4

I wouldn't admit I was planning another trip to that Starbucks. I even concocted intricate plans to make myself believe I was going to be busy, so busy, so that on the day of, the thought of traveling into the City wouldn't even occur to me. But I'd work better there; that was for certain.

Writing in a quiet house actually isn't easy, even though it sounds like a dream job. It's not long before you start listening to the creaking of the floorboards, the dripping water, dogs barking, the phone, the TV, cars in the street, airplanes flying over, Pipers and Cessnas that *droooone* past, their sound never seeming to fade.

There's peanut butter and crackers in the kitchen. Some great DVDs just left of my elbow. Unread books. Newly re-mastered recordings of *Time Out* and *Conversations with Myself*. When I go out, I can make sure I leave my earbuds behind.

I begin each day with the goal of getting ten solid pages done. Ten little 8½ by eleven pages. It sounds like a molehill, but any writer knows it's much closer to a mountain. Flaubert is said to have licked a page a day, when he wasn't distracted by his penis. But Melville banged out *Moby-Dick* in a year and a half. I have an advantage over both of them, though: I'm just beginning my yarn. The game is always the same when writing. Charge out of the gate, take no prisoners, and believe this one is going to be easy. When you hit the middle you begin to feel straitjacketed by your own creation. *This* mandates *that.* A character introduced *here* means something else can't happen till *there.* Something brilliant in the beginning turns out to lead nowhere. And then comes the ending, the hardest part, the moment to tie everything together, hoping not to arrive and find your audience already there, waving at you, or not show up at all, lost and confused.

I tried writing on the train to Manhattan, but that turned out to be impossible. I don't suffer motion sickness, thank heavens, but the chatter of the train distracts, my Toshiba is a blur, my fingers miss the keys. And the scenery is a constant distraction; other people's stories—flowery backyards, winding streets and intersections, beautiful front porches and abandoned shanties—interrupt as I try to write mine, or Absinthe's, which I try every day to *make* mine. I get notes from her, thoughts, emails, but never phone calls. We have not spoken since the day we met, and she has gone out of her way to let both Brooke and me know she is not to be disturbed, that the communication flow is one way. Even Brooke does not have her direct number.

Today it was raining when I left Callicoon, cloudy most of the way down, and sunny just as we approached Pennsylvania Station. The (not inconsiderable) walk to 48th and Park Avenue was giving me a burn, no doubt melting inches, which was another reason to be doing this, I told myself. I actually welcomed the heat on my skin against the November air; a woman with bare legs and stilettos hurried by, and I wondered how she endured the cold.

Inside the Starbucks I found a cozy spot and settled in. The people here were becoming quite familiar. Regulars, the 80/20 rule.

Most of them were dressed for business, but a few of those who I would discover were unique regulars populated the store like spices in a bland dish. They tried to sit at their favorite table, though that was more often than not impossible, because so many fancied the same real estate. If their preference was filled, they'd watch closely till it became free again, then slip in briefly even if they soon had to leave. I imaged a whole hierarchy of desired spots among the 13 or so tables in the room.

They were a cast of characters: Socrates, a shaggy man in his 20s or 30s, always reading thick esoteric books when he wasn't discoursing on ethical topics with whoever was at the next table. Next to him was The Dancer, a tall woman who always wore black tights and moved with grace. She usually favored a table close to the window, but today it was taken by The Professor, a gray-haired man who always wore a sloppy sweater and sported a goatee. Though he usually sat alone, at the moment he was talking to Raven, a tall, wiry woman with cropped black hair who had large bags under her eyes. Next to her was The Corporation—three serious-faced men in matching suits who tried, whenever possible, to pull a nearby table over to hold their printouts. A somber balding man with small eyes and attaché case earned the sobriquet of Putin.

I love to listen to people talking, not so much for the content as for the subtext and the delivery. Rarely do two people engage in conversations equally. There's always a Dominant Talker. The Dominant Talker steers the topic and doesn't take cues from others. A Dominant Talker is going to talk about what they are going to talk about. All you can do is nod and agree. They also know how to talk for half an hour without breathing.

Socrates, on the other hand, had been reading Kant when I came in, dog-earing certain pages and yellow-highlighting others. I remember thinking I had a crack at understanding Kant when I was in college, but after months of reading and rereading all I could do was quip, "I *kant* understand it," which elicited no reaction from my dad.

Socrates was now talking to several others who'd joined him, they leaning in to catch every word, then asking questions that sent him back to his blocky text. Although it could be and so often was quiet and detached in here, this afternoon's group was unusually animated, which led me to something else I noticed about coffee shops. The noise level and general business rose and fell like tides.

Something caught my attention. A pair of eyes fixed on me, hidden by dark, oval lenses...

The dog was with her. She appeared to be without makeup, again in a hoodie and beat up jeans. Unremarkable. A 20-something New York kid who unloaded trucks or worked in a stockroom.

She scanned the room for a nonexistent table. I stretched my leg and pushed the chair across from me toward her. She continued to look around. A spot by the wall cleared, and she started her move, but somebody else was quicker. I laughed to myself.

More head-turning. Once again I gave the chair a little push and a tiny wiggle. This time I thought I saw a faint smile cross her face.

But she remained standing.

Five minutes, ten. The crowd was here to stay. And who could blame them? Outside was uninviting; that rain from my morning was now threatening New York. Inside was warm. There were pastries and sandwiches and lots of outlets, and artwork on the walls—strange abstracts in bright colors; I planned to check them out more closely. But not now. I wasn't leaving my table. I knew it was The Dancer's favorite; she kept eying me for it.

So I stayed seated. From across the room, the actress seemed to sigh. "Uncle," she said quietly as she approached.

Welsey Shaw sat, sort of hunched her shoulders, and folded her hands around her paper cup, blowing on it. She tasted and made a face. "I told them no sugar. I always tell them no sugar.

Maybe I should get a shirt made." She gestured across her front. "'No sugar.' Well, okay," she said, casting the cup aside and wiping her tongue against her teeth. "So here I am. Make me glad I sat here. Entertain me." She fed a treat from her bag to the dog, who sat by her feet, like an angel this time.

And now the question of what the hell do you talk to Welsey Shaw about occurred to me. There she was. Here I was. I knew nothing about her that I could bring up at this table and expect her to stay. She knew nothing about me at all, other than her dog had bitten my hand, a subject best forgotten. "So what are you doing here?" I asked, and then added, "again."

She looked at me and frowned, or seemed to underneath the glasses. They were Gucci, I noticed, with a bluish tint. In their lenses I saw myself, looking fatter than I am, because the glass was curved. Somehow I was not happy about how I looked in front of the great actress in the hoodie. I should have been dressed better. Not better, but more stylishly, I thought as I looked at her tattered threads. Not more stylishly, but more unobtrusively, like she was, just a simple gray and blue combination. Then I noted I too was wearing gray and blue. But somehow her gray and blue looked more chic than my gray and blue, though I could not tell you why. I banished this daffy thought and concentrated on her dark shades instead. They looked heavy on her face. "It's drafty at this table," she half-rose, and I thought she was leaving. But she only readjusted her chair to angle her back to the door. "How do you sit here?"

"I don't feel a draft," I said, and indeed I didn't, though for some reason I felt at that moment like being contrarian, and would have said I didn't feel a draft even if I had. It gave me something to talk about.

"I'm very sensitive to these things. I feel a draft," she insisted. "What am I doing? I'm doing the same thing as everybody else. Someday that chi-chi girl with the wingtip eyeliner will get my order right."

"That's Yukiko," I said.

"You know them by name?" she asked with amusement. "You bothered to read, and memorize, their nametags?"

"Always know the name of the person who makes your drinks," I said. She laughed. I had made Welsey Shaw laugh. "Surely you can get any kind of coffee you want at home," I said, imagining a kitchen filled with the latest shiny gadgets. "You wouldn't have to go through the trouble."

"What trouble?"

"The trouble of coming here." I looked at her cup. "To drink—"

"...A grande non-fat double-shot extra-foam light-caramel latte with sugar."

"Wow." I silently pantomimed clapping. "And *you're* impressed I memorized a nametag?" She was smiling. But already the conversation felt like it was running out of steam. She looked at her cup and licked some of the foam. I unobtrusively closed my laptop and desperately tried to think of something to keep going.

"How's Enron?" I asked.

"*Chev*ron. He's fine." On cue she fed him another treat.

"Seems much calmer today."

"It's the Prozac. He's taking to it real well since his doctor adjusted the dose."

I nodded stupidly.

"So...that's that." She looked around. "Do you live nearby?"

"No," I said. "I'm fairly far."

"So what brings you here? I'm sure you could make any of these wonderful coffee drinks at home."

"Ha. Enjoying a change of place mostly."

She pointed to my Toshiba. "What do you do, if you don't mind me asking, and if you do, tough. You invited me over."

"I write. Places like this one are golden for writers."

"Why?"

"Anyplace different is a good place," I said. "Different is the key."

"That's the theory I've heard too," she said, leaning in a little bit. "But does it really work?"

At that moment I admit I had little proof that new places produced better writing, but I believed in it anyway. I had to. Everyone has irrational dogmas. Vladimir Horowitz performed at four in the afternoon on Sundays. A famous baseball player believed leaning on your bat while waiting your turn guaranteed a strikeout. My grandmother, a baker, never washed her bread knife on a Sunday. It brought bad luck, she insisted.

I smiled. "It helps. Working here. I can see it when I get home. My writing is better."

"Ah. And what do you write?"

"Anything someone will pay me for. I'm a gun for hire."

She gathered her things, stood, and started to wrap Chevron's leash around her wrist. "What? What's wrong?"

She ignored me until she was facing the door. "I don't do interviews," she said under her breath. "Especially these kinds."

"This isn't an interview!" I reached out. Her forearm was small, slender, light. Cold. Even though the thick sweater.

"Don't touch me," she barked.

"I'm sorry," I said, and we were both surprised how real that sounded. "I'm not out for an interview. I wouldn't have told you that if I were, now, would I?" Occasionally I can think on my feet.

"I have to admit that's a good point," she said grudgingly.

"I write novels nobody reads." Yes, I realize it sounds self-pitying and perhaps even calculated. But it wasn't. She may even have been curious.

"Like?"

"*Heaven's People.*"

She shrugged. "Never heard of it."

"And that's the most famous one."

Another outbreak of nervous laughter. She didn't quite sit back down but pulled the chair out, set one knee on it and leaned on the back. Chevron resumed his spot on the floor.

"Okay, wiseguy, you seem like the fool. And by fool I mean jester. Do you juggle?" she asked. "Fools juggle. Let's see you juggle your coffee cup, my cup, and this scone. Oh, and—" She yanked the flash stick out of my laptop. "This thing. What is this?" She turned it over in her hands. "It better not be a camera."

"It's not a camera," I sighed.

"Microphone?"

"It's a flash drive that's probably screwed up now because it was just jerked out of my laptop," I said.

She laid it on the table. "Oh. Shit. Well, whose fault is that? It shouldn't come out so easily. There should be like an electric shock or something to deter me." She picked it up and shoved it back into the port.

"Can't juggle," I said.

She looked at the table as if it were doing something fascinating. "Me, neither. Someone tried to teach me once. He could do eight. I started with two and kept dropping them. We were shooting a movie, working on an elevated set. Fun for the crew."

"What's an elevated set?"

"Built off the ground so they can fit underneath and get really low shots. I kept dropping bean bags onto people's heads. A disaster. They hated me. So what do you write then? Besides the novel, I mean."

"Freelance. Magazine articles mostly. Sometimes I ghostwrite books."

"Some examples?"

"Well, I wrote an article recently about people in New York keeping rats as pets. And I just finished a piece on people living in treehouses. Some impressive houses up there, too, hot tubs and everything."

"Water and electricity in a tree? Is that a good idea?"

"I don't know. Worked for him."

"What's your favorite story you've ever written?"

I wanted to answer seriously. In the more than ten years I'd been freelancing to earn a crust, few stood out.

"Possibly the 43-year-old elementary school teacher who won the state jackpot twenty years ago. She's still teaching. Hasn't taken one sick day. Pays for all her class supplies and takes her students on amazing class trips with her winnings."

"Okay, good choice. So, what else shall we talk about?"

I leaned back and took a breath. "I don't know."

She did likewise. "Me, neither."

"What can we talk about? What do two people from completely different backgrounds have in common that isn't trivial or clichéd?"

We thought.

"Isn't this tough, finding something in common? We're both from New York. We both come here. We're both going to get wet when we leave because neither of us has an umbrella." I looked out the window to see raindrops hitting the street so hard they bounced three inches back up.

"What's your name?" she asked suddenly.

"Daniel. What's yours?"

She smiled. "Lizzie Borden," she said. She tapped her fingers on the table. "This might be embarrassing."

"Agreed."

"But is it an indictment of our materialistic and class-obsessed culture, or is it an indictment of us?"

"Of us."

"Of *me*," she corrected.

"Really?"

"It is, in a way," she admitted. "Now would you believe I feel sort of bad about that?"

"Sort of bad?"

"Yeah. It's the best I can do. So, have you seen many of my movies?"

"Not really. We don't get first-run movies where I live," I said.

She frowned. "Where the hell do you live? What kind of town doesn't get *my* movies?"

"*Excuse me.*"

Yukiko was before us. Abundantly overdressed again, she seemed taller today. "That dog can't be in here."

For the next several minutes Welsey alternated between impetuosity and patience, explaining that the animal was a service dog. Papers and tags were produced. Claims of "a man injured in here from a dog bite" were offered in rebuttal. I was right there but the barista didn't seem to remember me among the thousands of customers she'd been indifferent to that day. Welsey kept insisting that no one had been hurt by her dog. I sat mum. Finally Yukiko gave in and walked away.

"Thanks," Welsey said, "for not saying anything. About being bitten. Normally he's not like he was that day. He's not used to the crazy people. He's a doll," she said. "An *aaan-gel.*"

"Even angels have scruffy paws." I held up my hand. The wound was all but gone.

Her faint smile vanished, and her guard seemed to go up again. She grabbed her bag. "I really should let you get back to work. Thanks for sharing the table. Come on, Chev," she said, no longer looking at me. And she was gone, leaving her plastic cup and her wrappers for me to deal with.

I looked at my watch. Twenty-two minutes. That's how long I'd spent with Welsey Shaw today.

Ann spent Thanksgiving at her parents'. She was apologetic for not bringing me to meet them, but she felt they "weren't ready yet," especially her father. Later, after I was introduced to him, I would understand. Jake Geyer—pale, serious, no discernable lips—drove the last white wall-tired 1989 Oldsmobile Cutlass I've ever seen, in immaculate condition, white with cranberry velour seats. Two bumper stickers, *Bush/Cheney '04* and *God Bless John Wayne*, were symmetrically stuck to the back bumper. Ann said he was so upset when Obama won that he refused food for a week, finally ordering a Papa John's pepperoni pizza on November 11, 2008.

His plaid shirt buttoned all the way to the chin. He had a collection of them, red and orange and rust and brown, and a green one he wore only on Saint Patrick's Day. It was impossible for me to imagine him smiling, or conceive that Ann came from intimate contact between him and Ann's mom. It was more like Erin came into the room and said, "I'm pregnant," and he replied, "That's wonderful. Did you read George Will's column?"

As it always is in situations like these, Erin was sweet and motherly. One would have to be to sustain 30 years of marriage. When I finally would meet them, I'd find myself spending as much time with her as possible and censoring myself continuously when around him. I hate to have conversations like that. You wonder what you said, if it matches what you're saying now. You take a breath to jump into the conversation, rethink, decide it's best left unsaid, and swallow your air. That tight smile stays plastered on through the entire day, and it starts to hurt.

Sometimes I wish sweethearts came without family. They make already difficult relationships more difficult.

Anyway, today Ann was in Providence, 240 miles away, and I was here, truly alone for an extended period for the first time since we'd met. I don't like Thanksgiving much to start with—it's the day restaurants get away with serving bad food, dry and tasteless. I wish the first settlers had dined on filet mignon and baked potatoes, pork ribs, smoked barbecue sauce and chocolate cake.

I made a reservation for one ("Just one?" said the voice on the phone) at The 1906. My own parents weren't coming for one day and the Volvo's ability to reach New Canaan was questionable. Or maybe I was just paranoid that a car with 255,000 miles on it was likely to break down in a neighborhood with a median annual income of $200K. So at three-forty, under slate gray skies and a raw chill, I walked down River Road amid an unworldly stillness—literally *nothing* moved. I stamped my feet and heard the echo; I coughed, and someone coughed back. The restaurant greeted me with warm yellow and brown, but was otherwise as lifeless as the outside had been. Had they kept it open just for me? I almost wanted to send everybody home and just help myself in the back.

The waitress tried small talk, hovering around my table when she wasn't doing anything, which, apart from taking my order, was all the time. Her mother had read my book once and loved it, she said. "Tell her I said thank you." "She's dead." If there was ever a time I didn't know what to say next, that was it.

Fortunately she retreated while I ate my turkey, gravy and horrible stuffing, wondering all the while what I would do with both my parents when they became too feeble to take care of themselves. Great Thanksgiving thoughts. I calculated that Dad had 15 to 20 more good years, max, mom less. Fortunately dessert came at that point.

I left a hefty tip on the bill, because EMILY, as her nametag called her, deserved it for schlepping in today, no doubt missing her own family, to be my server.

"They're all dead," she said as I thanked her.

Back home I shuffled around, utterly refusing to work on a holiday even though it felt no different from any other day at home, other than it seemed to go slower.

I poked through old magazines, weeding out anything that went back further than '08. I did this every once in a while. Ann thought magazines were snapshots in time, and should be kept forever. I was merciless, and thinned my own periodicals periodically. The first magazine I pulled out had the words WELSEY SHAW in large yellow caps on the front cover. Inside were candids in Cannes. Welsey and a boyfriend were getting out of a limo, were walking through glass double-doors with their heads down, were kissing in a pool. The article was all about their futile attempts at privacy. On another page they sat in a restaurant, their attempts at dining thwarted by photographers, their faces rendered pale and gaunt by the flashbulbs. She wore a beautiful sleeveless pink dress and covered her eyes; he wore a black suit jacket, shirt and sunglasses and looked away. "No wonder they're thin," crowed the caption. "Paparazzi won't let them eat."

I found features about Welsey in three other random magazines. They ranged from short paragraphs to cover stories. I stared hard at the photos. It was hard to believe I had just casually talked to this person, when so many reporters had to chase after her.

I threw everything else in the trash. But I kept those magazines.

I really wasn't walking faster than usual. But I was sweating and my clothes were damp. On the street my feet crunched crusty snow. Inside it must have been 80. I removed my coat but that was not good enough, and before I got to the front of the line off came the sweater too. Across the room, wedged in a corner, she was looking right at me, different sunglasses once again. No dog. Her attention went back to her phone while I ordered but as soon as I approached she looked up.

"Hello."

"Here you are again," I said.

"No, here *you* are again. Let's get it straight."

Welsey Shaw wore Michael Kors across her face today. These glasses weren't as large or heavy, didn't seem to be a shield to the world. And she was actually tucked into a table this time.

"Where's the pooch?" I asked.

"Aquatic therapy till three," she said. "Then canine dance class." I couldn't tell if she minded I'd called him a pooch or not.

"That's some big bag you carry," I said, jockeying for space.

"Never trust a woman with a small bag. You'll be sorry." She eyed my emerging laptop. "You're still coming in from two hours away to sit with me?"

"I'm writing," I said.

"I actually find that the most annoying."

"What?"

"The people who pretend they're not interested in me. I know I am famous and therefore, irresistible."

"Well, I'm not interested in you." I held my computer up and showed her a screen filled with tiny double-spaced words. "I don't really follow movie stars or celebrities. There are too many of you, for one thing."

She sighed. "Oh, God, that's true. Think of how it feels on this end." She drank some coffee and, for some reason, shook the cup slightly.

"The second most annoying are the ones who take the opposite approach. The serious geeks." She made a serious face. "'Your performance in *blah-blah* was *blah-blah-esque*. That scene where you did that thing.' They point out something to impress you with how carefully they've studied me." Or, 'The critics didn't like *such-and-such*, but *I* thought it was the best movie of the year.' Then they wait for a big reaction. What do they expect me to do, shove my tongue down their throat?"

"I'm not that way. I've only seen one of your movies."

She leaned forward, actually seeming to care. "Oh you have? Which?"

"Mystery at the creek."

"Oh, what a relief. I was afraid you were going to say one of the bad ones." She took a long sip from her cup, and pried off the lid. A long stare inside. "Does anyone ever do that with one of your plays?"

I didn't correct her. "Does anyone ever do what?"

"Come at you with all sorts of nerdy analysis. Things they 'noticed' to show off."

"No, they never heard of me."

"Then there are the really creepy ones who just stare at you from afar. They don't say anything. You don't know what they're thinking."

"So which am I?"

"I keep changing my mind. Just this morning at the nail salon I was thinking you were a pervert stalker. Now I think maybe you just moonlight as a pervert to make ends meet."

"Actually I've had worse jobs."

"So tell me what a typical day is like. A typical day that you have. Just tell me."

"Why?"

"None of your business. No reason. Whatever."

"You must have a reason."

No response.

"Well, I get out of bed and I write," I said.

"Back up."

"I pee."

"Go forward."

"I cook breakfast."

"Stop. Do you feel happy when you wake up?"

"I don't know. Beats not waking up, I guess."

"What do you cook?"

"My favorite is the humble soft boiled egg. But they're tough to do so I end up with a hard boiled egg and tell myself it was what I wanted anyway."

"You rationalize your failures."

"I'm a writer."

"Why are they so tough? The eggs?"

I took a breath. This was a serious question. "It's getting them to just the right amount of 'done.' A few seconds too much-ruined. A few seconds too little-ruined. Kind of like life."

"Hmm," she said, looking straight ahead.

"I'll bet you've never boiled an egg," I said.

"No," she admitted after a moment where she looked like she was contemplating a lie. "Can't bake a cake, can't boil an egg, can't cook a turkey. I'm learning. I sent my housekeeper to the store the other day to buy some turkeys for me to practice."

"Practice does make perfect." I had this mental image of a housekeeper hauling home a pile of turkeys on a handtruck.

"You really have no idea how helpless I am. I don't even know what she adds to the milk to make it taste so good. God I love it."

"Cinnamon? Vanilla?"

"Maybe?" It was a question. "I'm learning things, though," she said defensively. "Last week for example I made my first bacon and eggs. And coffee."

"Congratulations!"

"I hope that wasn't sarcastic."

"It wasn't."

"Good. Breakfast is hard. Harder than dinner, which I've already made, actually, thank you. But breakfast—you have to time everything right, or the toast gets cold, the butter doesn't melt, the eggs dry out. Breakfast takes real skill."

"It does."

"So I'm learning to use this machine, this big espresso machine

I ordered from Germany. Or was it Holland? I figured it would be easy to use because it's all automated and it's got the most buttons, right? Wrong. Very very wrong. It's a mystery."

"Don't look at me. I still have a Mr. Coffee."

She jumped in her chair. "Oh, I *love* Mr. Coffee! My parents had one. The original one, white with that fake wood front. Have you ever seen a coffee maker with fake wood?"

"So simple. Two buttons."

"They had theirs forever. It might still be in a garage somewhere. But my new espresso machine is the worst. It's got a seven-point-five inch computer screen, thirty buttons and comes with an instructional DVD. It *dares* me to use it, sitting there on my counter, taunting me. It knows it's the boss of me."

"You have an active imagination."

"Of course I do. It's an occupational hazard. Keeps my therapist dining on caviar."

"You just told me you go to a therapist," I said.

She shrugged. "So?"

"Isn't that a big deal?"

"Oh come on, you must have read that about me."

"Why do you assume I read about you?"

"Everyone who's been in show business more than a week goes to a therapist. I think therapy does a world of good."

"Really?"

"For his wife. Her car has shiatsu electric massage seats and an espresso maker in the dash. I did that. So, after eggs what rocks your world?"

"Waffles."

"Ooh, Belgian?"

"Kellogg's."

"Oh." She started to stick out her tongue, stopped. "Then what?"

"I start writing."

"Oh no you don't. I've known writers. They procrastinate for hours. You sit down, page through the paper, read every stupid thing online to put off the act of writing. You call people on the phone—*blah-blah-blah-blah*. Then it's almost noon. So you decide it's too close to lunch to start now. So you break for lunch. Then you come back from lunch, and you're really full, and so you rest for a while. Or look at porn. And then, when it's finally about, oh, two-thirty, quarter to three, you start to feel guilty so you start working. By five you're on a roll, but it's time to stop. And you swear you'll knock it out of the park tomorrow."

She leaned back and smiled.

"Like I say, I've known writers. They are the laziest people on earth. Daydreamers. Full of excuses. If excuses were currency, they'd be rich. You know, they say genius is one percent inspiration and ninety-nine percent perspiration. Actually it's one percent inspiration and ninety-nine percent procrasperation. —Hey, I invented a word. Not real but it ought to be."

"Thanks."

"You're welcome. So what else do you like to do? When you're not 'writing.' What's the name of that far away town where you live?"

"Callicoon."

"I've heard of it. Maybe. Why do you live there?"

I felt my face reddening. No one had ever asked me that question before, it was a strange question, and for a minute Welsey was replaced by an image of my dad.

I fumbled for an answer, "One has to live somewhere, right?"

"But how does it compare to other places you've lived?"

"I haven't lived anywhere else, really."

I didn't know what she'd say. But she merely raised her cup. "Well, here's to long roots." She tapped it against mine, took another long sip, and then looked inside it again. "So then, what's the weirdest thing you've ever drunk?"

I actually tried to think for a moment before saying, "Where in hell are these questions coming from?"

"Caffeine."

"I have no idea. What I've drunk, I mean. But I'm assuming you have something in mind."

"I do," she affirmed. "The weirdest thing I've ever drunk is *masato*."

"Don't remember seeing it in the supermarket," I said.

"Probably because it's made from fermented saliva."

"So maybe it's next to the yogurt."

She smiled. I was making her smile a lot today, and I could feel my heart beating every time I did. "Swished around in the mouth and then spit into a bowl." She raised her cup again and grinned like a small child grossing out a parent. The well-dressed elderly people at the next table glared at us, got up, and left.

"It's a *delicacy*," Welsey Shaw teased.

"Where?" I asked.

"In the Amazon."

"Oh."

"The natives there chew up a shrub, mix it in their mouths, and spit out the tasty result."

"And you drank this?"

"I kinda had to." She lowered her voice. "I was in Peru. With a madman of a director. Total psychopath, and that's when he was taking his drugs. Lots of downtime. It rained for like six months. One day we're sitting around, after, like, fifty days of rain straight, and we're crazy. We're slap happy and making no sense and drunk without the alcohol. You know how it gets when everything's just crazy and your world is totally upside down? It was like that.

"And we knew about masato. We'd seen Peruvians drink it. In the script my character drinks it. Now he told me he wanted me to. Getting into the part, see. I said, 'I'm an actress. I can act it.' 'Tough,' he said."

"So you did it?"

"I had to. He said I wasn't getting out of the jungle until I drank it. Being that he controlled all the communication and transportation out there I had little choice." She grinned. "I couldn't even call my agent and scream for help."

"Who is this director?"

Welsey made a zipping motion across her mouth. "Just ask yourself what movie director is the most insane one out there. Then you'll have it."

I wasn't sure how much of this to believe. Was she feeding me ridiculous information to see if it came out later on some website so that she would know who I worked for? Seriously, I *could* imagine this making a great story. It was tempting. This whole thing was tempting. Why *wasn't* I selling all this to someone? I decided it was because it might get better the more I came, so why ruin things?

"So if he's so abusive why do you work with him?"

She opened her mouth, stopped, and stared into space for a moment. "He—he may be a crazy person, but he's an amazing director. Where does genius end? I have no idea. But when he talks to me before a scene, it's like, like there are all these distractions I bring with me onto the set. Everyone does. And he comes over to me and closes the universe so that it's just me and him. And it's like he goes around me turning all these little lights off, all these thoughts, until the only ones left on are what I need for the scene. And as long as I'm in that room with him, with just those lights on in my mind and nothing else, I'll do the best work of my life." She came back down to earth.

"When does this film come out?"

"Hasn't." She sighed. "He's still messing and reshooting. It'll never happen. He's too much of a perfectionist. I heard my part's gone by now anyway. On the cutting room floor. He never liked me. *Bug Bites and Diarrhea with A Madman* is the title I suggested one day. I wound up on his shit list for it, pun intended. Maybe I did it on purpose. Who knows? At that point I'd been in the jungle for four months, going on five. Or was it five, going on six?"

"What if I find out there is no movie, no director and no drink?"

"You won't. And I'd better not either."

Suddenly we had nothing to say. We just stared at each other, and I pretended to check my computer for something. I figured she would probably disappear now.

"Nutmeg!" she finally said. "That's what Marlena adds."

"Ah," I said emptily.

Sure enough she said, "I should go now."

"So soon?" I asked feebly. She didn't respond. Once again she left everything on the table, everything being a paper cup, a stirrer, a wrapper and two napkins.

I glanced at my watch: 37 minutes today.

The first thing I checked on after she left was masato. That was real.

Then I tried to flag down the director. After an hour, no luck. I checked to see if there was advance buzz on the movie she described, based on keywords, because how many movies were filmed in the Amazon? Nothing.

I summoned her filmography and tried to figure out where in her busy schedule she might have had time to spend six months in the Amazon. Her list of films was so dense, but at the same time, there were gaps large enough to accommodate her. I'd never really studied a movie star's list of credits before, and I admit I couldn't fathom how Welsey Shaw could work so incessantly, even if most gigs were only for a few months at a time: finding her character, learning her lines, and getting to know a completely new cast of strangers had to be crushingly fatiguing. I tried to imagine "changing jobs" every few weeks. Even with breaks in between it must amount to a very chaotic, schizophrenic existence, one in which your must develop thick skin and become hardened early on. Welsey Shaw was like an army brat dragged from town to town, albeit a well-paid one.

But forming friendships must be nearly impossible…

The off-Broadway outing provided me the perfect excuse. Ann was in some sort of training class offsite, courtesy of suits in her dealership who had changed their minds about how they wanted to count money. I had assumed there was only one way, which is you add it together. Ann chuckled lightly when I said that and showed me that, no, there was a near-infinite number of GAAP–approved techniques to shuttle beans, sometimes counting them twice in the process, sometimes not counting them at all. "The way she explained it was fascinating, though I could not in turn explain it back to her. Ann said that was okay so long as her people could explain it to auditors.

So I would leave for the City that morning, to see if, on any day *other* than Wednesday at noon-thirty Welsey Shaw appeared at the 48th Street Starbucks. I knew one day out of ordinary meant nothing—perhaps Welsey was out of town, or had an appointment, or just didn't feel like braving the walk. But if she did enter, it would perhaps not shed light on her odd visits, but remove some of the mystery I was confronted with, which in a sense was just as important.

As I hiked up Sixth Avenue I checked myself in some windows and approved. Inside the Deutsche Bank building I was greeted by much the usual crowd. It looked like a Wednesday, even though it was a Friday. As I cradled my drink a lanky man with dreads smiled in my direction: "Mind if we share?" He raised a brick of a laptop and waved large hands over the little round table like a magician doing a trick. I smiled, with my mouth at least. Truth is, I did mind. I did not feel like company, unless it was Welsey Shaw. But I didn't want to be seen as rude, or worse, racist, so I would have company, at least for a while.

"I'm Ajani," he said. I told him my name. "What do you do?" he asked as he set up his laptop. He had a separate mouse covered in buttons and shaped like a running shoe.

I bristle when people ask me, right off the bat, what I do. Will my examiner subtly tailor their conversation to my answer? And how many people lie? I don't mean an outright lie, but a freelancer copywriter I once worked with introduced himself as an "advertising executive," which conjures a completely different mental image, not to mention year and model car.

"I'm a writer," I said.

"What kind of writer?" he asked. "News writer? Business writer? Financial writer?"

"I'm a ghostwriter." I expected he would ask me what that was. Instead his eyes lit up.

"I had a friend who was a ghostwriter..."

"Really?" I said. Looking past my tablemate, I witnessed a dazzling blonde strut into the store: brown jacket, jeans, boots and sunglasses. She shouldered a huge bag. I strained to see her face…

"Do you make money at it?"

"Yes, I do pretty well actually."

"He didn't," he said. "You don't mind if I ask you that?" he said. "America is a funny place. Some people mind if you ask them about money and some people never want to stop talking about money."

"Yes," I agreed. "I know the type."

The blonde was checking her phone and shifting from foot to foot. She flung her hair back, but not far enough.

"And what do you write about?" He trilled the *r*. "W*rr*ite."

"All sorts of things," I told him. "Fiction, nonfiction,

biographies. People with family stories who don't have the chops to tell them." Then I realized the word "chops" might confuse him.

"My friend wrote science fiction erotica," the man said. "Sex with futuristic robots."

"You know what?" I said. "I have to get another coffee." I held up my cup for emphasis, praying it looked emptier than it was. "Nice meeting you." He smiled as I stood. The laugh again. I couldn't tell if he was laughing at me or with me.

Another coffee meant I would not fall asleep no matter how boring tonight ended up being. I got as close as I could in line and still wasn't certain what dazzling blonde I was looking at. At that moment, she turned to me, peeling down her sunglasses.

"Do you know where Magnolia Bakery is?"

I didn't. And it wasn't Welsey Shaw.

But now a commotion had broken out at one of the tables. A few people were stretching to see over one another. Elbows jutted out from the center of the action.

My new acquaintance was also drawn to the scene. We squeezed through the onlookers to arrive upon two men—almost boys, really—neither seeming to notice the crowd, deep in a game of chess, oil-cloth board, dinged pieces on the table. "Ah, chess," Ajani said, as if none of us knew what it was. "The game of kings!"

It was blitz, just five minutes per side. They slapped down the pieces so fast you'd think the moves had been agreed to ahead of time, and as their clocks neared Armageddon their speeds only increased. Pieces fell, or were knocked over, and both players replaced them until one clock reached zero. There was a second of silence. They nodded to each other and leaned back. One got up and walked away.

The player still seated looked around, and his eyes fell on me. He gestured to the seat expressionlessly.

"Go on," Ajani said encouragingly. It never occurred to me to say "After you." It also never occurred to me that this might have been a setup. Were the two of them in it together? Maybe they'd entered, surveyed the room, and found me as their mark. Foolishly I sat. "Five dollars" I was told; I placed Abe on the table. We set up. I admit I had to look at his side to see how to place the king and queen. That probably told him all he needed to know.

He opened by pushing his king's pawn two squares. I did the same, because it's all I knew to do. I knew there were fancier openings, where you started with an off-center pawn or a knight, but I didn't know what to do after that. I was aware that chess players memorized books the size of bibles containing thousands of openings with colorful names that branched into complex trees of moves; I wondered if the man before me was one such person. I stayed out of his way and castled my king as soon as I could. I created a little pawn pyramid, a fortress of plastic. He attacked them not at the center but along the sides, marching his pawns and following with bigger pieces.

Gradually squares were taken away from me, until I had nowhere to go. Most of my major pieces were now huddled in a corner, useless. A glance at the clock revealed I had thirty seconds. My opponent kept his head down, thumb on chin. I was the one who had the problems, yet he stared at the position as though some even better slaughter might reveal itself, and he could move on to his next kill all the quicker. I noticed I was sweatier than I ever thought I'd get over a few dollars.

I decided to free up space with some captures; maybe then I could move my pieces into offensive positions. Or at least I hoped they were offensive positions. I sacrificed a *bishop*; I figured he'd decide I was someone to be reckoned with. His queen took control of the resulting open space, and now my king was in trouble. That hadn't been the idea. With less than ten seconds left, my monarch was trapped between a rook and a hard place! At least I could still be witty in the face of death.

The word "checkmate" has nothing to do with a sexual

encounter. It actually makes no sense at all, really. It comes from the Persian *shah-mat*, which means "the king is dead." And mine was.

"Play another?" my opponent asked. "No thanks," was my reply.

The circle parted as I made way back to my table. I noticed no one else immediately took my place.

"You played well," said Ajani, consolingly. He wasn't even a convincing liar. I shrugged.

"My four o'clock is late again. I do not like it when students are not on time. It shows a lack of commitment."

"Maybe he's stuck in traffic," I offered, assuming the pupil a he.

"If I offered a free phone to be here promptly, he would be. You can count on it."

I now had a headache thanks to the chess game. More blondes entered, blondes who were not celebrities but who were every bit as young, as attractive, perhaps as accomplished in their own way, yet I was not interested in them. Why was I wasting so much time trying to figure out why and when a movie star came into a coffee shop?

I circled the room, which elicited suspicious looks from some. I stared at the art on the walls. The price for each of the eight-and-a-half-by-eleven watercolors was three hundred dollars. I estimated I could easily paint five an hour. Not bad for a day's work. I bought another coffee, an iced latte. A latte was the only coffee drink that tasted good cold, in my opinion.

"My student is chewing on some problems," Ajani said, returning to my side. "I can't believe how math-challenged some of these young people are. This is high school trig. He's struggling. In my country we have eighth graders doing this work. We have high school students designing train stations and college freshmen doing the engineering for the water treatment plant."

"That's impressive," I said, curious what country it was.

"This one asks me what an imaginary number is. I do not understand the lack of comprehension here over mathematics. Psychological. That's what it is. Psycho*log*ical. But at least he apologized for being late." I was terrified he'd ask me if I knew what an imaginary number was.

"Psycho*log*ical," Ajani insisted. I think he liked the sound of the word. Then I remembered—

Dinner!

I wasn't just shaky in math; I couldn't tell time. I had been thinking of the start time for the play, totally forgetting I'd booked a table for five across town. Experiencing a sinking feeling, I realized 1) there was no way I could get there in time, and 2) Ann had probably gone on to the theater by now anyway, because she used her head more than I did in times like this.

Walking backwards, I scanned the room one last time to make sure Starbucks didn't have a secret back entrance for movie stars to slip past ordinary people. Convinced it didn't, I grabbed a cab, blurted the address, and started cursing every red light we hit. Arriving at the theater with ten minutes to spare, I paid and thanked the driver, explaining the reason for my haste.

"Blame Amtrak," he said. "Always works."

Concerned faces peered at me from behind glass doors. Roz was smiling as if to say to Ann *I told you so*. Ann stuck her head out, breath rising into the night air and disappearing right below the marquee.

"We were worried!"

"Sorry. Amtrak. Someone jumped," I said, scratching my nose.

"Suicides are common in the winter," a voice to my left replied. The owner of the voice nodded, as if acknowledging thanks for his opinion.

"This is Ron, and this is Karin," Roslyn said. "They're new to the area. Our area, I mean."

The man nodded again, rocking a bit, hands in pockets. The woman, considerably taller even in nub heels, held his arm, a bit awkwardly I thought, but I always think that when the woman is attractive and the man is short. And she was attractive. And he was short. She looked like she was propping him up. "Hi there," she said.

The voice was throaty. Full and a whisper at the same time. A smoker? Didn't seem like it, yet God had endowed her with a sexy voice. She had auburn hair, a smattering of freckles, high cheekbones and green eyes. Her date had a flat brown haircut from the 1980s, a stocky body, and an annoying drone to his voice that said 1) I know everything and 2) I know *everything*. Yet she was thoroughly enmeshed in him. I found myself disagreeing with Einstein. God was malicious, not subtle.

"I've been wanting to meet you," she continued. "I love your books. Roz loaned them to me." Was she flirting? Her hands were wrapped around Ron but her eyes were burning a hole in me. Something about both of them screamed *We want to be noticed.* Mostly, it was how they kept looking around to see if people were looking at them. When Ron wasn't looking around, he'd stare at his loafers or check his diver's watch repeatedly.

"Ron's here buying up real estate. With the fracking going on he figures this would be a great market to get into."

Ron added, looking past me. "Do you know anyone looking to sell?"

I shook my head.

"Maybe you'd want to consider," he said.

Another shake.

"Where do you live?"

"River Road," I said vaguely.

"Nice property. You should sell."

Shake shake shake.

We were led to seats by a senior woman with a snow-white

mannish haircut, wearing a tuxedo. She said she hoped we enjoyed the show. Ann snuggled close and smiled. Ron balanced his left leg on top of his jiggling right knee, threatening my dress pants with his shoe print. He also smelled peculiar, like dust. He and Karin whispered throughout the first act. He apparently said many things that amused her. She rubbed his leg; he touched her arm. He didn't seem to be paying attention to the action on stage; then again, neither was I. I was noticing the blonde in front of me, six rows down, twenties—possibly the youngest person in the place. She was with a darkly handsome man who sported trimmed stubble and the kind of disheveled hair that no doubt required hours of attention in front of a mirror. He wore black on black, and checked his phone or the program notes every few minutes. The blonde rested her head on his shoulder throughout much of the first act, though at one point something on the screen of his phone seemed to amuse her. She also caressed the back of his neck incessantly, drawing slow circles with her index finger. When I looked back at the stage, the scene had changed, perhaps more than once. I'd missed a lot. Who were all these new people? Were we always in Chicago? And when had the man with the bow tie died? The audience roared at some line that made absolutely no sense to me. I laughed anyhow. The lights came up for intermission and I was lost, completely lost.

"What do you think so far," asked Ann.

"It's great," I said bravely, and Ann smiled.

My attention returned to the blonde, who rose to stretch. She was the right height, five-eight. She was the right build, thin but curvy. She whispered into the ear of the man as adoringly as Karin was doing to Ron next to me. But when she turned around to look up at the balconies, her eyes momentarily making contact with mine, I realized it was someone else, someone who looked not a whit like Welsey Shaw.

5

Welsey Shaw was strategically covered in clinging, wet sand. She was naked in the ocean. She licked ice cream cones in a way that threatened to make ice cream illegal. Breast shots: firm, round, oiled. More ample than what was suggested under the gray sweatshirts and green sweaters I had seen. I found myself enlarging some of the photos to check on the size and color of her areolae—

"Not my nipples! Too big. Wrong color. Mine are nicer, really."

I jumped. "I was just—"

"Please..."

"I didn't see you."

"No shit, Sherlock. Happy Me-Wednesday." She smiled and got in line, head down, hunched over her phone, whether for real or for cover I couldn't tell. She wore sleek Ray Bans today and had her hair pinned back. Instead of the standard uniform hoodie a long white man's shirt covered her down to tight leggings and ankle boots. These small changes somehow made her utterly unrecognizable.

"Of course you didn't see me," she said when she returned. "I'm good at hiding. Otherwise I'm like a deer standing in the path of buckshot."

"Have you ever gone hunting?" I asked.

"Yep. My dad took me. I can drop a deer at 300 yards."

"That's impressive, I think."

"Damned right it is."

"I don't know much about hunting," I said, "despite growing up with many people who do." I looked down at the bags she'd toted to the table. "I see you've been Christmas shopping."

"I have. Stop trying to peek."

I suddenly entertained the absurd fantasy of getting Welsey Shaw a small but amusing Christmas present. I'd give it to her at our next meeting, and she'd laugh. The question arises: What do you get Welsey Shaw? There's no way of knowing what she has, where she's been, what she's seen, so the default is to assume she has, has been and has seen...everything and everywhere.

"Can I see what you got? I'm kind of curious what celebrities shop for."

She looked inside the bag. "You'll have to stay curious. Presents are deeply personal, like showing someone your diary. Or your nipples."

"Well, I wouldn't want to peek at your diary," I said.

"If you knew what I had in here and who it was for, you could sell that information, and then you wouldn't need to come here anymore."

"I doubt it."

"I don't."

"Are Christmas presents that personal?" I asked.

"For me they are. I feel presents are a kind of test. A test of how well you know people. How well you listen to them throughout the year when they talk to you. I find the worst present buyers are self-centered. If they can't buy me a good present that's a clue to ditch that person," she said with satisfaction.

"That's an interesting philosophy," I said. She shrugged and looked away, watching someone outside get a parking ticket.

"I'm terrible at buying presents," I continued.

"Well," she said pitilessly, "you're a writer, learn the fine art of observing people and then you'll know what to get them. For example, I know someone who is always talking about gossipy mysteries: the disappearance of Amelia Earhart, that base in the desert where they keep frozen extraterrestrials. So for her birthday I got her an actual lump of coal from the boilers of the Titanic. I picked it off my barbeque. Got a calligrapher to make a 'certificate of authenticity.' And now she's my best friend. The moral of the story is you have to be observant of people and then you can play them like a piano." She rolled fingers across the table.

"Is *that* the moral of that story?" I asked. She nodded.

I looked over at The Duchess. She was a new addition to the 48th Street Regulars, a tall sixtyish woman with grayed hair pinned high and reading glasses attached to a chain. She always wore dresses, usually red, sometimes black.

"What would you observe about her?" I asked.

"You mean Elisha?" Welsey asked.

"That's her name?"

"It is. I heard it called for a drink order. I'd say never married. Probably has had very few if any lovers. Lives on Park Avenue, very high up, in an old building that's secretly a fire trap. Season tickets to the opera, even though she doesn't care about opera. It's the going that matters to her."

"That's pretty good."

Welsey leaned back and pondered her lunch.

"I have little names and identities for all of them," I confessed, wondering if she would decide I was uncomfortably eccentric or bond with me through her equally-fertile imagination as an actress.

"Oh, so do I," she said.

I pointed to The Dancer. "Her. She's a dancer. Ballet or tap. Look at those legs."

"Of course you see the legs right off," she said. "But I saw her sleeveless once and there's some nasty scars on her right arm. I wonder what that's about." She gestured over my shoulder. "What about him?"

"Mr. Feltsman."

"Who?"

"He was the family's tax accountant when I was growing up. He'd come over once a year, do my dad's taxes, tell me I was cute and give me a lollipop. Looks just like him," I said, looking at the morbidly obese man in the suit who was thoroughly engrossed in *Le Monde*.

"Okay," she said, gesturing to my right. "What about that guy?"

"That's Socrates. Comes in here with these huge books and spends all day reading them. Then he holds court with a bunch of followers who hang on to his every word. And when he doesn't have them, sometimes he talks to himself."

"What kind of books?"

"*The Poetics, Symposium, Beyond Good and Evil.*"

Welsey raised her eyes.

"You've read those guys?"

"Hell, no. I tried once. But there's usually some pretentious guy on the crew with stuff like that, to say to everyone he's just slumming it with the rest of us. Or there used to be; lately it's a competition to be the biggest nerd and so they mostly read comic books now. *I* read romances. Sue Grafton—I love Sue Grafton. But I can't claim to be a really big reader. I see those thick books and I think how long it would take for me to read just one. And there's hundreds. It's like dieting. Struggling to drop two pounds and after a week of sweat there's like 30 more pounds to go. So I just fall in front of the TV with a pepperoni pizza and watch *Sex and the City*. Good times. They can make me thinner with CGI. Fuck dieting, this holiday I'm eating all the cookies and candy I want."

Welsey's phone chimed. She answered, cupped her mouth, then went outside for a few minutes, hunching her shoulders and leaning against the building.

"Where are you going?" I asked when she returned.

"What do you mean where am I going?"

"For Christmas."

"What makes you think I'm going somewhere for Christmas?"

"Celebrities always go somewhere for Christmas. Somewhere tropical and completely devoid of the Christmas spirit. They bring their kids, so that the poor tykes never learn that Christmas is celebrated in snow by a fat guy in a red fur coat."

"Oh really?"

"Yes. Private islands. Magic places. Places where they stop the outside world, just push a button and it stops."

"Tell me where this is."

"You already know. You go there."

"What if I told you I don't?"

"I'd have a hard time believing you. Celebrities go away to far-off vacation spots where they're tended by obsequious staff who roll out red carpets and sprinkle them with rose pedals, and make a trail with salt water taffy to your room, which has a giant revolving bed with silk sheets and little plates of foie gras on the pillows."

"It's Debauve and Gallais chocolates, not salt water taffy. Jesus."

"What about the foie gras?"

"That part you got right. Nobody knows where I'm going. Haven't breathed it to a soul. Last time I told just one person, and there were paps camped outside my room when I arrived."

"Paps?"

"Paparazzi. Those little shits with cameras. So this time it's classified. Not even my assistant knows. Or my boyfriend. All me. All alone."

It was the first time she'd mentioned the boyfriend. Last I'd heard it was some financial guy, about her age, middleish 20s, movie-star looks even though he wasn't one. My information, however, was old. Opinion was split as to whether they were still together.

"Who's the boyfriend?"

She smiled broadly and made that zipping gesture across her lips again. "God you're nosy today."

"Is it that hedge fund guy?"

The zipping gesture once more.

"What are you going to do wherever you're going?"

"Run around naked."

She let that sink in as she gathered her things.

"Just keep that picture in your head till I get back. No packing. No unpacking. Can't beat it. I have to go now," she said. "But I'll be back in exactly two weeks, and—" she bent over me and whispered, "—so will you."

I left New Year's Eve planning all up to Ann. I never like planning for New Years. You normally have to start thinking about it by Thanksgiving, if you don't want everything to be either booked-up or extra-pricy. I never remember to think about it by Thanksgiving. Since Ann loves to take care of details, I left it to her this year. And she decided on Matthew's on Main.

Matthew's on Main looks like a barn on the outside. Indoors it's dark and removed from the rest of Callicoon, which is already pretty removed. On weekends I'm a regular because they serve breakfast until four in the afternoon. Ann was unenthusiastic until she tasted the vegetarian burger. There's no better way to hook Ann than with a vegetarian burger.

On this night she was taken with the bar, sitting with her back to me, talking up a storm with whoever was on her left as she finished her third Sweet Tea Vodka Lemonade. I chatted with the new bartender, a collection of vertical lines named Sammi, until she was monopolized by someone at the end, an older-looking truck driver with a young blonde in a shock red dress.

That left me with the guy to my right, the owner of a sporting goods store called Al's. I asked who Al was, since his name was Gene. He said no one; Al's was simply the friendliest name he could think of for a sporting goods store. Gene sat with his girlfriend, Bree, a middle-aged woman with long, streaky hair, who couldn't seem to take her eyes off the TV for a single second.

Gene was one of these small business owners who could not stop talking about their small business. For forty-five minutes I learned about inventory, purchase orders and requisitions, and distribution channels. I decided when I was about twelve I did not have the entrepreneurial spirit my dad valued so much in America and Americans (even though he never started a business, not even a weekend hobby one). I took turns with two friends once running a lemonade stand, and I was bored. I also didn't charge enough, they said. I soon crept away and went back to my room and started writing a story instead, which I never finished. "We made fifteen dollars," they said when I came back, "but since you didn't do anything you're not getting any." They then split fifteen whole bucks between them and went away happier than I'd ever seen them before or since.

Maybe in a way being a ghostwriter is akin to entrepreneurship. Lord knows I have to make excuses all the time about why a "shipment" (my manuscript) hasn't arrived yet, fix (revise) something defective and even cancel accounts (throw up my hands and say I can't work with this person or that person). All-in-all, I'd rather leave the business end of this business to someone else, and much of it is handled by Carla Vanderhoof, my long-suffering agent. I talk to her as little as possible. She probably thinks I don't like her. Not true. I just don't like the business side of what I do, or talking incessantly about it, at least.

When I refocused my attention to Gene he was now talking about an article he'd recently read, "Celebrities Who You Didn't Know Fished." "You never know who's going to walk into your shop who's an avid fisher," he said, although for some reason he pronounced it with a long A, *aay-vid*. "He could be wearing a striped suit, don't matter. Some people you can't stereotype. Most people, I'd say."

"That's true," I said. "In fact you won't believe this, but I've actually chatted up Welsey Shaw in Starbucks."

No reaction at first. Then a squint. "Really?"

The bartender, who'd returned to a spot in front of me and started getting out champagne, looked doubtful. "She's like, totally antisocial. Don't' know much about her but I know that."

For some reason that made me feel defensive. "No, she was alone. And I've seen her and talked to her—quite a few times since then actually." I expected a question but instead got silence. All eyes went back to the TV screen.

"How would you know?" the bartender asked after a minute went by, while the camera was panning over the crowds in Times Square.

"What do you mean, how would I know?"

"Well, has she ever said to you, 'Hey, I'm Welsey Shaw'?"

Actually, come to think of it, she hadn't. Ever.

"*Aha!*" Sammi seemed to be reading my thoughts.

"Isn't she in Italy or somewhere shooting a movie?" The lady in red at the end of the bar spoke up.

"That was, like, four, five months ago," said Sammi. "They don't work very long."

"I heard once she went to some restaurant, demanded they

close the place just for her and her people, and then after three hours left a ten percent tip," said the trucker.

I felt a nudge. I turned to a smiling Ann. "Hit me," she said, shoving her glass forward.

"Another *STVL*," I said to Sammi for Ann, who for some reason couldn't say it for herself.

"You should talk to Duane here." Ann motioned to the man next to her. "He and his wife run this couples retreat in the Catskills." The glass slid back to Ann. "They bring couples closer," Ann said.

"Really?" I said. I glanced over at Duane the Couples Counselor, wondering where his wife was right now.

"People go there for long weekends," Ann said. "You sit on a floor, stare at your partner, and really notice them, sometimes for the first time. It's to get you to notice each other. You touch, but it's not naughty touching." She touched my nose. "Like that." She touched my ear. We should maybe try it some weekend. They have a steam brunch and everything."

I saw myself at a steam-table buffet, sitting in a heart-shaped hot tub with Ann under one of those faux-stars ceilings, and engaging in intimacy exercises with 20 or so strangers who probably all had camera phones.

"Doesn't she make her assistant sleep in her room with her because she's afraid of the dark or something?" the woman with the trucker asked as I turned back to my conversation on the right. "What a piece of work."

"I don't remember that," said Sammi, mopping up a spill on the bar. "But I do remember when she said, 'I'm just different from other people, and I can't pretend I'm someone who lives an ordinary life with an ordinary income.'" Sammi affected a snotty high-pitched voice.

Gene shook his head, and his companion took her eyes off the TV while a commercial flashed by. "Did she really?"

Sammi nodded, adding, "She rolls her eyes too much when she acts."

"She does," agreed the trucker's woman.

"Makes her own travel arrangements, though," said Bree. "Bully for that."

"She said once her idea of a perfect night is staying in and playing a game of Pictionary." Everyone laughed before conversations drifted away to other subjects, Gene back to his store, the trucker to something about changes in federal highway laws starting tomorrow, Bree back to Times Square.

"It's time for champagne!" Sammi announced, overly upbeat. She grabbed the TV remote and cranked up the volume.

"Have you ever noticed you have interesting ears?" Ann said to me. "And I'll bet you've never noticed mine, how this one," she brushed her hair away from her left, "has a closed loop around the top and the other one," she tilted her head to show me a differently shaped ear, "doesn't." She was having a little trouble focusing her eyes.

"No, I'd never noticed," I confessed.

I turned to see Sammi filling champagne flutes lined up like soldiers, drizzling bubbly in one expert motion. A pro. At that moment I thought about all the New Years that were different from mine, and how most were surely better.

"Raise your glasses! There's only one shot to get this right," Sammi said as she nervously handed me my flute. With all of us ready, we turned to the television to watch the countdown.

"What's she like?" asked the truck driver.

"Who?"

He made a face of annoyance. "Welsey Shaw, who do you think?"

I had known who he meant but didn't want to talk about it anymore. I gave a vague shrug and turned away. He seemed miffed now. To my left, Ann was so engrossed in her conversation that I had to wedge a glass into her hand. She turned to me and smiled.

"Okay," said Sammi, lifting her own glass. "Eight. Seven. Six. Five. Four—"

I always spend moments like this thinking of all the things I hadn't accomplished and how the next year would be different.

"—Three. Two. ONE!" Cheers from everybody, a lot of noise from such a small group. Sammi whooped the loudest and smiled the most. Ann planted a very wet, very forceful kiss on my lips, then another, then another, nearly pushing me off my stool. "*Happy New Year,*" Sammi yelled. A few people blew noisemakers. Ann gave me yet another deep kiss and squeezed my cock.

"How come you don't ever visit me at work?" she asked, her alcoholic breath on my face.

"I don't need a new car."

"Yes you do." She laughed. For some reason so did Duane. Then she said, "I wonder what New Years is like on other planets."

6

"'*Parabéns a você* is happy birthday in what language?'" Welsey read.

"Portuguese," I said.

She looked at me, astonished.

"How on earth did you know that?"

I grinned like a Cheshire cat.

"Can you speak Portuguese?"

"A little," I said.

"Really? How much?"

"Enough to say 'Happy Birthday.'"

"Har-har. Your turn." She pushed the deck of cards at me. I shuffled them.

"Hey, I put an easy one on top."

"I know you did. Here we go. 'What's the only sport that was ever played on the moon?'"

She rolled her eyes. "Get out of here. Nobody ever played sports on the moon."

"Apparently someone did."

"Who?"

"I'm thinking it was some astronaut, probably."

"Oh, you're so funny today. I don't have the faintest idea. What was it?"

"Golf."

"Really?"

I showed her the card.

"'Apollo 14 commander Alan Shepard hit golf balls on the moon, February 6, 1971.'"

"I'm pretty sure they all landed in sand traps. All right, ask me another." I drew the next card. "'This aircraft set a speed record of 21 days when it flew around the world in 1929.'"

"Charles Lindbergh?"

"Charles Lindbergh is not an aircraft, Willamina," I said, using the name we'd agreed we would say in public.

"True."

"Does that mean you give up?"

"It does."

"The *Graf Zeppelin*!"

"Never heard of it. Okay, I'll get you." She shuffled. "'He was the first African American boxer to achieve world recognition.'"

I stared at the ceiling.

"Ha!" she grinned fiendishly. "Sports. Your Kryptonite."

"I surrender."

"Daniel Louis. —Ever hear of him?"

"Nope."

"Me neither." She handed the cards back.

I read. "'How much does a paperclip weigh?'"

"Formal protest—that's a ridiculous question. There are all sizes of paperclips." She moved her thumb and finger from half an inch to an inch to two inches.

I read from the card. "One gram."

"Move to strike that one."

"Denied. You've already passed your quota of strikeouts. Three per game."

"Okay, then game over. I won."

"How's that?"

"Because I said I did." She regarded the battered deck. "Where'd you get these?"

"Somebody left them here."

She put them in her bag. "I want to see if my friends are as smart as you are. How do you know so much shit?" she asked. "I mean, were you the teacher's pet? Lord of the nerds? Did all the other kids hate you?"

"Yes, yes, and yes."

"Ha! I probably would have beat you up in phys ed. Ripped off your gym shorts and pulled them over your head."

"Probably."

"I was pretty tough."

"I don't doubt it. Where'd you go to school?"

She might have slightly rolled her eyes. "Well, I was in—I had private tutors, obviously. There was no other choice, I mean." She said it almost apologetically. "I don't know what it's like to go to high school. The only prom I've ever been to was in a movie."

"You're kidding," I said.

She shook her head. "I didn't know how to kiss. The director told me to practice on the flabby part of my hand between my thumb and index finger."

Her phone rang. She fished it out of her bag, cupped her hand around it, and spoke, though she did more listening than talking, and her responses were mostly mono syllables. After a minute she tossed it into the Louis Vuitton, a bit violently.

"Did you like your childhood?" she asked after a moment. "Guys never admit to liking their childhood."

"Well," I said, then I paused. "I liked my childhood. Of course it could have been better. Whose couldn't have?"

"Mine!" she said. "Mine was perfect, absolutely perfect. I feel like my life exists in two parts. Part one: Fade in on the child, little blonde girl running though a grassy field, spinning and blowing bubbles. Second part, a few years older, in an alien world. No friends. That's why I did so bad at school. I hated my tutors, because they were the ones who'd taken me away from my friends. So I was determined to make life as rough as possible. I abused them. I knew my mom would side with me. She always did.

"I do regret one thing, though. One day," and she smiled, "I was really mad at this tutor, Miss Hutchinson. She always came to lessons with this giant thermos of apple juice, and she'd slurp it while I was doing work. So while she was away I took it out of her bag and emptied it into the sink. Then I refilled it with something else. But it overflowed and I made a mess all over the kitchen floor and she came back and saw everything and I started crying.

"I had no idea an eleven-year-old's bladder could hold so much."

"Did your mom side with you there?" I asked.

"Oh yeah. Miss Hutchinson got fired."

Welsey's phone rang again; this time she let it go to voicemail.

"You were a bitch," I ventured.

"Oh, God. Served me well where I was going, my mother used to say. But I do feel bad about Miss Hutchinson. A while ago I wrote her a letter, not apologizing exactly, but kind of asking how she was and what was she doing and if she remembered me." She laughed. "Never heard from her. Probably for the best, actually. I wouldn't talk to me again either. As it is, I don't get why people want to talk to me now, except for the obvious." She looked at me.

"Don't you like yourself?" I asked.

"Depends."

"On what?"

"A lot of things. Who's called me today. Who hasn't. What I've had to drink. Who sits next to me here…"

"Do you think you're a good person?" I asked, wondering where I was headed with this.

"That depends." She seemed to take the question seriously. "I don't know what a good person *is*. I mean, what's good? Who's good? Someone who says they are? Someone others say is? No one's good all the time. Sometimes I think no one's good at all, really, because you can't be. It's just a zero-sum game: good here, bad there. More niceness over here, less of it to give over there. It really has no meaning," she said almost defensively. "'Good what? Good why? Good how? But think of this: the bar isn't set the same. People expect more from certain people, for reasons they have no control over."

She took a swig of her coffee.

"All right, I'm a miserable shit."

What if it really *wasn't* her?

She looked like Welsey Shaw, made the requisite career references, had the appropriate neuroses and phobias. But she'd never actually said she was Welsey, never introduced herself by that name. She'd mentioned movie titles, benchmark moments in her life, facts known to everyone. What if she was some blonde taking me for a ride, having fun at my expense or the expense of others?

My doubts became so sharp that I actually got out of bed and did a search on the internet for celebrity impersonators. The sheer number of people who got off pretending to be somebody famous was simply mind-boggling. For some it was identity theft and material gain. Others seemed to have more "innocent" motives: They simply wanted to be the person they worshiped.

For half an hour I studied images of people who thought they resembled someone famous. One woman with thin lips and small eyes believed she was a dead ringer for Angelina Jolie. A battered man claimed to have won a Clint Eastwood contest, but he seemed at least 30 pounds too heavy. Gwyneth Paltrow's doppelgänger had brown eyes and a pug nose. I didn't think they could fool me. But who knows? I really wasn't sure what color Gwyneth Paltrow's eyes were.

I found a very large close up of Welsey Shaw and magnified it as much as I could, staring into it as though I were having a conversation. Did it look like the Welsey I sat across from?

Yes.

Exactly?

Yes.

No.

Those eyes, like cat's eyes, eyes that were impossible to see behind. The curve of the cheekbones. The long neck. The wide eyebrows.

How could it be anyone but Welsey?

I cropped the photo, enlarged it, and made it my computer wallpaper. Then I deleted it.

Then I put it back.

Then I deleted it again, and went back to bed.

"Are you insane?"

I didn't answer her.

"I'm not going to show you my driver's license."

"You can cover the address with your finger."

"My finger's busy right now."

"Well, how do I know you're really *her*?"

"Why the hell should I care?" A slow suck through the green straw. "If I act like her, if I look like her, if I'm the same, what difference does it make? Really?"

"Obviously you know it makes a huge difference," I said.

"Life is an illusion, Ferreira."

I opened my mouth before realizing I had no answer. What was I looking for? What was anyone that chased her looking for? It struck me they were looking more for themselves, for a reflection of themselves in her, rather than for anything that was her. How many Welseys were there? Could there be? The characters in her films? The spoiled brat who was popular in the entertainment press? The figure before me? The "real" Welsey?

"If you're not really her it makes a big difference."

"Why? I've got to have some secrets."

"So you do admit it matters, then."

"Sure it matters. That's what I hate. If they found something new that looked exactly like gold and had the same characteristics as gold, but chemical tests proved it wasn't actually gold," she said, "it wouldn't matter."

"Sure it would."

"No."

"Absolutely."

"Definitely not."

"Would you wear it?" I asked.

"I'm not stupid, Ferreira. There's good and then there's good. There are only a handful of people who know, who really know the difference. And I am one of them. I have to be. Most people don't. *And to them it doesn't matter.*"

I shook my head.

"Look at it this way. I'm DNA, just like you. I'm hair and skin and teeth and a few freckles and a freakish blemish somewhere you'll never know about. It's the same stuff everyone else has, except for the blemish. So what do you care if there's more? I'm what's in front of you. You're entitled to nothing more." She looked over to the watercolors hanging on the wall, one of which had a small SOLD dot now on it. "Take it or leave it."

"I should know if you're real," I said, thinking, just briefly, of how much these train tickets, every week, were costing me.

"No, Ferreira, I'm a fucking hologram."

"Why such a bitch today?"

"I thought you'd never get around to asking."

"I'm asking."

"I'm on *Late Night* tonight."

"Congrats?"

"I've been puking all morning."

"Puking?"

"I hate going on those TV shows. *Hate* it."

"Why?"

"I'm totally not in control in situations like that, and one misstep can put a third-degree burn on a career."

"Even one like yours, established and all?"

"Especially one like mine, established and all. That's what they want to derail."

"Who?"

"The 'celebrity journalists.'" I could hear the quotes of disdain around the phrase. "They love to build you up. That's how they make money. Then they love to tear you down."

Her phone rang. She took it outdoors, pacing the street in tight circles, head down. Then she dialed a number and talked for another five minutes.

"My dress is all ready," she said with mock excitement when she returned, sitting down again and hurling the BlackBerry into her bag. "They want something 'new.' A new story, a new anecdote, a new revelation: I'm afraid of spiders. I hate goat cheese. I have a huge crush on the lead guitarist of some band, but can't bring myself to approach him. They love it. But here's the thing—I can make them think they got something new without really telling them anything. I can sell fake intimacy. That's what it's all about, really.

"A manager once told me the point of it all was to make every male thirty-nine and younger fall in love with me every time I appear. Oh, really, he didn't say that," she whispered. "What he really said was to make them want to *fuck* me. I just don't feel like playing the game tonight."

I just looked at her, and she looked at me.

"Of course not all of them want that. They want to see you 'let your guard down.' We spend lots of time coming up with things I can say to make it seem like I'm letting my guard down."

She looked at a point past me, to the street outside.

"What they don't get is we never let our guard down. Ever."

I said nothing.

"But it can still make you puke, the fear of it."

"Of what?"

"Messing up."

Her eyes returned to me.

"Look, I can do mirror handwriting—you know, like Leonardo da Vinci."

"Never read that about you."

"Of course not. *That's* my revelation for tonight. That or my tipped uterus. My publicist vetoed the tipped uterus."

She produced a piece of cream stationary and started to write strange glyphs, smoothly and effortlessly. After a moment she got a mirror out of her bag and leaned it against the paper.

I am really, truly Wellesey Anne Shaw.

Then she wrote,

I was born July 25th in the year nineteen hundred eighty-four.

Then she wrote,

I would not lie to you.

The woman who appeared on my television that night was not Welsey Shaw.

All grace and fluid lines, eyes made to look several sizes bigger by expertly-applied makeup, she kissed Dave and shared a personal laugh in his ear. And watching the woman in the silver dress—chatting easily, telling funny stories, enjoying herself even when the camera wasn't on her—I began to wonder who I was looking at. The woman up there was taller, she definitely was taller. Her hair was longer and it was thicker and more flowing and *honey* blonde; it seemed it would glow if the lights went out. When I first met the person I took to be Welsey, I was struck by how different she looked from the movie star; now, watching TV, I was struck by how different the movie star looked from that woman. My worst fears were coming true. This was all bullshit. They were laughing at me; they were right.

How could I think I'd be sitting with a real, famous actress week after week for almost two months now, talking about *this* and *that*? Hearing revelations about her childhood? Was I that *stupid?* Yes. Did I feel like the dumbest fool I knew right now? Yes. Served me right. Jesus Christ, just look at that face. The difference was more than makeup and hairstyling could be responsible for, I told myself. I was clearly as dumb as they come.

Then we came back from a commercial break, and she started demonstrating her mirror handwriting...

7

How did Welsey not see me? She seemed oblivious. I stood, trying to attract her attention without drawing looks from others. I tried a small wave. I tried a larger wave. I tried staring straight at her with great intensity. I heard this worked for Rasputin.

She looked past me, face a blank mask. Then I saw her hand, folded into that of the guy behind her. He sported that stylish stubble that annoyed me so much and the sculpted features of a catalogue model. His body language telegraphed boredom, and hers mimicked his. This wasn't the curious being who watched everything and scribbled in notebooks. This was the movie star, too cool for Starbucks.

He gave her ass a pat, and she advanced in line; the casualness of the touching of her derrière sent a jolt to the pit of my stomach. Even I was surprised by its intensity. He just *did* it; it didn't seem…right.

I realized I knew that face but couldn't place it. Whoever he was, he was cutting into *my* Welsey time. And I was furious when he touched her ass. The surge in my gut actually surprised me. I knew her first!

They reached the front of the line, ordered, and blended into the wall until their drinks were ready. I tried one last time to catch Welsey's attention, even as I wondered why I was doing this. I love a challenge, I guess. But she was oblivious, talking to him. I so wanted to know what she was saying; he in turn was not saying much. A curt nod, a slight smirk, a quick glance at what I thought was me. I thought another ass-pat was coming, but instead he just reached for a napkin.

Now Welsey and her interloper were eying the paintings on the wall, the displays on the counters, the piles of napkins and straws. For some reason the sugar packets amused him, then her, as he showed her something about them that made her laugh. Hard. She'd never laughed that hard for me, though my comments had produced some impressive expressions of hilarity. She'd told me I was entertaining time and again. But as I looked up, she was still in hysterics. I wondered what you could observe about a sugar packet that could make someone laugh so hard. Sugar packets were boring, a dime a dozen. She had to be faking it. Had to be.

He grabbed a napkin and blew his nose into it. Welsey turned to the wall for this, pretending she didn't see. Mr. Cool then looked in my general direction again, and I put my head back down, pretending to be fascinated by something on my computer. My screen saver. Fish swimming.

He was probably ten years younger than me. More Welsey's age. Was it odd, some sort of ongoing interest between a 26-year-old and me, thirteen years her senior? No, because it was platonic. I wondered about the details of the definition, which gave me something to look at on my screen. Google told me my relationship with Welsey wasn't really platonic either, because I could hardly claim it was "intimate." I didn't know *how* to describe it, what to type into the computer. I tried "meeting actress for coffee once a week at coffee shop" and got directions to dozens of cafes and headshots of dozens of actresses, past and present. After a moment I decided there was no way to describe what went on, assuming it was still going on after today. Which I guess was why I kept coming back.

Welsey was disguised even more than usual, I noted, covered with a large knit cap as well as sunglasses, and a long black scarf. The guy, on the other hand, appeared to have no concerns with recognition, staring patrons in the eye with amusement and even smiling at and talking to a few, giving an elderly lady a gentle nudge and a smile, saying something that made her laugh just as Welsey had at the sugar packets. I decided he was too much of a jokester.

Welsey's drink required minutes of special instructions to the barista, a patient new guy with neat black combed-back hair and a huge earring. She made no conversation as he worked on her creation, leaning crookedly on one foot and checking her phone. Then, cup in hand, straw inserted, she made her way outside without another look in the direction of the tables, even though I foolishly tried yet another wave. Her guy held the door for her, and then for another couple just entering.

Was that it? Were our Wednesdays over? Was Starbucks just a quick stop now? Would she soon master that imperious coffeemaker from Holland?

Lying in bed that night, I remembered: Brett Davison. That's who he was. He was an actor, also had started as a child star, and was currently riding high with a TV show where he played a hunk of a surgeon from the future who traveled through time to save present-day people who had no cure for their ailments. To accomplish this he had to fake his identity and, of course, was nearly discovered at the 45-minute mark every time. For some inexplicable reason I'd watched it once, and thought it mind-bogglingly stupid. But I'm sure the show's demographic didn't notice the gaping plot holes, the improbable coincidences, the repetitious storylines; they just wanted Brett to escape back into the 23rd century unharmed and with his hair perfectly in place…

…Which he always did.

Welsey Shaw was showing me her butt. It was packed into a pair of skin-tight, ridiculously sexy jeans boasting a *WS* in glittering Swarovski crystals across the back pocket. They were "inspired by her," the creation of a big time fashion designer who said she was his "muse." The "Welsey" would sell for five hundred dollars starting this spring at exclusive you-have-to-be-buzzed-in boutiques, followed in the fall by the department store blitz, beginning in New York and L.A.

"There will be a bargain version where my initials are only stitched," she said.

I was still smarting from last week's encounter with her dreamy boyfriend-apparent but delighted that today she was displaying her lovely crystals for me.

"I put them on this morning, even though I'm not yet supposed to just wear them out. I should be careful. These were hand-made by the designer himself. There's markings inside that reveal the difference. It's one of only five." She pulled a bagel apart and crushed a piece of it, much like a child playing with food. "But screw it. I put them on because I needed a pick-me-up."

"Tough day at the office?"

"I just heard a rough cut of my latest movie is not what they were hoping for. That's how they put it. 'Not what they were hoping for.' Or as I put it, Oh fuck."

"The more direct translation."

"And someone spit on me the other day…"

I raised my eyebrows.

"…I think."

"You think?"

"Well I'm not sure if it happened or it was just in a dream. After a while, it's hard to tell what's real and what isn't," she said, turning the rest of her lunch into Play-Doh. "It can be scary sometimes."

"So what was the deal last week?" I asked.

"What do you mean?"

"Just what I said," I said.

"What do you mean?"

"Who was that person you were with who was so fascinating and distracting that you didn't even notice me?" I said.

"What do you mean?"

We watched a man empty about ten packets of sugar into his coffee.

"Future diabetic," I said. She nodded.

"And the week before that you were gone, away."

"It was Christmas week."

"You said you weren't going anywhere."

"I lied. Actually, I was vague. Throws bloodhounds off the scent."

"Where were you? Am I allowed to ask?"

"Havana."

"Havana...Cuba?"

She gave me a stare. "No, Ferreira, Havana Delaware! Yes, Cuba."

"How'd that come about?"

"I was invited." She patted her jeans.

"Just you?"

"A bunch of us," she said.

"He lives in Cuba?"

"No, he lives in Brazil. But he has a yacht that for two weeks was anchored off the coast of Cuba."

"Go on."

"What do you want to know?" —Coyly.

"What do you want to tell?"

"Let's see, I was picked up by helicopter."

"Helicopter?"

"A luxury helicopter. One of those jobbers with the propellers"—she made whirling motions with her fingers— "that can rotate vertical or horizontal, up-down or sideways. Had couches, TVs and a minibar inside." Huge smile. "That's something I'd never done before, flown in a helicopter, never mind one that's like a flying Ritz-Carlton. By a pilot in a tuxedo." A grin. "Andres. He said it's extra hard to fly a helicopter in a tuxedo. Who was I to argue? Everyone was flown in like that, by Andres and four other chopper pilots, from wherever they live."

"Who's everyone?"

She started ticking people off on her finger. "Fashion bigshots. Music bigshots. Piero's favorite singer—"

"Piero?"

She patted her knee again.

"Oh."

"—Several studio execs and their wives. Tech gurus he's partnering with. A few Wall Street types—" She rolled her eyes and flung her hands. "People who bored, bored *bored* the shit out of me. You have no idea how socially-backward the nerds were. The Wall Streeters think they know everything about everything. I think even Piero found them insufferable but he needs them."

"Poor Willamina."

"But there were a few cool people. The lead guitarist from a band I love. He gave me an autographed guitar. Red. I look hot playing it."

"You play guitar?"

"No. I said I *look* hot. —Oh, and there was an architect. I told him I want him to build my dream house someday. With my favorite frivolous necessity."

"Which is?"

"A car elevator."

"Do you have a car in New York?"

She leaned in a bit. "*Frivolous* necessity. We actually made some sketches of my perfect house! I just spitballed it. But I might have them framed, they're so good."

Did Brett Davison go with you? I wanted to ask. "So what did you do once you got to Cuba?"

"I drank. I ate. I drank some more. I danced to burn off what I ate and drank, but it didn't work, and I had to go lie down. Oh, and I smoked. Cuban cigars! Why the surprised face? I'm actually quite a cigar girl if they're good. We went down Paseo del Prado, where there are these great old buildings and shops."

"What's it like there?"

She thought. "Everything was old but everything was so beautiful. More beautiful than if it were new. You could forget who you are. It was a fantasy, albeit the fantasy of the very rich at the expense of the very poor. I drove! I barely ever drive, and I drove in Cuba. A 1957 T-Bird, blue with white vinyl seats! It's the first American car I've ever driven. Isn't that weird? They're from before the embargo. They lovingly restore them and polish every inch, and put American flag decals on them.

"The locals were so much fun. They'll just invite you into their house for some rum after they check you out for about five minutes. Can you imagine that here?"

I smiled.

"I danced with some Cuban guys at a small and incredibly hot night club." So Brett *wasn't* there… "I thought I would pass out. A kid and his dad. Both hit on me. The dad was sweeter. The kid was the better dancer. He could move! I was so clumsy next to him that eventually I gave up. I told him it was because of the heat, that I was normally a much better dancer. Oh, I wore a red dress that would have killed you."

"I don't like red dresses."

"Right."

"Did any of them know who you were?"

"Hell no. My films are banned there. But I could buy them on the street corner." She held up a blurry picture on her phone of a faded bootleg cover. Her name was spelled *Wesley*. "I could be anything to them. The young ones were the friendliest. I played street games with them. Soccer. *La rubia* they called me."

"The redhead?"

She frowned. "*Blonde!* Red is *roja*. Of course there was the one who called me *La rubia oxigenada*." Sly smile. "He thought I didn't know what that meant."

I didn't. "Didn't they wonder what you were doing there?"

"Nah. They didn't care. They just wanted us to buy stuff. I got to thinking one night when I was just wandering around that one purchase can mean the difference between eating and not eating that week. It's scary. It made me want to buy everything in sight. I bought things I had no interest in. I left most of them on the yacht. Piero laughed at me. He said I'm a bleeding heart, like his French wife."

"Most people might be surprised to learn that about you."

"Oh, Christ, most people would be surprised to learn so much about me, even people who know me well."

"Like Brett?" I wish I hadn't said it, but I couldn't stop in time.

"Like Brett," is all she said in reply.

"So he's in for surprises?" I wish I hadn't said it, but I couldn't stop in time again.

"Maybe with someone, but not me. We're done."

"Done?"

"Yesterday, as of three P.M."

"Why?" I heard myself asking.

"One of us was just a fling for the other. But I can't remember who was who" she said, affecting boredom. "Okay, enough of your nosey questions. Really, I talk to you way too much."

"Why do you put up with me?"

"Been askin' myself that a lot lately."

"Oh really?"

"Oh really. And it's way past time for me to go."

I decided to extend boundaries and see what would happen. Until now, I had never spoken to her, seen her, stood next to her, outside of the confines of this room. So I got up with her—synchronized standing. She looked a bit startled for one second. I walked with her to the door, a little awkwardly, as if I'd only recently learned how to put one foot in front of the other. She seemed to be looking for something in her pocket and I was trying to find some excuse to stay at her side. I wanted to see where she'd go. The wind blew. A truck's brakes squealed. Two women passed, one saying, "I should have *known* better than to trust that contractor with our bathrooms."

Approaching us from 49th was a slender, bony, pony-tailed woman walking an animal that could have been Chevron's body-double. She seemed in a hurry.

"That dog looks exactly like yours," I said. The thespian looked at me sideways, and shook her head slightly. The pony-tailed woman was maybe ten paces away when Welsey stuck out her hand and took the leash; the woman continued walking without breaking stride. After giving Chevron a quick pet, Welsey departed in the opposite direction without another word to me, digging out the BlackBerry and pressing it against her flowing yellow locks.

"Every Wednesday," the tall, dapper conductor said as he punched a hole in my ticket. "You're on my train every Wednesday."

I hadn't noticed him before. Indeed I'd thought different uniformed, flawlessly groomed Amtrak employees took my ticket each time, when I bothered to look. I particularly remembered a woman—tight ponytail, bee-sting lips—who effortlessly managed to eroticize her silly uniform with the men's necktie and make straight-legged loose pants look sexy. So I wondered how the current conductor, who strikingly resembled Neil deGrasse Tyson, had remembered me among the hundreds of faces he saw every week. But I liked how he personalized this vehicle as "his train." He felt a connection to the larger things around him, something it seemed to me was an increasingly rarer thing. Once upon a time baseball players made their careers with one team, symphony conductors with one orchestra, executives with one company. Today people changed allegiances regularly and had no attachment to anything. But we were supposed to believe in their loyalties that didn't exist a short time ago.

"Enjoy your ride," said the conductor as he ambled away.

Today's train was a tomb, even more so than usual. Usually I had some company; this time I was the only one in the car, save for an attractive woman wheeling a suitcase and several enormous binders of what looked like fabric samples. I'd said hello to her when I passed but she ignored me, instead pulling out a silver laptop and popping her gum.

The scenery slid by slowly.

"Just me. No reason to be alarmed," said Dr. Tyson, reappearing an hour and a half later behind me. "We'll be at Penn Station in about fifteen minutes. Make sure you take your umbrella, if you brought one."

"I didn't," I said.

"Well, it's only water. A lot of it this morning, but it's only water." Big laugh, as if he knew what I was in for and I didn't. Then he said, in a lower voice, "I sure hope she doesn't leave gum under her seat." He gestured around. "You wouldn't believe how much gum is under here."

"When I was ten my family threw me a big birthday party," Welsey was saying as Bottega Veneta tortoise shell sunglasses stared at me. "This huge cake, just huge, with jimmies and tons of icing. When I got to the west coast later that year we'd go into a bakery and ask for a cake with jimmies and they'd be like, 'What the hell are jimmies?' They call them sprinkles there. Wrong.

"All my friends were at this party. I got tons of presents. A Barbie townhouse. G.I. Joe, which I wanted because Barbie needed a boyfriend, one her dad wouldn't approve of. Ken had too much of a suburban sensibility." Welsey made twisted paper sculptures with sweetener packets as she talked.

"That party lasted all day. My dad could do magic tricks better than anyone you could hire. Years later I tried looking them up in magic books, and I even asked a real magician once, and he didn't know. Really, I never have found out how he did some of the tricks he did.

"My dad was amazing. Still the smartest man I've ever known. Not college-smart but smart, holds a bunch of patents, can fix anything. He came up from Raleigh to be with us every weekend. We were living in South Jersey at the time. This was after New Rochelle."

"Why didn't you all go down to Raleigh?"

"My mother didn't want to leave the shore. That was kind of the beginning."

"The beginning of what?"

"Of the end for them."

"Can I ask what broke your parents up?"

Welsey shrugged and stared at the table in front of us. "Me. They both wanted something different for me. And for themselves. I don't know. What breaks anybody up? Anyway, the party, the birthday party, went till evening. It was supposed to end at eight.

That's what we'd told all the parents. But my dad said, 'We're going to a movie!'" She laughed at the memory. "So all twenty of us piled into something like four cars. We owned this old station wagon with wood paneling—" I smiled; my family had the exact same car. "He was feeling so good that he bought a ticket for everyone in line and sodas and everything, and we saw a double-feature monster movie that lasted till midnight. When we got home some of the parents were calling us in a panic, wondering why their kids weren't back yet. They'd been watching the news reports. Dad called every one of them back and made them laugh with the story of how we all went to the movies, and it was longer than expected because the film broke. Seriously, can you imagine the last time you were in a theater and the film broke?

"When my dad put me to bed that night he gave me the biggest kiss and just said, 'Happy birthday.' That was it. That was all he said, but I still remember exactly the way he said it. It's still one of the most special things anyone's ever said to me.

"The next afternoon the phone rang. It was really hot that day, and we had this window-box air conditioner that was barely working and then the power went out and there was a kind of creepy silence, you know, that you get when the power suddenly goes out, and it's summer and there are no other sounds because nobody is outside since it's a hundred degrees. And then the phone rang and that made me jump. Somehow I just knew it was something big, something life-changing, something scary. My mom answered. I remember how nervous she was. Someone from a studio wanted to meet me. Next week I saw my first palm tree and read a scene in a script and cried on command while people kept being brought in to see how well I did it, over and over again.

"And it was years before I realized what a great, really fucking great birthday party that had been."

She took a long sip and looked at me.

"Maybe it really wasn't. Maybe we didn't all go to the movies.

Maybe he sucked at magic. But that's how I remember it."

Her lips tightened and she flicked at a piece of paper with her finger. "I don't know why I'm telling you all this."

First it had been soaps. Lots of them, each of which did different things, scrubbing away different parts of skin. They were joined by moisturizers, then shampoos. An electric toothbrush appeared. Lint roller. Sponges. Her contact lens kit. Her other contact lens kit. A slanting stack of *Working Mother* magazines (which made me do a double take) leaned against my sofa. DVDs of *The Jane Austen Book Club* and *Bridget Jones's Diary*. Her dog-eared copy of *Eat, Pray, Love*. Hand sanitizers. Vitamins. I never knew there were so many types of vitamins. Ann did.

Then it was clothes. Cassettes. (Ann still listened to cassettes, most of which she got from Goodwill.) Her little tins of tea came over and joined my five pound can of coffee. Free space went the way of the dodo bird. The shelves in my living room, dining room and spare bedroom were already bowed from albums, books, movies, and magazines, because, despite the thick-but-fragile cable in the back of my computer that opened onto the world at large, I held on to physical artifacts, still got much of my information from print and paper, still collected vinyl, because these hold memories in a way that bits on a screen do not. So that I understood.

But Ann...Ann saved mash notes from grade school, homework assignments that had earned gold starbursts at the top of the page, clothes she'd long outgrown, books she no longer liked, dolls she played with when she was eight. The pockets of her coats were filled with ticket stubs and movie receipts. A Canadian coin received in change on the day she'd met the man she'd married for five years (Michael Cleary, now a professor at Michigan State) was still, even after the divorce, a keepsake.

I on the other hand enjoyed the wholesale purging of my life on regular occasions. Each ride to the dump was a joyous journey, because of the ease with which I could eradicate memories. I didn't like looking back. On my last sortie I even nearly tossed that high school yearbook ("*I expect big things from you*") but it got a reprieve. I'm still not sure why. Maybe it was Mr. Reynolds' smiling face.

Ann was away for the weekend, helping Roz prep for some musical event. I got to rattle around the house alone, using the quiet time to root through old boxes and blow dust off of those really high shelves I rarely delve into. Outside, the roads had frozen over, and both Roz and Ann had decided to splurge and split a hotel room rather than venture back home. If the weather reporter on TV turned out to be right they might spend tomorrow there as well. I pulled back the curtains of the big picture window to look at frozen water droplets on tree branches lit by a full moon. Cold air from outside seeped in. The snow sparkled like sugar. The lawn, River Road, the frozen Delaware—it was all gorgeous, far more gorgeous than it should have been; Callicoon, like New York, looked better dark, highlighted by moonlight. Many people's front doors, I would find out later, had frozen shut. With much effort, I pushed my own open to a perfect stillness. "Hello?" Nothing, not even an echo came back. Times like this made me feel as though my life's deadlines were being extended. There was no wind, no movement, so time had stopped, right? The cosmos was begging me to stop thinking, stop doing, and be a spectator.

Such dreaming led me over to my bookshelves. Those four pieces of furniture dominated the room, stuffed so tightly I sometimes feared they might snap. No knickknacks, because serious bookshelves do not have knickknacks. Among the titles were my four remaining copies of *Heaven's People*: I still loved the cover, which I felt hadn't dated a bit. The dust jacket was made of thick, glossy paper and was very beautiful. I stared for a long time at the title, then opened to page one: *This is the story of four people—John, Angelica,*

Paula, and Cornelius. At the beginning of this story, where you are and where I am, neither of us knows what's in store for these four people. Normally the author has everything planned out, but this time you will learn what happens to John, Angelica, Paula, and Cornelius when I do; we will discover their destiny together. There are no notes. No plans. No roadmap. Because life isn't like that, and stories shouldn't be either.

I kind of felt that's how my own life had been. No plan. I didn't need one; plans were for lesser people, those who mapped out every twist and turn at 22 and followed each one until, at 30, they were married, had two kids and a house with a hot tub and barbecue out back, a 4Runner in the driveway and a DVD player that never got a rest. I'd also ignored all the planning others tried to do for me, thinking by dint of IQ life would serve up something special. It had to. It had for all my heroes.

And maybe it had, and maybe I held it in my hands. I sat in my leather recliner and stared out at the white-on-black stillness, before starting on *Heaven's People* for the fifth time in my life. By 3:00 A.M. I'd gotten nearly two-thirds through and jammed a Peck's receipt inside chapter 20, tossing the book into the dented cushion of my chair and stretching stiff legs. I suddenly realized the house was freezing.

The next day, roads still frozen over, neighborhood still paused, I finished the book.

The ice and snow in Callicoon had translated to rain in the city. The sidewalks were still tricky as I watched a man carrying his lunch in a paper bag slip and fall in spectacular fashion, ejecting a sandwich and fries into the street; the birdies now had something to eat.

Where was Welsey this time? Maybe the rain had slowed her? Maybe, once again, she wasn't coming. Maybe it was over. She was tired of me, tired of this. Our last couple of conversations had been a little boring: too many pauses. Now there'd be no way to contact her ever again. I kept thinking about that as customer after customer entered, none of them Welsey.

Outside, New York hustled by. The rain made everyone move at double speed; it was like watching a movie in fast-forward, as umbrellas flapped, trench coats blew and loose newspapers flew by. But the figure that moved past my window still was not moving fast enough so that I did not recognize it as the assistant, the dog-walker. I think she was wearing the same beige outfit as the other time I saw her. Her hair was tied in the same pony tail.

She was headed up East 48th. With nothing better to do I jumped up and was outside, trailing behind her. Perhaps she was headed toward Welsey. Perhaps she would solve the mystery of where Welsey was today, on *our* day, after I'd come a hundred miles to see her. Her walk had purpose like none I'd ever seen before. Perhaps she was shopping for the boss; what sort of errands would the slave of the world's most famous actress be running? What would Welsey want, and would they be the same as other people's wants—dry cleaning, groceries, a drugstore run—or extraordinary wants, the wants of the special? Could they even be ordinary if they were for her? Did the very fact that she was who she was make her assignments different?

I slowed; she crossed Madison and continued along 48th. On the off chance she'd notice me, I decided I'd hide behind the abundant construction scaffolding along the way. She jaywalked across Fifth Avenue, doubling her step; indeed it was tough keeping up with her. Walking past high-end stores I expected her to enter, she instead headed through Rockefeller Plaza and cut a right into Dean & DeLuca.

Inside, the fat lady was singing. Italian opera played while ceiling fans did a choreographed spin at just the right speed for the music. Suddenly my mouth found itself watering for all sorts of edibles I normally don't care for: glazed hams, oyster stew, Tuscan table olives and anchovies. The way they arranged the merchandise just *made* you want it, as though the store generated some sort of magic field that increased desire. I looked at the assistant, who concentrated on her task as though she were Garry Kasparov pondering Deep Blue. She nabbed black truffles in olive oil, various smoked meats, about eight different kinds of cheese, Beef Wellingtons, and boxes of some very fancy iced butter cookies. I stayed just behind and tried to peer over her shoulder, but she turned and looked right at me. I reached out and pretended to grab a tin of cocoa as though it were the find of the century. She continued on her task without regarding me further. Welsey had expensive taste, if it was Welsey she was shopping for, and everything came in the smallest of containers.

Finally the tall and efficient lady blew past me to the register. After a moment $586.94 appeared, and she swiped a card.

I ditched my can of chocolate powder. The clerk kept his eyes locked on me as I followed the woman out the door. I imagined a phone call as soon as I left, "A strange man came in here, didn't buy anything and is now following you," a courtesy they probably extended to their best customers.

I followed the assistant back down East 49th to Park, where she crossed and went left. I had to step around plastic garbage bags strewn across the sidewalk; later Welsey and I would be brought closer by, of all things, garbage, and I'd have the most memorable night of my life, one I've told no one about since, because no one would believe me. But that's months away. Today her employee and I walked up Park for nine blocks, winding me while she bounced on thin legs. I was sweating, feet throbbing from walking so far so fast. Finally at the corner of 59th the sleek silhouette entered a building, nodding to a doorman looking ridiculous in white gloves and a matching bow tie. The building was old, very likely from the teens or 20s, ashine with gold, glass and, above the street level, brick. Impressive as it was, it also needed a good scrubbing.

After about five minutes, the assistant reemerged with Chevron and began to walk down Park.

From relative safety across Park Avenue I continued to watch. I don't know what I expected to see. I was not thinking clearly. I was not thinking at all. I was just staring at the place where I realized Welsey Shaw, one of the most reclusive celebrities, spent her day-to-day life.

People came and went in an almost constant stream; where were so many residents going in the middle of the day? To each inhabitant the doorman gave his same smile, nod and hat-tip, touching the brim with his first two fingers. Eventually he noticed me staring from across the street. He looked at me with a partly defensive, partly curious expression. We exchanged glances for several stoplight cycles.

Then he went back to nodding and tipping his hat.

I now owned seven Welsey Shaw DVDs. Ann would wonder why, so I hid them, ingeniously. A master thief with a resume of purloining the Louvre couldn't find them. There was a spot, see, between two walls, a gap, in the spare bedroom hidden by wood trim. When I was young, porn went there. Kids today can hide downloads on their computers, cake; they aren't as ingenious as I. Ann would never find my stash.

Where to keep all the tabloids when Ann was over was more problematic.

Buying them was equally tricky. I knew every cashier at Pecks, which wasn't hard to do, and they all knew me. And Ann. In small towns, everyone knows everyone's business. That's how it feels, anyway. So I had to target either stores outside Callicoon or Peck's cashiers who didn't work the shifts Ann and I were typically there, so they wouldn't wonder why I was buying a half-dozen trash papers about Welsey Shaw topless at Waikiki Beach after she'd just dumped boyfriend X or had an abortion. I finally settled on Sundays, when Betty Lau typically worked the first checkout lane. She did everything with her eyes closed.

I knew what Ann thought of tabloids, and the people who wrote for them, and the people who read them. "My dad says that's why America's in such decline," she'd said once. "I'd never date a man who read them." I confess with shame I really wanted to know how much of the gossip was true. I now watched the supplements on all of Welsey's DVDs, something I never used to do, to see her praise colleagues I knew she disdained. *Kissy-kissy*. Often the featurettes contained better acting than the movie. "I was astonished by the range of ---'s genius," she said of a writer-director she considered a total hack.

The silence this evening as I cooked and Ann sat in the living room was a mystery until I saw her with some of the tabloids, pulled out of hiding and unfolded on the coffee table. She looked up, looked at me, and I was unable to hear anything for several seconds.

"What are these?"

"Just junk I should throw out," I said, going back to the kitchen.

After some minutes Ann asked, "Who do these people think they are?"

I poked my head out the door. "Who?"

Ann was reading one of the papers, stretched out on the sofa, pages raised above her head. "'I would rather smoke crack than drink soda from a can.' So someone mailed her a bottle of Pepsi. That was witty."

"You don't like me to drink soda either," I pointed out.

"Yeah, but she's different. She doesn't have to worry about the things you do."

"Why not?" I asked.

Ann folded back the page, nearly crumpling it in the process. She was never very good with maps either; she'd mutilated several of mine, managing to tear them at the folds as she put them away. "Say, what's your favorite movie? You've never told me."

I emerged from the kitchen again. "I don't have a favorite movie."

"Everyone has a favorite movie," Ann insisted.

"Not me."

She kicked off a powder pink shoe and watched it fly across the room. "Remind me I need to get new shoes from Payless this weekend. These are killing me."

"Noted."

"Well my favorite movie is *Singin' In The Rain*. Good mornin,' good *mor*nin'…" she began. I always hated that song.

"That's my favorite movie," she announced.

My favorite movie was now *Mystery at Alessandro Creek*. But I couldn't tell her that.

I knew today's time with Welsey would be short.

She was in a rage about something. About what I knew not, but every few minutes her phone would ring, and she'd step outside and shout into it.

She returned and threw the phone into her bag so hard I thought it might break. I decided it might be best to ignore her, and work. Yet when I opened my laptop she seemed irritated by that too.

"Am I boring you?" she asked, pushing her hair off her face. Well, too bad."

The BlackBerry rang. This time she didn't leave. For five minutes she cupped her hand and leaned away from me, doing more talking than listening. I strained to hear until, call finished, she turned to me: "There are some people who should go straight to hell," she said. She threw the phone into her bag again.

—Only she missed. I felt it hit the top of my shoe, bounce silently, and land next to my foot.

I didn't react.

"I'm gone," she announced, not even really talking to me. She heaved her bag over her shoulder, took a last sip, and threw her cup at the trashcan the way she'd thrown her phone at her purse. "Fuck," was the last thing I heard her say.

I waited a few minutes, expecting her to reappear, expecting her to ask about the phone. I would pretend to look around, pretend astonishment. "Lucky you came back," I would say. That's what I would do.

But I didn't have to.

She didn't reappear. Not a minute later, nor five, nor ten. So I reached under the table. Slowly. Casually, or as casually as you can reach under a table while you're watching people who may be watching you. My fingers found the power button, pressed and held; the screen went blue, then black, then blacker. I looked behind me. Nobody there. I looked out the window facing 48th. Nobody there either. The phone slid into my bag easily, as if it wanted to be there. Then I sat and worked a while longer, no longer thinking about what I'd done, as if that could divorce me from having done it. Then I pretended to notice the time, packed my computer, and walked out. I practically sprinted down Park Avenue to the train station.

8

First came the photos. Hundreds of them. Welsey on countless sandy beaches. Welsey on the water: sailboats, motorboats, yachts. Welsey in England, the London Eye over her shoulder. Welsey watching a bullfight. Welsey with a group of men in lederhosen, holding beer steins. Scuba diving with friends. On a hotel balcony. With many tuxedoed men in front of some building. With the same men inside, grinning broadly. Attending a fashion show, seemingly with every famous person on the planet, in a form-fitting red leather dress. In the Bahamas. St. Barts. Maui.

At some tropical port of call. A stock car race. In front of a fancy building—some sort of fundraising event. Trying on wigs in a shop. Riding a Vespa. Posing between two mannequins. Sitting on a fuchsia sofa (hers?) eating a bag of corn chips, crumbs on her lips. Holding Chevron. Playing with Chevron. Lots of pictures of Chevron.

Pictures of other people: Musicians. Lawyers. Political figures. People I didn't recognize, but who were probably important. A famous chef. Another famous chef. A third famous chef. There were lots of famous chefs.

Then there were just pictures of what appeared to be ordinary friends, mostly female, mostly doing nothing.

More photos, these inside her gorgeous apartment, or inside somebody's gorgeous apartment: Welsey sprawled out on the couch, coffee table covered with all manner of drinks, Welsey the only one in the group not smiling. Pictures from some sort of costume party, people wearing paper headdresses and posing like Egyptian statues. In another set of shots, she stood clutching her Oscar, flanked on each side by friends who bowed down to her.

I had Welsey Shaw's BlackBerry in my hand.

Then I discovered the nude photos. Real ones this time. I don't even know why they surprised me, but somehow they did. And she was right: her areolas were nicer. In one of them her hands were loosely cuffed in front, a dog leash between her teeth, face fierce. Another appeared to have been taken at a ski resort. The naked actress cupped her breasts in front of a frosted picture window, icicles hanging outside, snow piled high. There were also a bunch of stunning black and white shots in half-light, apparently taken by a professional, that managed to be erotic as hell.

Because it was Welsey Shaw's, it didn't seem like an ordinary BlackBerry. Somehow the keys looked bigger. The chrome around it appeared brighter. It felt heavier. After some navigational cluelessness, I found and opened the address book, scanning it for names of famous people. Nothing. I wondered if they were really under made-up names. Maybe she had a key somewhere, a cipher that would reveal incredibly powerful, important people. Who would answer if I dialed the number at the tip of my thumb? Would it be perhaps Steven Spielberg? His assistant? His housekeeper?

There were dozens of routine listings, too. Six doctors. Four pharmacists. Three vets. Several nail salons and a pet groomer who made house calls. Event planners. Catering companies, florists, chocolatiers, travel agents by the dozen. Every major department store and boutique. Specialty food stores. Lots of restaurants that delivered, everything from deli to sushi. Dry cleaners. Two personal assistant services. An obedience school called The Bow Wow Wowhaus. The Las Vegas and Los Angeles Chambers of Commerce. Photography studios. Cosmetologists. Spas. Two astrologers. A note under one: *Do not use again. Not accurate!!*

A video showed her lip-synching and dancing around the room with a friend. In another she was trying to play an old piano somewhere. Next she was driving in a hilly location with an ocean view, the video taken by someone in the back seat. Rounding a turn, she nearly sideswiped a van; there were screams followed by nervous laughter. She blew out candles on a cake; she fired a gun on a rifle range; she played Pictionary with unseen friends.

There were two videos of a garden tour and one of one of those famous chefs whipping up a salmon mousse. At one point the man says, "A cooking show, Wels. That's what you have to do with me, a cooking show." "The first cooking show from someone who doesn't know how to cook!" was her off-camera reply.

I'd been sitting in my armchair for hours, exercising little more than my thumb. My thighs were numb. I shifted position and nearly got a cramp. The bathroom called. I pulled myself up and realized I was clammy. My clothes were soaked through, my body smelled dank. I hadn't turned on any lights since I got home, in late afternoon, and as the sun set her tiny screen became the only source of illumination in the house.

I might as well state I didn't feel bad about what I was doing. I hadn't stolen her phone but merely picked it up after she dropped it; had another person found it things would have been infinitely worse for her. Someone else would sell her information. With me, it was safe.

Welsey apparently loved games. Dozens of them were on her BlackBerry. Her calendar, on the other hand, was surprisingly bare, at least this year, which is as far back as it went. Aside from doctor and salon appointments, lots of vet visits, and a few trips, her days were largely empty weeks at a time. She was an avid writer of short emails. There may well have been over a hundred. Marlena the housekeeper received the brunt of the short ones, most of them either neutral or curt—instructions or, mostly, criticisms, none of them devastating but the cumulative effect when reading through the list was that Welsey was impossible to please.

There were folders for many places and people. "Dr. Bradshaw" stood out because it was in all caps. I clicked. Inside were other folders as well as files galore, many of them invoices. One was labeled "Checklist." Another read "Exposure Practice forms" and still another said "Panic identifiers." "Exercises" was written with a space between each capital letter, E X E R C I S E S. But what really caught my eye was the one labeled "Ferreira."

I just stared at it. Yes, there was a folder in Welsey's phone with my name on it.

Ferreira.

I actually didn't want to look. What if it angered me? Or disappointed? What if it couldn't compete with my imagination? Maybe she knew another Ferreira. Maybe she utterly hated me.

I stared at the folder for maybe a minute. Probably closer to ten seconds.

Ferreira. Ferreira. Ferreira! I swallowed and clicked.

That's when everything went black.

The closest store was in Jeffersonville, a brick and aluminum structure that used to be a house or maybe still was a house. It's easy to miss if you didn't see the very small, barely-visible-from-your-car wooden sign. Fortunately I'd Google street-viewed it in the morning, and I knew exactly what to look for.

I was on a bridge out of Callicoon when I lost road feel. The Volvo slid right. Or the road slid left. I jerked the wheel. Nothing. I positioned the wheel straight ahead, which I'd read was how you got out of a skid. Nothing. I hit the side of the guardrail, pinballed past the ROAD FREEZES WHEN WET sign and ended up facing the direction from which I had come. I cautiously did a U-turn and maneuvered back into my lane. That's when I heard the sound—*bup-bup-bup-bup-bup-bup*—that seemed to come from my wheel well. I tried to imagine how bad the damage was. Then I tried not to.

I parked and inspected the car. The right fender was bent, and it scraped against the tire. That was the source of the noise. Other than that things seemed okay, not counting the mangled hubcap.

I entered the store, noticing for the first time that I was shaking. A bird-like man sat behind the counter next to a space heater, eyes closed, head bobbing to Paul Desmond's airy alto on a boom box held together with duct tape. The whole store actually, was held together with duct tape. "I need a charger for this," I said. He squinted at the BlackBerry, picked up the phone, and started dialing the police. "This belongs to Welsey Shaw," he said, locking the door so that I couldn't get out. "I'm calling the police." When my mind snapped back, I saw him rifling through some bubble packs on the back wall. "This one," he mumbled. "Are you sure?" He gave me a cool look, to say I shouldn't question his many years of standing behind the counter. "How much?" He pointed to the Day-Glo orange sticker on the front. "Twenty five. Just like it says. No credit cards."

On the return trip only one headlight reflection greeted me when I turned into the garage. I wondered how much all this would cost to fix and decided not to think about it. I'd get used to the *bup-bup-bup* eventually.

In the house I connected the charger before even taking off my coat, reviving the phone back from the dead. The folder with my name on it was still there.

Ferreira.

Welsey Shaw had a folder on her phone about me.

I opened it.

Dec 9

Day 1. Just trying to get comfy for now. Don't know who I'm going to approach yet, I keep looking but don't know why, know what I'm looking for. Know I'm not supposed to look for anything, but I keep finding reasons each person isn't right. Who knows. This is hard. This is not fair. Why did I say I'd do this? Oh, that's right, because I'm your bitch at $450 an hour, that's why.

I can't sit still when people pass me, look at me or in my direction, even if they're really looking at someone passed me. Sometimes I get so scared around people I don't think I'll get back to my apartment without help. Today was one of those days. I even tried calling you. One guy appeared again who I met last week. We had a little dustup and then he became a total asshole to me. Today he was back and I think I handled him well. I tried to tell myself he's not typical and I'm sure he's not, so mostly I ignored him. He tried to pretend we were real familiar. A for effort. He's not afraid to talk to me, and I mean as a person not as a movie star.

Dec 16

Went up to a grand total of three people today. It got harder each time. Felt like a pretty long hour! Most people aren't friendly beyond basics. I made the most progress with the guy from last week. We actually sat together, just briefly. It definitely feels funny, though, because I know absolutely nothing about the way anybody lives even though I watch them and pass them and make small talk with them every day. What shall I talk about? And how do I come off? Could I survive in the world that everyone else lives in? I don't know. I've never filled out a job application. Really. I went to a store that sells handbags the other day and asked for one. I had no idea they asked so many questions for a stupid part-time job. And then they never called anyway. People go through this to work in ordinary jobs anyone could do? It's insane that this is what the people out there around me all go through. Until recently I had no idea. Fucked up.

Dec 30
Sat w/that same guy fr 2 weeks ago. Wasn't unpleasant actually. He made me laugh a few times. Place was packed and after a while that made me uneasy, claustrophobic, and it just got worse so I cut it short and left. Halfway to the goal. Half is something.

Jan 2
Woo-hoo! Freezing outside. I knew right off the crowds in Star$s wouldn't leave and finding a table would be fucking impossible. But I talked to him for nearly 3/4 hour! (Of course he was there.) Said he just likes to work here. Then he spent the whole time watching me! What did it feel like? Good! Was able to talk to him without any panic. We talked about pretty normal everyday things, I think, and I think I actually enjoyed it. It may have been the one true conversation I had all week. Kept thinking about it for days.

Jan 6

This time I invited him over to my table. How's that for progress??? Aren't you proud?

His name is Daniel and he's from like 2 hours away and he comes all the way here. He's a writer. Didn't get the impression he was married or had a family. Pretty smart, I think. He knows all kinds of silly shit but he's socially clueless.

Jan 13

Me and Daniel again. Didn't need my dog with me or my bag on the table between us.

This guy is awkward in the extreme. But he does makes me laugh pretty hard. He can be funny the way dad can. Funny makes me weak. I actually enjoyed today, felt like I belonged, stress-free.

Jan 20

We talked about many different things this time, all of it deliciously normal. Its not a total normal conversation. He pretends to be cool, but he's not, and his attempts to hide his unsophisticated ways are amusing at times. And I think he maybe pretends to be less impressed then he is. He's never mentioned my movies or asked for an autograph, but I know it's in the back of his head. I sort of want him to ask, but that might mean I'd have to move on to another person, right?

Feb 10

Gradually I've become more comfortable in situations where I am not the one in control. This came to me after sitting with D today (we people-watched and he made some pretty amusing jokes) where I went into an elevator with crowds of people and rode up and down for like 15 mins while people crowded all around me, getting on, getting off, brushing against me, asking me to push the buttons, etc. Was all good. I liked it, liked being out of control was almost sexually arousing. Afterward I was sweating but it was a good sweat, like an exhilarating sweat.

Feb. 17
Sweetheart, I can't give out my phone number, show you my driving license, or tell you where I live. Get real!
But that was the only down thing today. Truth is we had a really fun convo in which I relaxed quite a bit. Took the train and sat next to people, deliberately bumped some of them even, asked a few for directions to places I already knew. Talked to a cop for ten minutes and he had no idea it was me even though we were standing in front of a movie poster with my face on it.

Feb 24
What the fuck are people all doing charging their phones and computers? Am I the only person who's got electricity at home?
Another day. Another Daniel. I am really becoming too accustomed to this.
We talked about my life today, about his life today (about mine more), and really enjoyed ourselves. He makes me laugh and I think I have finally had a day where I felt like what I believe a normal *person would feel like in the outside world, walking around, not on guard, not being afraid all of the time.*
Sometimes, when I'm a paranoid star, which is to say all the time, I feel like every thing I do is being recorded. So I am scared. Scared when I go out. Scared home alone,

because there are cameras, cameras in the building, in the elevator, how do I know they dont save the videos with me in it and watch it themselves? This is a fucked up way to live, but its reality. I would like to have the courage not to give a damn about anything. The funny thing is, this is what people already think I do, even though I feel like I am careful with everything I say, every word I utter. Words no longer disappear into the air. I imagine coming home and finding investigators standing around my stuff and they say "we have reason to believe this computer was involved in criminal activity" and they take it away and look through it. And they see my whole life, these strangers, and I can't take it back because it's out there. And tomorrow everyone else will know it too and my life will be a total open book and people will use innocent things against me in ways I cant even imagine now. Jesus H. Christ…

Mar 17
Talked much longer than I intended today. Almost missed appointment w a lawyer. Why am I doing this? The anxiety I use to feel about the outside world has vanished. That doesn't even make sense, but its true.
He understands me well…not that Ive told him this, and I wouldn't tell him this. I can't tell sometimes where our thoughts begin and end. Cant imagine him outside this environment, but maybe that's the point of it all. Maybe I need to hit the reset button, dont you think? Next weeks the first day of spring…

Mar 24
We're getting into things I never told anybody about before. I guess that makes it a success to you but I'm getting a level of intimacy ("Intemessy" my friend Persephone liked to call

it. God I miss her.) I never intended and I dont have the slightest idea why *my damn tongue is so loose when, its only hours later when I go home and recall all the stuff. I have to check myself: I'm starting to really care about what he thinks.*

Since we're not supposed to go into my real world with him, maybe I should start this whole thing again with someone new. Probably my fault, since I made the mistake of losing sight of the point of this whole exercise. I didn't set out to really become his friend, and while these conversations across the table are fun, really how far can they go? So maybe I need to find some way to break it off. I know I should. We both know I should, right?

9

Well then, fuck you too.

I didn't go back to the City the following week. Instead I sat in my kitchen and watched an egg boil, Mendelssohn and Sarah Vaughan keeping me company. I have no idea what she did. Maybe she went. Maybe she didn't. Maybe she talked to someone else, another adjunct to her head-doctor's experiment on anxiety suppression.

I was no less guilty. I'd been so eager to part the celebrity shrubs. I had been thinking she'd have this complicated life—like latticework—but maybe she didn't.

I thought about this after eating my egg, staring out the kitchen window watching a neighbor fueling up his mower for the first official grass cutting of the season. I thought about it as I procrastinated cutting my own. I thought about it over the weekend, while Ann knitted a sweater for Matt & Audrey's toddler (they both worked at the dealership, he in service, she part-time at the front desk). I still thought about it as I stared up at the otherwise unremarkable building at 59th and Park. I stood for fifteen minutes and let my imagination pour through those walls, not caring what my brain told me about Welsey Shaw, myself, or anything else. Sometimes brains should shut up. Movie stars were America's royalty because we live in a land where we're told we're all equal, yet we're constantly flogged to "get ahead," and measured by the size of our toys and the toys of our acquaintances.

Welsey Shaw was in that building somewhere, doing things unique to her and her life. It was funny: she was rich, but had no lawn to mow. She was famous, but was in a small concrete box up there cut off from the world. Ann's comment Sunday, "Oh look, Naked Ladies," causing me near-whiplash as I turned my head, was something she'd never experience, unless she ordered a botanical garden shut down so that she could have her own tour. Maybe she didn't want to see flowers, unless they were in St. Bart's.

I put my right hand on my hip and was immediately bumped from behind. "Sorry," a voice said to the pavement before I realized. Hoodie and sunglasses, but no dog. I gritted my teeth and started following. Halfway down the next block she stopped at a window display. A truck passed between us, and when it cleared—Where'd she go? I hovered between rushing forward to find her and staying back so she wouldn't see me. Rushing forward won. I reached the store and saw her inside looking at luggage along a back wall. The sales clerk, a young, impossibly-tall olive-skinned woman of exotic origin and delicate cheekbone, didn't see me, and neither did Welsey. The actress examined everything thoroughly, taking a lot of time with the straps and zippers. Then she moved closer to the window, which made me step to the curb. She fingered a brown wallet, studying it with furrowed brow. She asked the girl something, first pulling up her glasses so that there'd be no doubt who she was. They talked a while, the clerk nodding a lot, before the younger woman picked up a phone. A moment later a second clerk emerged from a back room with a few other wallets, in brown, black and tan; the three conferred, heads bowed, like surgeons over a body. What one could talk about for ten minutes regarding four wallets I couldn't imagine. In the end Welsey whipped out a card, bought all four, and watched as each was wrapped in tissue paper and set aside with tags and brightly colored boxes.

I hid myself some distance away as she emerged, redonning her shades and resuming her walk at a faster pace. Next stop was a jewelry store. I circled across the street, even holding my fist to my ear so that I appeared to be on a phone call. When I crossed back and looked toward the window she was discussing a timepiece with a bearded man. Again lots of nodding. An assistant by his side—twenty if a day—appeared to be taking notes. Welsey concluded her business and turned quickly, sending me into a crowd of passersby. After she was gone I entered and went to the same counter, trying to look casual as I located the watch she had been handling, a watch with intricate detail, sparkling in the light. "Can I help you?" the bearded man said in a tone that said he was doubtful. "I wanted to know, I was wondering about the pricing on that one," I said, trying to come off somewhere between casual and sophisticated. I doubt I hit even that broad target.

"One hundred twenty," he said. I was certain this shiny, rose-gold alligator-band watch with asymmetrical dials and a diamond where the "12" should be did not cost $120. Of course I was meant to understand there was a comma followed by three more zeroes.

"Thank you," I said. Eyes followed me out the door and into the street. Amazingly, within two blocks I'd caught up to Welsey. She would tell me later she had many techniques for disappearing into crowds. She would attach herself to a group—of tourists, say, where no one would think to look for her. Or she would duck into certain restaurants or other buildings she knew to have back exits. Subways were a great way to disappear, though they were fraught with their own special difficulties.

She crossed the street and entered St. Bart's Church. I couldn't possibly follow her there; my only option was to wait, wondering what she could be doing. Welsey had never talked about religion. I'd just assumed she thought about it as much as I did, which wasn't much. But she was thinking about it now, it seemed, so for a full half hour I paced, afraid to let my attention wander far lest she slip away. Even so I nearly missed her exit. I expected her to cross 49th to the Deutsche Bank building. Instead she made a left down 47th, walked some, and entered a wine shop. I crossed and stood between a pair of brown postal drop boxes. A few doors down some guys hooking a red Fiat to a tow truck looked at me curiously; I pretended to be waiting for someone until even I grew tired of the ruse and decided to cross to her side and sit on the front steps of a nearby brownstone.

Those steps led to a psychic reader's colorful door, and a thought jabbed at me. I leaped from the stairs and ran back into the street, hiding near the end of the block. A minute later Welsey left the wine shop sans bottles, and as I predicted headed right to the psychic's steps. But she did not stop inside; she passed within three feet of me, on her phone, oblivious. After another right turn and another stop in a store that sold ugly antique lamps with insects on them, she reversed direction and headed back to Park, me far behind her.

Welsey was able to both keep her head down and scan around her when she walked. She would stop and change direction abruptly. At one point someone, some tourist taking random video of New York, came at her sideways, and she dodged his camera, walking quickly toward Park.

Several more blocks, several stops, one phone call, and she arrived at the door to the 48th Street Starbucks, stopping for one final glance behind before going in.

I waited ten minutes from half a block back and then followed, pretending not to notice her till I was in line. So the game continued.

“I lost my fucking phone.”

“Wow,” I said, being careful to say nothing more, distracting myself by eying the smudge on her forehead.

After a pause during which she stirred her coffee and stirred her coffee again, she repeated, “I lost my fucking phone.”

“I heard,” I said. “Wow.”

“Yeah. Wow.”

“Where?” I heard myself say.

Her pause lasted eons. “Don’t know exactly. Somewhere around here.” She eyed me. “I do know that.”

If only I could keep this face when I played poker.

“Somebody stole it.”

“Stole it?” I asked. She nodded.

“I thought you said you lost it.” She waved her hand around vaguely.

“How do you know?”

“What?”

“How do you know that someone stole it?”

“I know.”

“Maybe it’ll turn up,” I said. “Maybe it’s not lost. Can’t you dial it?”

“You think I didn’t try that? It’s lost. *Stolen*.”

She twisted the straw in her drink like she was twisting someone’s neck.

“Okay,” I finally said.

“The police are investigating.”

“The police?”

“Of course. It has all sorts of confidential information.”

“True.” My mouth went dry.

She twisted the straw tighter. “Fuckety fuck fuck. This has not been my week."

"Do they have any leads? The police?"

"Can't talk about it." Another twist.

I should have kept my mouth shut. "I think you probably just lost it."

She looked at me. Long.

I maintained eye contact. *Never look away*, I remembered reading once in an article written by a retired FBI agent.

"You don't know about it, right?"

"No," I said. "What makes you think that?"

She didn't answer. I wondered if she could hear my heart beating, because I could.

"All this time, and I've never even tried to take your picture," I said.

She stared past me.

"You could at least cut me a little slack."

"Fuck your slack," she said.

I looked at her. I don't know why I was in such a mood, but I felt like pushing, provoking her: "People give you things just because you're *you*." I was surprised how loud it came out; she didn't react, or if she did, the sunglasses covered it. "You can do anything, go any*where*, have any*thing*," I continued. "A private plane, limo to the airport, no line to wait in, a private bar stocked with your favorite everything? Another limo to the hotel. Your feet didn't even have to touch ground until they were on the sandy beach. Heated to precisely your temperature.

"Do you know how many people would kill to be you, to have your life?" I said, even though my brain was telling me to shut up. "Every day planes coming into New York and L.A. dump out hundreds of young girls who have gambled everything they own for the improbability that they will be the next you. What you pay is small, it seems to me, all things considered." I just couldn't stop. "You can escape, you can afford to run away, to buy an island and live on it, lord of all you survey. Or commission your own island, every tree and rock and koi fish exactly how you want it."

She put down her cup and looked at me. I thought she would bolt. I thought she might throw coffee at me. I thought she might upend the whole table.

Instead she settled back into her chair and took a slow breath. She smoothed her straw. Amazingly, she was still able to suck her drink through it. After a moment she leaned back a little and folded her hands in front of her. "A couple nights ago a fan tried to get into my apartment while I was sleeping," she said in an even tone. "No one knows he got in. He made it all the way to my floor before they caught him. George. A really brave security guard. George caught him."

She finished her drink and pulled out a new, shiny phone, which had just chimed, to check on something.

"Oh," she said, "he had duct tape. And a gun."

This is all the internet said about Dr. Leonard M. Bradshaw, Ph.D.: *Dr. Bradshaw specializes in treating individuals, couples and families using conventional techniques combined with his own tested approach, distilled through more than 20 years' experience in a comforting, completely confidential environment. Areas of expertise: Social anxieties. Fears and phobias. Clinical interest in life transitions and identity struggles. Doctorate in Clinical Psychology, Boston University, 1989.*

He didn't seem to have a website of his own. Dr. Bradshaw was middle-aged, at least in the photo, which I suspected was probably from a while back, because it was low-res, because they always were. He looked easy going, with thin sandy hair, a beard and glasses, dressed in a mock turtleneck under a blazer. Ordinary, really. You'd never imagine Welsey Shaw could be his patient.

There were pictures of a Dr. Leonard Bradshaw online,

snorkeling and riding dune buggies with his wife (middle-aged, blonde, athletic, stunning, with skin that suggested she spent most of her days outdoors) and two boys (also blonde, athletic, cute). I was unable to tell for certain if this was the same man. He looked older in the outdoor photos. Another website showed a Dr. Bradshaw at a conference in Toronto—a small figure in a group shot of about 20, with no first name given. The figure wore glasses but did not sport the beard. Still another site showed several photos, taken from far back in the audience, of a Dr. Bradshaw on stage, giving a lecture, but the figure was too tiny to see any details.

More searching uncovered that Welsey's Dr. Bradshaw owned property in Oyster Bay. Google revealed it to be an impressive, rambling structure with two pickup trucks, some all-terrain vehicles and several cars. There may have been stables for horses as well, toys for when everyone got tired of the cars.

I sat in my underwear as my microwaved dinner cooled, channel-flipping while thinking about how one's problems would become more important by virtue of telling them to someone while stretched out on a thick leather couch, far above the cares of the street, the air conditioning whirring softly, rubbery indoor plants softening the décor, stylish black and white posters by famous photographers lining the room, thick carpet deadening any noises.

"What's troubling you?" the psychologist would say.

"I cannot figure out how to make the extraordinary in me break out."

"How do you mean?" he'd say, sitting up slightly in his Eames replica chair.

"What I mean is some people have extraordinary talents. But more than that, they're put on earth knowing how to bring attention to those talents. Others can't figure out how to get people to notice them. No matter what they do, they're at the mercy of other people."

"So?"

"So true autonomy is impossible."

"I see," he would say, scratching his beard, for any therapist of mine would have to have a beard. I have no idea what he'd say after this, however. That's the problem. But I'd sure like to be there to hear it.

The movie star squinted through her Diors and slopped latte right onto the table top. What her napkins failed to stop was soaked up by her Welseys. "They look better stained anyway," she said, after contemplating. "And calm down. I was just away a week."

"How was I to know?"

"You weren't," she said, blotting her thigh. "Why do you think you should be?"

"Common courtesy."

"Shut up. You're another one. You think you own me."

She looked over to another table.

"You can own me for two hours, for ten dollars. Six if it's a matinee."

The woman at the other table—a Millennial conservatively dressed in gray sweater, black slacks and boots—was watching a movie, one of Welsey's it turned out, on a tiny screen in her lap. She paused it every few minutes to check her phone.

"It's wrong to watch movies that way," Welsey said. "What the hell is wrong with people? Movies were meant to be seen in big dark rooms with other people. Lovers, strangers, it doesn't matter, but other people. Now my films compete with video games, YouTube, and twelve other films in the same Cineplex, all of which will be gone in a week. People don't see a film all at one time anymore so they can't talk about it Monday morning. They can't talk about anything Monday morning. What's the last movie everyone can remember where they were when they first saw it?"

She looked at the girl again. "That's blasphemous. Does she *know* how many people worked on that movie? She pauses it, she talks on her phone, she has it on as background while she checks her social crap. Then she goes online and rates it and tells me what I could have done better." As if on cue the girl switched off the movie mid-scene, answered her phone, and walked out.

"You're in a mood," I said.

"I am. And no jokes about why that might be." She pointed a finger.

"Wouldn't dream of it."

We watched the crowd inside for a while.

"Do you believe in reincarnation?"

I tried not to make a face. "I'd have to have some proof."

She rolled her eyes. "Typical."

"Typical what?"

"Typical *man*."

"Do *you* believe in reincarnation?" I asked.

She looked at me as if it were a stupid question. "Of course I do. Why else would I ask?"

The Dancer rose and smoothed her short skirt, very stylish over black tights. I often wondered why she wore heels when she already towered over almost everybody. Maybe you can never have too much of something.

"I have a feeling like no matter how many chances the Goddess gives us, we just keep blowing it," Welsey said. "That's why I have to believe in reincarnation."

"Who's the Goddess?" I asked.

"Shut *up*, Ferreira."

"Just asking."

"Maybe if we lived a very long time, as long as tortoises or bowhead whales, we'd be able to work all the mistakes out of our lives and we'd finally be enlightened."

"Some koi live up to two hundred years."

"Get out."

"They do. Look it up."

"You're on Ferreira." She seemed to scribble a note to check it out. "Seems like a waste for a fish. What can a fish atone for in life? How can it improve?"

"Well, what can I improve? What can you improve? But we believe that we can. We have to fix our mistakes. It's why we get up every day. To fix yesterday, in some way or other."

"Is that why you get up?"

I thought for a bit.

"I get up every morning..." I stopped myself. "...Because I'm hungry."

"So witty."

"I'm serious. I eat like a pig in the morning. I'll have two eggs, and then cereal after that. Then two pieces of toast with butter and jelly."

"Forgetting your belly for a moment, how do you *feel* when you wake up?"

I drew a breath. "Lost," I said. "Utterly, completely lost."

She leaned forward. "Go on."

"It's the most—" I paused for the right word, "—vacant, really vacant feeling. When consciousness starts to seep in—"

"Oh, God, don't you *hate* it when you're coming to, your comfy dreamworld is fading away, and you remember where you left off when you went to bed last night and you're like, 'Oh God, I can't deal with this shit, not today. Let me have a day where I don't have to deal with shit'? I'm sorry, go on," she said, patting my hand.

"It seems like every problem, even the smallest, is insurmountable. I really have to fight the urge to just stay in bed. Even a shower seems herculean. I'm convinced birth and getting up are very close experiences. You're warm and secure in there, and you don't want to come out."

Welsey smiled.

"Then I climb out of bed," I continued, "hating every bit of my life, dreading something as simple as the fact that I have to open a new bar of soap, that I have to find a new bar of soap, did I remember to *buy* a new bar of soap? I stretch for five minutes and walk into my dining room, which leads to my living room. I stare at everything, stare at the chair next to my computer, then at my computer, touch a key, it wakes back up, and yes, all my anxieties from yesterday are waiting for me, along with new ones in the form of emails."

"What do you do then?"

"I put off starting my day. Sometimes I don't start it. I'll do that for weeks...

"What I do not understand is why, once I begin, it's not so bad. But oddly, the very realization that it's not so bad can make it feel depressing."

"Why do you think that is?"

"Because I *should* think it's bad. But I don't. That's more pathetic."

She seemed about to say something, but stopped. "Interesting. Okay, go on."

"Lately I've been thinking about exactly how my life came to be—"

"Didn't they teach you that stuff in school?"

"—And how much I had control over, if I could have controlled it. My life wasn't laid out like yours was. It was a series of accidents. It's like I slipped and slid and tumbled randomly down the street, to land where I landed."

"And if you had it to do all over again, what do you think would happen?"

"The same thing? A different thing? I don't know, really. That's why I don't have much interest in the whole reincarnation thing. Life is dice."

Welsey bristled. "Life is not dice."

"Life *is* dice."

"There's a reason things happen."

I felt like that was an insult, hurled at me. "You're telling me you believe so many things, so many seminal things, that happen in your life aren't just luck?"

"I don't believe it, I know it. I'm proof."

"The first person to really love your acting and want to cast you, what if he'd randomly died the day before? Hit by a truck that was overdue for brake inspection because the owner cut costs. The editor who rejected my novel, what if she'd never been hired, and someone else had been hired instead, someone who liked it, who liked me?"

Welsey shrugged. "It evens out, eventually."

"Have you ever heard of the concept of the bell curve?"

She rolled her eyes. "No. Should I have?"

"It shows a distribution of something, anything, from the people who get it the least to those who get them the most. Most people land in the middle—average—and so they form the bulge of the curve. There are people who land on the edges, however, and they get disproportionately more or less of something."

"Okay."

"So you get it."

"I get the *curve*. What I don't agree with is how you land on it."

"You're saying you choose your spot?"

A nod.

"Look around. People don't choose their fate. That's an illusion."

"And I'm saying I'm proof they do."

"On what do you base this?"

"Life."

"And what if someone else's life is completely different?"

"Then they're different. But we all live in the same world with the same rules. I was just watching this science program last night about how the laws of the universe are the same everywhere. So the way I see it, that pretty much invalidates your theory."

I shook my head and leaned back in my chair. Stalemate.

I was now subscribing to a satellite TV package that tonight offered a veritable Welsey festival: *Leaving My Life Behind*, *Cold Love*, and *Jane Callahan Where Are You*? This would take me deep into the A.M. I fell asleep during *Gods*, not because the seventh viewing wasn't as enjoyable as the others but because it was 2:00 in the morning when it started.

The phone startled me awake. I squinted at the clock. Quarter to noon, and I had to pee.

"*Happy birthday*," my dad's voice boomed.

I rubbed sand from my eyes. "It's not my birthday, Dad."

"Yeah, I know that. It's mine."

"Sorry. I knew that, Dad, but I've been insanely busy lately," I lied.

"Yeah, I understand," he lied. "I'm going to Pontchartrain's tonight for steak and lobster."

"That's great." I wondered if I could pee quietly.

"I love steak and lobster."

"I know," I said, getting off the couch and edging to the bathroom. "They're your favorites."

"So how's Ellen?"

"Ann."

"That one."

"She's fine."

"A keeper?"

I thought for a second. "I guess so. I don't know."

"If you have to guess that's bad."

I did not want to talk about Ann. "What's that screaming?"

"The hot water for the tea's ready. Now I just need to steep and add the amaretto and chilled whipped cream."

"What is it?"

"Breakfast."

"No, I meant...Never mind. How are you feeling, Dad, on your, your—"

"Sixtieth. The big six-*oh*."

Sigh. "Happy birthday, Dad, really."

"Yeah. Matthew's still open?"

"It is."

"Frieda still there?"

"Frieda?"

"Yeah. Frieda Farmington."

"Don't know her."

"Sure you do. Petite, black curly hair, mole on her left cheek. Always gave me extra toast with my eggs. No one else ever did that. She knew I couldn't stick a slimy egg in my mouth without toast. Still can't. Tell her I said hello."

"I will, Dad. How's mom?"

"Who knows? She does her own thing, has her own friends. She goes out with Vicki and Alice and Carol. Sometimes Albert goes along."

"Who's Albert?"

"Carol's husband. The one with the lazy eye. There's this restaurant that has a bar out front and they all drink there. Sidecars. Theirs is called the Twin Turbo Sidecar. Extra booze. The servers wear racing gloves when they bring it. That's the gimmick.—You peeing while I'm talking to you?"

"Running the sink."

"I'll bet you're not even dressed. You fell asleep on the couch after watching TV all night. It's noon and you're in your underwear just now getting something to eat."

"Nope. I'm dressed," I said, looking down at my clothes from yesterday.

"Okay, okay. I was wrong about that," he said mopishly. "So what are you doing? Still up to writing for other people who put their name on it?"

"That's basically it, yeah."

"Hmph. And anything else?"

"Spending lots of time in New York City these days," I said.

"Doing what?"

"Having lunch with publishers. Editors. A few famous people thrown in."

"I've always found the City to be overrated. Really in love with itself. Has to constantly be told how great it is."

"Maybe. Doesn't hurt any of us once in a while, Dad." I made my way into the kitchen, opened the refrigerator while trying not to rattle anything.

"You can't drive there and I hate to go anywhere where I'm not the one driving."

"I understand that," I said.

"Remember when you were a kid, and you'd stay up all night writing whatever it was on that typewriter we bought you?" I did, but I didn't feel like participating in this conversation. "I'd open your bedroom door and say, 'Turn out the damn light and go to bed, Steinbeck. It's keeping me and your mother up.' And you'd say, 'How can it be keeping you up with the door closed?' Always had an answer." A laugh. "Still do."

"Yup," I agreed, trying to figure out what to eat. An aroma that reminded me to clean out the fridge more often wafted out.

"What was all that stuff you were writing, at three A.M?"

"Stories, Dad."

"About what? What the heck can a kid write about at three A.M?"

"All sorts of things. Night is when I get inspired."

"Yeah, I remember. You would never go to bed. Then you'd

never get your ass up in the morning. You still have them?"

"Have what?"

"Those stories."

"I think so."

"Ever try to sell them?"

"I was just a kid. They're not that good."

"A lot of bad stuff makes money," he said. "Don't you go to the movies?"

I didn't make a sound. Instead I pondered eating breakfast out somewhere.

"Can I read them?"

"They're kind of private, Dad. I wrote them for me."

"Oh. I see."

"You could always read *Heaven's People*." I must have gotten used to it; I couldn't smell the refrigerator anymore.

"Too long. Isn't that something like three hundred pages?"

"Two hundred fifty-eight," I said.

"Yeah. TV's more my speed. Have you ever thought about writing for TV?" He cleared his throat. "So, I don't mean to put this indelicately, and I'm really not trying to ruin your day on my birthday, but I mean, don't you want to move on? Isn't it time to admit it isn't really working out and do something else? What do you make a year? Twenty-five thousand? Hello?"

"I'm here," I said.

"I'll let you sell the house. You'd get one sixty for it. One sixty-five."

"What could I buy anywhere else for that?"

"Parts of Philly are nice. Those colonials."

"They're beautiful, Dad. Can't afford them."

"How do you know? Have you tried? Really tried?"

"Yes, Dad. I've tried."

"I'd like to know you're good before I die."

"You're sixty, Dad." I lunged to the back of the refrigerator and grappled for two eggs, putting my finger through one and jarring the other loose. It rolled to the front, past my elbow, and onto my foot.

"People *die* at sixty. And I figure it's going to take you a full ten years before you become self-sufficient."

"I am self-sufficient, Dad, thanks."

He was silent for a second. "It seems like for the last 30 years or so, you need more money than ever to be happy. That's just the way it is. People who say happiness is not about money don't have any. That's why they say it. That's why they put those happy-sappy sayings on refrigerator magnets. You don't find them on refrigerators in rich people's houses. You just find kick-ass big refrigerators. Years ago you didn't have to pay for TV and radio. You didn't need a burglar alarm and motion cameras. You ate chicken, which cost a buck a pound. Today they raise them in air-conditioned condominiums before they cut their heads off. Your phone used to be stuck in the wall, it was yellow with a curly cord and lasted thirty years. Now it's obsolete every year and costs seven hundred bucks to get a new one. Car insurance costs more than the car. So you have to have so much more money today than you used to just to be okay, forget about happy. Remember that, if you only remember one thing."

I picked eggshell off my toes and thought about Ted's in Jeffersonville. Only fifteen minutes away and I was suddenly craving their sucuk and eggs.

"It's good advice. Ann would think so. You're pushing forty. I may have just turned sixty, but trust me, forty's a bigger one. You know why? You're not young anymore. Your life's not unfurling. That's when people start getting material-oriented. It's not the receding hairline and the spreading waist that makes you want shit. It's the fucking realization that this is all there is in life. *Shit.* Time to get yours. You still there?"

"I'm still here, Dad. I'm listening to you."

"And dammit, it's nice shit. They outdid themselves. With this stitching. That leather. Those cool dials that glow. Those doors that close with just the right amount of soft. The packaging that's more beautiful than the thing itself. That's how they get you, with the *packaging.* Kitchen drawers have little lights in them now. You know how I turn on the torchiere lamp? I touch the glass shade with my finger. I never loved turning on a light before. And you know why I love it? Do you?

"Because I'm going to die soon! And it's going to suck. It'll be painful and miserable, and your mother will probably cry a lot and then be left alone for the rest of her life. And there used to be religion for that. But nobody's got religion anymore. Not even religious people. In fact, they got it the least. So they got soft-touch lights and glowing drawers and window blinds that rise and fall with a push of a button. Because all this shit takes my mind off death. That's the real reason it's there. To make me forget what's real.

"You know what I'm saying, right?"

"I know Dad, I get it."

"That's why people really want things. You know what would be the biggest hit to the GDP? If nobody ever died. Then we'd all be sitting in hammocks, not doing anything, not wanting anything, because why bother?"

"True," I said.

"That's why people want things. That's why—"

"That's why I want to write," I said.

"That's why you want to—"

Long pause. It seemed we'd run out of conversation. And for some reason I had to pee again.

"I'm going to let you go, Dad," I said, clearing phlegm that was suddenly in my throat. "Happy birthday. Say hi to mom."

"She's giving me the silent treatment."

"Why?"

"I don't know."

"Well, say hi to her anyway?"

"Sure thing," he said in a way that made me think he wanted to say something else. Then without another word he hung up.

Welsey stood before a man wearing a fleece jacket bearing the name of a well-known investment firm, one whose television ads informed us of its humility and ethics. He was camped out on one of the Starbucks tables while using another to hold a stack of loose-leaf binders, two cell phones, a wifi "hotspot," his suit coat, a thick accounting manual, pens in shades of red, yellow and blue, and a second, smaller laptop with Chinese characters that bore the sticker "Not to be used outside the office!"

"I would really like to sit at that table," said Welsey Shaw, politely, sweetly. He ignored her.

She peeled down her dark glasses. "I think every customer is entitled to a table," she said.

He looked up momentarily. "Sorry, I'm working," he said, and went back to one of his phones, speaking German to whoever was on the other end.

"Wow, that big investment firm with the skyscraper doesn't provide you with an office?" Welsey said. "One with electricity? Wait, I know it does because I have about nine or ten—my apologies, I haven't had time to check my portfolio lately—million dollars invested with you." He looked up at the bluejeaned kid with the tangled hair. She pulled out her phone and did a little tapping. "Sorry, I exaggerated. Only eight-point-five million. You shitheads are down today."

He took another look and possibly realized who stood before him. Or maybe he was just not in the mood for the argument.

"Here, Merry Christmas," he said, logging out, slamming shut his laptops and stuffing everything into a (beautiful) leather briefcase sporting his initials, the middle one larger than the other two. He hastened out the door but left his cup and about ten opened sugar packets on the table.

"Can't even pick a fight anymore," Welsey said, sitting down. "They give up so easily. I miss film crews."

"You suck."

"I do." She pulled a twisted magazine out of her bag; it had another celebrity on the cover, but featured an article claiming to have delicious new dirt on Welsey. "It's official. See? It doesn't bother me anymore, really. I'm immune. But, I mean, why lie? You've already got stuff. I never even did any of that shit."

The story claimed Welsey was seeing an actor, who was already happily married and with three kids, and that his wife, an actress herself, was none too pleased, leading to violent scenes. "Driven to suicide!" the subhead screamed.

"Why do they always pair me with dark-haired men? Always dark. And long. I hate long hair on men."

I involuntarily felt at the locks on my neck and decided I was okay.

"So I spent this morning looking at real estate."

"Oh?"

"I was out of ice cream."

"Oh."

"Hideaways."

"Off the beaten path?"

"Off any path. No easy access. Not many windows. That's important. You can't have windows in a hideaway. It can't have a postal address, either. Must be a P.O. box."

"I think I could help you with that part." I looked out the window. A bus narrowly missed a bicyclist crossing against the light. Putin paced on the sidewalk, nervously smoking a cigarette. He looked like he was about to order up a war against someone.

"But I would want to go under a fake name," she continued.

"I've even got one picked out. *Gary G. Fitzsimmons.* He was the neighbor who cleaned my parents' pool." She waited for a reaction. "Well, nobody would ever guess it's me." She seemed suddenly struck by an idea. "Let's play a game." A piece of paper appeared and she started scribbling: *Couch. TV. iPod. Shampoo. Conditioner. Soaps and Oils (counts as 1). Tampons. Deodorant.* "On second thought who cares about deodorant?" she said, scribbling over it. "I'm all alone there. What do you think so far?"

"You get three more."

"Really?"

"It's the tradition."

"Okay, I like that. Well, my comb."

"Why?" I asked.

"Says the short-hair guy."

"It's not that short."

"Speaking of which, is there a salon in these here woods?"

"Better bring scissors."

"Really?"

I nodded.

"Okay, we're at nine. Now, can I get something pre-furnished? Because if I can, I can drop the couch and TV, and I'm at seven again."

"Okay, let's say it's furnished."

"Cable, right? And a whirlpool?"

"Nothing like roughing it."

"So three more. I'm alone, so I don't need clothes."

"Can I come over?"

"There have to be vegetables in the back yard, place for a bike but no car—I hate cars. I suck at driving."

"You'll need a car."

"I'll bike. And I've been wanting to start skateboarding again. Now, I'll need bean-bag chairs because I love those. Porch is mandatory—a big one. Well, big compared with the rest of the house, anyway. The swing has to squeak. I've never had a porch swing. Never even sat in one, except for a scene in *Leaving My Life Behind*."

She finished her list.

"Okay, what would be your ten things?" She shoved the paper at me.

"Are you done?"

"I am."

"Okay." I thought. "iPod, just like you. You need music in the middle of nowhere. Laptop. No clothes either. My books count as one item, even though there are hundreds."

I thought.

"What else?"

I shrugged. "I don't know."

"You only picked three."

"I have no idea. Silverware."

"Hadn't thought of that!"

"Does that count as one or is a knife, fork and spoon three?"

"God, this is complicated. One, let's say. You have six left."

"Soap."

"Five."

"Mouthwash."

"For who?"

"There's dating there."

"Oh. Damn. I didn't realize." She started rewriting her list.

"A copy of *Heaven's People*. A copy of *Mystery at Alessandro Creek*."

"Aww, that's sweet. And the tenth?"

"I don't know. I want to keep the tenth option open. You should never close all your doors."

Welsey thought for a moment.

"That sounds reasonable."

"So where is it?" I asked.

"What?"

"Your hideaway?"

"Well, where's yours?"

"Concord, Massachusetts."

Welsey nodded with polite confusion. "Okay. Why?"

"Have you ever been there?"

"Yeah."

"Okay, so where would your hideaway be?"

"Puerto Vallarta."

"You can't have a hideaway in Puerto Vallarta."

"Why not?"

"Because that's not a hideaway. It's not a hideaway if John Travolta can visit."

"But he never comes. I always invite him. I love his movies."

"Hideaways have to be hidden."

"You can be hidden in plain sight." And she spread her arms a little.

"Maybe, but it's not a *hideaway*."

"Yes it is. Now shut up. A hideaway is psychological."

"Okay, it's psycho. Just like you."

"Whatever, Ferreira. I don't want to be cut off. I need to know there are people just past the wall, the door, the window."

"Look up 'hideaway.'"

"Ferreira!"

"Okay, so who would be allowed at your house? Let's say there'd be only one guest pass. Who would it go to?"

"That's pretty restrictive."

"But let's say..."

"I don't know," she said pointedly.

"Am I invited to your hideaway?"

She shrugged noncommittally behind the shades. "Maybe. You're pressuring me. What about you? Am I invited?"

"Naturally."

"Who else?"

Think of someone quick! Ann? I still wasn't sure, even after all these months. Maybe Dad was right. Who else? Friends? Relatives? Definitely not relatives. "John, Angelica, Paula, and Cornelius," I said finally.

"That's four," she said.

"John and Angelica are twins," I tried.

"No."

"Okay, you're allowed to have four, too."

"Great—"

"As long as I'm one."

"You may come on a trial basis, provided you take off your shoes at the door. Also you can't stay over." She grabbed my computer and spun it around. "What's the name of that town you're in?"

"Paris," I said.

"So funny." She typed a bit. "Ah, *found it.* Jesus Christ, Ferreira! Houses under two hundred K?" She started typing frantically into her phone.

"What are you doing?"

"Calling the realtor." She spun the computer back to me. Rosie Ackerman's thumbnail was on the screen, smiling at me, navy blazer, a three-time "Broker's Circle" winner. Below was a phone number. "Um, hi, yeah, is this Rosie? My name's Julia. I would like to see the property you have listed on Country Road 164. Yes. Yes. That's the one. Yeah. Great. You're awesome."

She got up and started gathering her things, balancing the phone on her shoulder.

"Where are you going?"

"I'm on hold. But she can see me in three hours."

"Hang up!"

"Which train goes to Callicoon? Never mind, I'll ask at the station." She started talking on her phone again, making straight for the door.

Suddenly I was crossing 48th. I caught up and Welsey looked

over her shoulder. "I'll check out more real estate when I'm there," she said, and at that moment it dawned on me that I was not dreaming, because this is something I could not have dreamed of. As we skirted trucks and busses, attracting honks and at least one expletive, a sun shower burst on us. I was in a scene from a movie, me chasing a famous actress through the streets of New York while light glistened off the wet roofs of cabs. Thunder boomed, bouncing between buildings. Soon a rainbow would even oblige and form in the distance. The wind howled; umbrellas inverted. Most people were just roughing it, running with bags or newspapers over their heads.

Welsey was much faster than me. "Lard ass" she called back, encouragingly.

"Why aren't we taking a cab?" I shouted up the block. People looked.

Welsey leaned against a building, breathing deeply but easily. "Lungs burning, legs hurting?"

"Yes," I managed.

"That's why we're not taking a cab!"

"You're in shape from that green screen movie you did."

"That was three years ago. Come on, I'm a *girl*," she taunted, taking off again.

"You're lighter," I hollered ahead.

I was afraid we'd get separated as we reached the train. "I'll hold it for you," she hollered. Maybe she thought this was like the movies, where the conductor waited patiently for lovers to board. By the time we reached the terminal building I was hobbling badly. Welsey sprinted inside, shook her hair dry and shouted to no one, "Which track?"

We started down the escalator—Welsey so far ahead of me she was at the bottom before I reached half-way, pausing just long enough to thumbs-up a digital billboard of one of her movies. Embarrassment now overwhelmed me. I could imagine her looking at every house for sale within a twenty mile radius of mine, able to buy them all, probably putting them on that fancy credit card. She'd bring macarons from La Maison du Chocolat to potlucks—adorable or amusing at first, but obnoxious when you keep doing it.

On the platform I got in front and nearly blocked her with my body. "You're really not going to do this."

"Get out of my way," was her reply, and after shouldering past she was aboard. I followed. Where was Neil deGrasse Tyson now? I wanted him to see who was on "his train." *Hey, check this out—Welsey Shaw.*

Just as I was looking for him Welsey's phone rang—this new one had a different ringtone, a hip-hop thing that meant absolutely nothing to me. "You can buy tickets while you're riding, right?" she asked as she shook her head and tucked the BlackBerry against her ear.

I turned and was about to answer when we collided; I was headed deeper into the train and she suddenly was headed out. I nearly knocked her down, the glasses almost came off, and real anger flashed. For a split second. Then it dissipated.

"I totally forgot," she said, pointing to her phone. "I have an event at six o'clock. Some other time." And before I could even make sense of any of that, she turned, slipped through the closing doors, and ran back up the escalator, two steps at a time.

10

Nothing says June in Callicoon like the annual tractor parade. The event is attended by hundreds of residents, hundreds of visitors and hundreds of tractors. And as usual one guy—or this year, a pony tailed, baseball-hatted, buff woman from the local paper, armed with a camera and a tattoo of Ceres, the Goddess of Agriculture on her arm—was here to chronicle it. Between taking snapshots of giant diesel-belching contraptions, she told me she had just covered the annual Trout Parade in Livingston.

"They had basset hounds dressed like trout," she said, digging an attachment out of her bag. I told her we had to work hard to keep ahead of the Livingstonians. Ann had gone off to talk to a couple that was having a baby while I wondered if it was a good idea for the mom-to-be to breathe so much diesel smoke.

Ann and I awakened early for the traditional pancake breakfast of the tractor parade. It's served every year by the volunteer fire department. I actually look forward to this for days. Butter sinking into a stack of pancakes just might be my favorite smell.

"That's a tall plate," Ann said.

"Message received," I said, but I ate it all anyway. Ann looked at me; I knew she was mentally counting calories.

At the moment we were standing in the crowd watching tractor after tractor roll down Main Street like steampunk supermodels. People waved American flags. A twangy voice announced the make and year of every machine. Two hundred eighty-two tractors—a record I would later find out—made up this year's show. I knew Rosalyn wouldn't be around because she didn't like the noise and the exhaust.

The newspaper photographer's name was Seera, and she fired off photos at lightning speed, evidently a pro at photographing tractor parades. She got as close as was safe and took photos from as many angles as she could, then dashed behind me to climb onto a wall for some higher shots from behind. I asked her why she was taking so many pictures for a newspaper article. She said she'd sell some online to other outlets, and some were for her portfolio. Was there a lot of demand for these photos, I asked. Oh yes, she said. "Definitely." When one guy got in her way (deliberately, I think) she squatted down and took the shot between his legs.

The PA system announced, "*A 1960 Oliver 880 Diesel.*" People erupted in cheers.

"*...a 1955 Ferguson TO-35...*"

More shouts and whistles. Ann stuck her fingers inside her mouth and made a shriek, which caused my ears to ring. "*Make way for a 1959 Farmall 340 Utility...*" said the voice. More cheers. Someone pushed behind me and almost burned my skin with her coffee. "*...A 1939 John Deere Model B...a 1970 Allis Chalmers...a 1967 International Harvester TD-20 Series B...a 1960 John Deere 4010D...a 1962 IH Cub Cadet.*" The play-by-play ceased, and then a correction was issued. The 1960 John Deere and the 1962 Cub Cadet had been announced in the wrong order.

I looked for Ann again. She was talking to a couple pushing

twins in a stroller. For days she'd talked about this morning and now she was hardly paying attention to the giant machines before her. I wasn't particularly interested either. They're loud, and I don't like loud. They're sooty, and I don't like that either. Nor am I interested in old machinery.

"*...a 1951 John Deere MT...*"

I started over to Ann and noted that the back of my neck was burning. It wasn't even noon. I began to think of the closest place I could wade to that sold sunscreen when I saw her: Welsey Shaw was standing across the street! I felt the juices bubble up in the pit of my stomach. Here she was at the *tractor parade*, of all things. I wondered if she'd check out the machines up close, go to the barbecue fundraiser later, participate in the raffle drawing for an "antique" dining room set.

There she was, talking to some white-haired guy in shortalls. (Why do men look so dorky in shortalls while girls look so cute? A mystery for another time, I decided.) Welsey wore what looked to be a silk tee, crisp as a brand new twenty dollar bill, designer logo above the small left breast pocket and sleeves crisply cuffed. Her perfect hair was in a perfect pony-tail and of course sunglasses shrouded the face. She cheered on the tanks that rumbled by, attracting the attention of one operator enough to get a nod and a toothy smile.

And I was sure she had already seen me.

She was directly across the street, headed to the end of the block. She crossed at a break in traffic and turned toward my direction.

I tried to put a few people between us, but they'd all seemed to move away on cue. She was now about thirty yards to my right, looking around at houses in the distance, on the hills, and checking her phone occasionally. She paused to applaud as a particularly large tractor passed, clapping louder and longer than anyone;

whether she was being patronizing or sincere I couldn't say. She turned back to me and smiled.

A few minutes and she resumed her walk, occasionally stopping to chat people up. I turned to where Ann had been standing but now she was gone, as was the couple with the stroller. So I turned to face the actress head on as she walked right up to me, smiling, tiny nose ring glistening in the midday sun.

"Excuse me," she said with a smile. I turned to watch her walk away. It was not Welsey Shaw.

"Come check this out," Ann said from behind me. She was now with a different couple that also had twins. "Another set of twins in strollers. Can you believe it? What are the odds?"

"How about that."

"Aren't they cute?"

I've never known how to respond to this. No, to me babies are not cute. Babies are drooling, loud creatures that require more maintenance than a vintage Fiat. So sue me.

Sometimes I feel guilty that I didn't make the requisite sacrifices and bless my parents with adorable grandchildren. I surely would have risen in their esteem for it. But I've always feared I wouldn't make a good father. I don't understand kids and feel helpless and stupid around them, unable to decipher what they want. A three year old can flummox me effortlessly just by being a three year old. What did I want when I was that age? How did I think? I don't have the faintest idea. To me babies might as well be alien beings.

Except that...sometimes, I start thinking having a family to call my own wouldn't be so bad after all. I meditate on only-child status and realize I would like to pass my genes along. My father had no brothers or sisters. The Ferreira line would end with me. A sad terminus if ever there was one.

But right then I was staring at two cross-eyed kids with sticky faces and matted hair. Believe me, I tried. They just didn't look cute.

"Adorable," I said.

Ann grinned from ear to ear. A lot of funny baby talk in a high-pitched voice followed. I just stood. The couple eventually wandered on, after telling Ann all sorts of details about their newly-minted family members' digestive and bowel habits.

"I thought you wanted to look at tractors," I said, maybe sounding a little irritable.

"I am looking at the tractors," she said. "I liked that really big one."

"I liked that really big one too," I said, wondering.

"The one with the big smokestack."

"Yeah."

"Did you see the little boy who ran into the street?" Ann asked, squinting towards the tractors. "His mother wasn't even looking!"

"No, I didn't see. Was he all right?"

"I grabbed him."

"Good for you."

"His mother didn't even say, 'Thank you.'"

"I am not surprised," I said.

"You rubbed on sunscreen, right?"

"I forgot."

She opened her bag and removed some. I turned and she slathered goo on my neck. "You're red."

"Now I smell like a beach."

"Hey, that sounds like a great idea," Ann said.

"Mind if I go see Roz? You know she won't come out here. I haven't heard her play in ages."

She made an "A-OK" sign and disappeared back into the crowd.

"*...a 1948 Farmall H...*"

All of Rosalyn's downstairs windows were open so I just stood on the porch and listened. Her fingers seemed to be able to hit more than ten keys at once. Yet her playing was effortless. Technique was merged seamlessly with expression. I wish I could write like that.

With Roz you didn't listen to notes. You listened to the total effect, a glorious blur that had both a fey quality and a seriousness that implied its creator knew more than she was revealing to you. I often wondered why so many other people didn't seem to hear it. They'd smile and say she was good. She wasn't good. She brought pianos to life. It was impossible to tell where she ended and the instrument began.

The playing ceased. A bench slid. The floor creaked. A door shut.

I knocked tentatively.

"*It's unlocked, Daniel.*"

I entered. A scruffy cat with a bob tail pressed its face into my shoes and left saliva as its greeting. "How do you know I'm not a burglar?"

"The piano's too heavy and I don't have anything else," came her voice, from where I wasn't sure.

"Where are you?" I called.

"In the bathroom. Take a seat anywhere that's clear."

I looked around. "A hint?"

The toilet flushed, the sink ran, and the door flew open.

"I'm still bleeding," she said, cinching a worn belt and looking around. "At my age. Can you believe it? Move something."

You know you go way back with someone when you can casually talk about bleeding.

"How did you know it was me?" I asked.

"Your knock. Has a distinctive rhythm. Everything about you does. You really missed your calling. Drummer. Bop combo. *Ferreira's Ferocious Five.*"

Roz's living room managed to be sparse and cluttered at the same time. Nothing was put away. Books lay open, music was in piles, chairs were strewn about. The hardwood floors were delightfully creaky. Bookcases served as walls, or at least room dividers. Roz's watercolors hung around the perimeter of every room—brightly-colored abstracts mostly, with a few landscapes and whimsical animals thrown in. Some were mixed media, which meant Roz rubbed real dirt and foliage into the paint of the landscapes. Many of them looked unfinished. One featured a tree with leaves and branches only on one side. I'd once asked her about this. "I couldn't see the other side," she said.

The magnificent piano—the 1907 Blüthner—squatted in the center of the main room. At one time Rosalyn had owned three pianos: a Steinway, one whose make I can't remember now, and this. She'd sold the others, with much regret, when she needed cash.

The last one, however, was "untouchable." It may or may not have been owned by Claude Debussy. There was conflicting evidence on its history, which I'd spent one summer tracing just for fun. I liked to believe it belonged to the man who gave us *Clair de Lune* and *La Mer*, two of the most arresting and original pieces of music ever composed, and two I'd want to hear one last time before I died.

Roz reversed direction and went to the kitchen. "I'm having warm lemon water," she said.

"Of course you are."

"What would you like?"

"Well, a Mountain Dew, but you don't have that, and Ann would probably smell it on my breath anyway. So I'll take what you're having, only with lime."

She emerged with two glasses, sporting green and yellow wedges. We tapped them together.

"What is new in your world of words and ideas?" she asked.

"Nothing. People still don't want to read me."

"Oh well," she patted my knee. "As Mahler said, someday your time will come."

"No, that was Snow White, and she said, 'Someday my prince

will come,' though I don't know if he did. I never watched that far. Always hated fairy tales. I think they're dangerous for children, speaking of which, Ann wants some."

"Fairy tales?"

"Children." I looked over at the music propped up on her piano. *Études* it said at the top. *Debussy* it said at the bottom. "Don't let me stop you," I said.

For the next half hour I was somewhere other than Callicoon. The sounds that cascaded over me are impossible to describe, and you can't even play a recording to get the experience, because there's nothing quite like hearing a piano live, there's nothing quite like hearing Debussy live, there's nothing like hearing Rosalyn Sommers play Debussy live. The tones were the purest sparkling water; visually they reminded me of Seurat's pointillism. Aurally they were like raindrops on a roof—multicolored raindrops. Emotionally they restored a feeling of wonder in life I'd thought I'd lost long ago.

That's why I had to come visit her every now and then.

"Why do you suppose," I said some minutes later, "we devote so much of our time to making things like this perfect, things like music or writing or even just thoughts, when most people won't even notice the difference. I mean, that time could be put to use doing other things: doing good, making money, having children... Instead, we waste our limited time perfecting things nobody but us cares about. Or if other people do care as much, we'll never meet them or they won't even be born until we're dead. Dead. I've been thinking about dead a lot lately."

She stopped playing, rose, and went to a closet. I knew what was coming next.

Rosalyn ran a healing program, a sort of holistic practice, in the Catskills. I scoffed the first time. I scoffed publicly. But the one thing I never admit is it seems to work. I think. Sometimes. At least it does no harm.

She grabbed a huge rolled-up mat and dropped it onto the floor with a thud. Two pillows were tossed in the same direction. They landed haphazardly, one on top of the other.

She resat at the piano. I bent down and smoothed the mat, grabbed the pillows and propped my head on them. I had as my view the underside of the Blüthner. The first time she'd put me under there, Roz had said, "Isn't it amazing?" I didn't say anything, but I'd begged to differ. I felt, if anything, like I was underneath an el train, looking up, my view of openness and light blocked by big pillars and criss-crossing underside. Hardly amazing.

But then something amazing happened: she played chords. Deep ones, that began to settle on me. They had weight; they had color. The air felt charged. So help me, I began to vibrate from within. I crawled out for a second, to see if I still felt that way when I was not surrounded by wood and metal and strings. I did not.

"At that point I thought I'd lost you, that you were going for the door," she said to me later.

I returned to my spot and embraced the feeling, a feeling of total isolation and comfort, where my senses, rather than being diminished, felt heightened by being where I was.

"I was saying—" I started.

"*Shhh.* No talking, Daniel."

"But I agree—"

"Not even to agree."

Deep chords. With lighter sounds from the right hand sprinkled on top, like rain. Raindrops again. There was something about the right hand on a piano, something that made me think the world could be purified. If only…

I think this is what the womb must have felt like, and I think we spend our whole lives longing to return to it. Security. The Blanket. That's what this all is.

I know it's not my theory. But down there, listening to what sounded more like an organ than a percussion instrument, I experienced something sensual no "extra-pianistic" experience could match. We see recurrences. Nuance gets lost in the noise. I thought about the time I observed some finance guys in action setting up retirement for my dad. They were closely matched, not just in haircuts and suits, but in grammar, vocabulary, movement, complexity of thought…They laughed at the same jokes, eyed the same girls in the hallways (skirts got noticed but pants were off the radar), drove the same cars right down to the color. Every chord under the piano was part of a battle against that.

Rosalyn started a new melody, with the right hand, winding it tightly around itself, faster and faster. I saw a figure skater spinning, and drawing her arms in (it was a her) tighter and tighter until they were folded at her chest and she was a blur. Surely she would drill through the ice. Then, just as evenly, just as perfectly, Roz began slowing the phrase down, and the skater reappeared as a distinct figure in my mind.

"The reason you want to get art perfect," she said then, "is because you can't get life perfect."

"That's obvious," I said, maybe a bit annoyed. "But why bother? Who cares if I can't get either perfect. Put it out there. How is it useful to go in circles about things that don't matter anyway?"

"Because very little of what we do is useful, strictly speaking. We convince ourselves it's useful. We create whole universes around it. Those finance monkeys with your dad, do you think they're useful?"

"Yes."

"Ever watch a Brazilian soccer match? Now that's some serious meaning. Kicking a ball into a net. Making a canvas with a splotch in the middle of it. Run across the country. Swimming across the English Channel. Climbing a mountain because it's there. Someone did all those things. Why?

She built a tumultuous climax from thick chords that sounded like fudge would sound if fudge were chords. I'd had my eyes closed for some time now (what is there to look at under a piano?) but now I opened them and everything seemed brighter. I sat up and looked out the window.

"Some people devote their lives into sinking a little ball into a *hole* in the *grass*," she said. "And then other people devote their lives to building whole industries for people who devote their lives into sinking a little ball into a little hole in the grass. And other people devote their lives to serving those industries built for people who spend their lives sinking little balls into little holes. And to all of them, that is the most important thing in the world. Think about that sometime. I mean really think about it."

I did. For how long I don't know, till I realized Roz wasn't there anymore. I called out three times.

After hearing nothing but silence, I did something I wouldn't dream of if Roz had been there. I went over to the Blüthner and sat. I touched the piano that Claude Debussy might have run his pudgy fingers across once. I made an ugly noise. Debussy would have made a beautiful one.

I wish I could play. Never had a lesson. It always seemed so formidable; all those keys that look alike. How do pianists play without even looking at them? How does a cellist know where to find an E on the fingerboard? How do you get a note out of the flute?

I produced a cluster of random dissonant notes that despite being nonsensical gave me a thrill, as I remembered what it felt like at age nine to touch typewriter keys and want to create something even though I hadn't an idea what to create nor the vocabulary to create it. I played some random "chords" and "runs" and listened to the notes vibrate. It sounded like some modern compositions. Maybe I should be a composer of "difficult" music, and be the darling of university professors. My colorful bursts of sound circled back and sort of "recapitulated," ending with—quite accidentally—a consonance. It might not have been bad, actually; there could have been something there. I smiled, got up, and went outside, back to the world of tractors, tourists, and families. I found Ann and we spent the evening talking about what we would name kids, if we had them.

The young woman was hard to shake. She was in her 20s, dark hair, boyish glasses, in a tight black T-shirt that said, *They're Not Comic Books They're Graphic Novels Dammit!* And she would not leave our table.

"You're Welsey Shaw." She said it with an *Aha!* quality. Welsey smiled, slightly at first, then with a thinner, tighter grin.

"Nope. I get that a lot, though." I sensed her tension even as she acted cool.

Welsey had surprised me today, facing the world without her glasses and letting her hair down, more typical of the way she appeared on red carpets, though of course not nearly as glamorously attired. I couldn't figure it out—was she so relaxed she was forgetting who she was?—and of course couldn't ask her, not in public.

"I can tell," the hipster confidently declared.

"People do say I look like her, but..." and there was a shrug.

"Come on, would you sign this? Please?"

I strained to see what "this" was. People at other tables were starting to look, too.

"Sorry, I'm not her. Really."

"Oh, I forgot, you won't sign autographs," the girl said in a sulky tone. Nevertheless, she kept the sheet of paper extended and proffered a felt marker as well. The smell from the marker was strong.

"My name is Elizabeth Armstrong," Welsey said, "and I'll sign that if you want, but I'm sure you'll be disappointed."

"I loved the *Caged* movies," replied the girl, in reference to the only horror franchise Welsey had ever done (to help her afford her penthouse on Park, she'd told me). "You were awesome as Julie Martin, just amazing. Welsey Shaw!" she said again, louder. The paper and pen remained extended.

The actress leaned closer. "I'll sign it if you don't say anything?" she asked in the voice of a co-conspirator.

"Sure," the girl answered brightly.

"That okay?" Welsey pointed to a spot on the paper. She scrawled a line across the page, a large W followed by a twisted spring, then an S that I thought resembled the snake on the Don't Tread on Me flag, followed by a shorter twisted spring.

"Thank you," she mouthed, taking a rushed flash picture with her phone before retreating to another table.

Welsey closed her eyes at the flash, then opened them slowly. The sunglasses came out of the bag and went back on her face.

"How are things otherwise?" I asked.

"Whipped cream with a fucking cherry on top." Her voice remained low.

"Care to talk about it?"

She raised her head. "Is twenty-six too young to retire?"

"Depends how rich you are."

She pursed her lips. She looked like she wanted to kiss me. Somehow all the hairs on my neck and back stood up. "I could leave. I could sell my apartment, move from New York, live like a vagabond going from place to place. I'd like to start the day by opening beautiful French doors on the island of Capri."

"That's an interesting definition of vagabond."

"The wind whips the sheer curtains and my sheer top." She giggled. "Imagine my sheer top, Ferreira. Tell me what kind of sheer top I'm wearing."

"Hmm. It's white, just like the curtains. Has a neckline like…" I made a shape, across her collarbone.

"Boat neck? Jewel?" she asked.

"I think so," I said. "Or maybe—" I reached out.

"Halterneck? I like those," she said.

"Halterneck it is. And loose pants, also sheer—" She raised an eyebrow. "You're wearing underwear, don't worry. Cut off like—" I stuck out a leg and gestured, feeling like I was playing charades.

Welsey grew excited. "Oh, white sheer chiffon smock-waist gaucho pants!" she exclaimed. "I love those and don't own a pair." She started searching on her phone. "Go on, what about undies?"

"They're white too," I said.

"Shoes?"

"Gold sandals. Or bare feet."

"I callous easily," she said. "And how did you know I always wear gold sandals when I'm on vacation?"

"I didn't."

She looked at me doubtfully. "Uh-huh. Okay, I open the French doors onto this amazing ocean view. What happens?"

"The wind whips your hair," I said. "It ruffles your chiffon. It flutters along your arms and legs, emphasizing your toned and tight body underneath."

"I like this," she said. "Then what?"

"You walk onto the balcony, take in the view, and breathe the ocean air. You pull your hair from your eyes and your bangles jangle."

"No bangles. Not with chiffon."

"Okay. No bangles."

"Now you're there. What do you do?"

This surprised me. I thought for a moment, trying not to smile. "I grab you. You're irresistible in the wind. I push you back inside and press my lips against yours. I push you down onto the bed and *fuck* you. Hard." I stopped, looked up.

She threw her head back and laughed. For a long time. I didn't know what to make of it.

"I *love* it, Ferreira! I would go there."

I didn't know what to make of that, either, but I didn't have time to think about it. "Welsey Shaw's over there." The sound floated through the air and landed on us. I turned, to the table where the T-shirt chick was sitting, it turned out. Welsey buried herself in her curtain of hair and tensed.

"She signed it," came coarse whispers from the other table. "It's *her*."

We were now attracting a commotion. Welsey said something to me without seeming to move her lips.

The group across the room got up and came over. The original girl trailed in the background.

"Welsey Shaw," said one, as though she were telling the actress her name. Then a curious glance at me, for maybe a tenth of a second, to register there was ballast filling the other seat.

Another girl, also in a novelty T-shirt, said, "You're really great."

She smiled politely, mouthing "Thank you" without emerging from her hair.

Others were approaching now. A camera flashed. Then another. "Who's over there?" I heard.

People walking in started noticing the little scene by the corner table. A few started taking videos. Of her. Of us. Of her. After a moment a man maybe my age brusquely slid a napkin and a pen in front of us. Then he moved it closer to her.

Time seemed to slow down, and at the eye of the storm, around us, everything was quiet. Welsey sat there, almost appearing to be in prayer. Maybe she was.

"Would you sign my shirt?" a young man asked.

"Could you pose for a picture where you, like, have your arm around me?" requested another. Somehow he made it sound so reasonable.

"Welsey, Welsey!" pleaded a woman, "my sister loves you and

she has cancer. Could you do her a really, really big favor and record a greeting on her answering machine?"

Others just stood, not wanting her to leave. They formed a human barrier around the actress; I feared for what might happen next. She rose, not looking at me or anyone, and managed to back into the crowd. I stood, too, and tried to get to the door with her, but she was the master of escape, and I was clumsy in crowds. She managed to make her way outside without even touching another body; suddenly I was surrounded by people who regarded me with hostility. "Thanks a *lot*," I heard, along with "What a dick." I stubbed my toe and kicked over a chair before getting into the sunshine, where there was absolutely no sign of her, not left, not right, not straight ahead. After five minutes of standing around I trudged away, wondering yet again if, now that she'd been discovered, I had perhaps seen Welsey Shaw for the very last time.

11

"What's that noise?" Ann hollered from the bedroom. "Oh God, is there a fire?"

"Printer's jammed," I said, opening the top and removing a crumpled page. Crushed up against the machine were dozens more eight-and-a-half by eleven sheets, which became maybe a hundred down on the floor, beside my desk. Notes, questions, corrections, new notes, new corrections, general exhortations…

Ann rubbed her eyes, looked at the dresser clock, and sat up. "You need to set it further away from the wall. Otherwise it gets backed up." She shuffled into the living room and flipped on the ceiling light, blinding me.

"Her," I said, blinking.

"Who?"

"The one person who doesn't realize people sleep at night."

"Why do you have it set to print everything out?"

"So I can read it in the morning over breakfast. It's my morning reading assignment. Every day."

I straightened the pages, struggling to remember a dream I'd been having. Oddly, it involved real estate, and a fantasy I'd briefly entertained shortly after college. In my dreams I often drift back to the past and imagine other roads, other outcomes; I once rewrote a chapter to *No Room for Coincidences* in my sleep, overcoming several flaws in the narrative, only to forget the improvements recalling the dream in the morning. I've since kept a notepad near my bed, ready to write down thoughts the moment they aroused me. But they never came after that one time.

I'd been dreaming of Rachel Hoffman when the printer woke me. Rachel Hoffman had worked at Moffat Realty back in the day. A real stunner, five-foot-eleven of energy, sexiness and optimism. She was the star broker, and never despaired even when incredible obstacles were put in her way. Rachel was the top producer in the company every year.

For a while she wanted me to break away with her to start our own full-service realty company: Hoffman-Ferreira. Why not *Ferreira-Hoffman*, which is alphabetical? I asked. "Because reverse-alphabetical is the trend now," she answered. I concluded this kind of fast bullshit was how she made so many sales and afforded handbags that cost more than apartments. We never started *Ferreira-Hoffman* obviously, but we did once, when the boss went home early, shove the bric-a-brac off her desk in an effort to satisfy her curiosity if firm, hard surfaces really do make the act of coming more intense. (They do.) Afterward we broke into one of the drawers—somehow Rachel knew the combination—and ate some of her fancy chocolates intended only for clients while drinking Gevalia espresso made from a cute little machine. I didn't have another chance to see Rachel, who ended up, just a few short months later, in Long Island, buying and selling trophy properties (or what would someday be trophy properties).

Rachel was one of those perfect employees, desk assignation aside. She managed to look fresh no matter how late she stayed at the office. She urged me, subtly sometimes, directly other times, to quit my writing and do something that made more of a "return." My arguments invoking Salinger and Tom Wolfe were in vain. "You wind up loving whatever you do if you're good at it," she'd say. "This whole there's-only-one-thing-I-was-meant-to-do-in-life is bull." Rachel claimed she found me "erudite" and livelier than the "dullards" she mostly worked with. But we had different definitions of what we wanted out of life, ultimately, and hers centered around velocity. Speed. Once, while giving me a ride in her car, she powered through every radio station on the dial over and over, bored after the first few seconds of every song. When she listened to audio books she would increase the playback speed till the narrator had a Donald Duck timbre. She took speed-reading courses and ordered all her food "to go" because sitting in a restaurant waiting for waiters ("Why do you think they call them *waiters*?") wastes time.

She was action-oriented, with no time for the theoretical. "You think too much," she loved to say. "Nothing comes out the way you plan, so don't plan." That may as well have been her mantra. For her it worked.

At the same time she'd ask me things like, "Daniel, what does 'demonstrative' mean?" (Only she pronounced it demon*stray*tive.) She misspelled "mischeveous," "independant," and "seperate" repeatedly, and was hopeless when it came to "principle" vs. "principal." In high school she'd paid a college student to read her assignments for English class. For 35 dollars per Signet Classic, she got a neat two-page summary. And a spot on the dean's list.

After she left Moffat we exchanged emails, but they became increasingly superficial: a few lines about what she was doing, a new car, new possessions, vacations, attempts at hang-gliding and parasailing, her struggles with dieting and quitting smoking, which she'd started again after moving to New York City.

So a couple days ago I'd picked up the correspondence, after more than a year and a half of silence, deliberately laying it on thick, telling her that I was ghost-writing a novel for a major name and that it might have a shot at the big screen, or at least of being optioned for the big screen, which is pretty damned good itself. Google had revealed that Absinthe's restaurant-designing daddy was friends with at least one prominent Hollywood producer, and that producer liked Absinthe tremendously…

The next day I received a reply. It was written late, probably just as she was winding down to get her usual four-and-a-half hours of sleep.

> *Daniel ~~~*
> *Was thinking about you JUST this morning. Imagine that? Was talking at work to a broker-partner whose wife inked a big deal on her first novel, something YA about a girl who discovers she has magic powers but only between the hours of midnight and eight AM.*
> *How are you? I'm married and living in Alexandria, VA. Jeff is a strategist for the Republican Party and works in D.C. We just bought a three-story colonial and we're having it refurbed. He's leaving that all up to me. But I don't know anything about it so I just hired a decorator and told him to do anything he wanted.*
> *I'm also pregnant!! Due in September, so excited.*
> *~~~ Rachel Golding*

In my dream Rachel hadn't left for Long Island and then New York City and then Alexandria, Virginia. She'd stayed and we'd indeed started Hoffmann-Ferreira, though at some point in my dream it switched to Ferreira-Hoffman. We had a first-floor office facing the Delaware, white-painted shingles on the outside, medium-sized, bright and homey on the inside, filled with New England-y furniture, with wood floors and walls that were painted light green. Our twin desks faced out and were slanted slightly toward each other, she on the left, me on the right. Even though I haven't seen her in years she still looked the same, with short black hair that curled around her ears, pale skin, and black dots for eyes. Our desk chairs were those sorts you see movie directors sit in, and the desks and credenzas were all white ash, and beautiful. Dual flat-screen computers sat on our desks; piano music—CDs of Roz's—filled the room from small cube speakers atop file cabinets flanking a beautiful picture window. For our clients, plush colonial chairs and gourmet coffees and teas on a silver tray with both bleached and raw sugar. It didn't feel like a realtor's office but rather a bed and breakfast that sold homes, but what was wrong with that? Ferreira-Hoffman was the boutique place to go for premium properties, and it would never get bigger because we wouldn't want it to be bigger. I poured a cup of coffee, cream and sugar in a dark roast. I then reviewed the morning's mails and read about the latest in the Sullivan County real estate market. Rachel had the *Times* spread open on her keyboard. The phone was ringing.

We were married and had three kids, two boys and a girl. We lived in a spacious house with a garden, although Rachel wasn't much of a gardener, considering it a waste of time. So we'd hired someone, because I liked having a garden, as well as a library with bookshelves built into the walls. To me that always says "classy."

The phone at my desk would not stop ringing. Even after I picked it up, the raw buzz kept going. *I have to say hello*, I thought, *for it to stop ringing*. I said hello to no avail. Now Rachel was picking up her line, and still the ringing continued. She did not say hello, though. "Say hello," I kept urging. "It didn't work for you," she said, annoyed. Suddenly she grew panicky. "What's that noise? Oh God, is there a fire?" I smelled burnt dark roast coming from the Gevalia machine, saw smoke in the corner of the room.

"I'm going back to bed," Ann announced, straightening her rumpled pajamas. "I have to be up in two hours."

Now I was waiting for Brook's indefatigable assistant, Debra Austen, outside Aquavit. About thirty yards away a round-faced woman with gray eyes and cropped cinnamon hair approached, not quite five feet tall, clad in a thick leather trench coat and black Mary Janes. Debra looked at least a decade older than twenty-four, by design it seemed to me, and walked as if her coat were weighing her down. She was on her phone, a pen in her mouth, so engrossed in conversation that she walked right past me and lugged at the door.

"Hi," I said.

She looked up. There was no smile or indication of pleasure or even recognition. "Call me back," she said to the phone before stopping and leaning against the wall. She sucked on her pen and disappeared inside a cloud.

"E-cig," she said to my curious expression, holding it out an inch from my nose. A stream of fog came from her mouth and formed a storm cloud overhead that soon vanished.

"Is that fun?" I asked. She didn't answer. "I thought it'd be a way for smokers and nons to live in peace and harmony, but it's not. They seem to accuse you of blowing smoke and ruining their meal anyway. People just like to complain."

Without waiting for a reply she put the device in her pocket and grabbed the door out of my hands. Once inside we were efficiently led to the middle of the dining area, where Debra wiggled awkwardly into a tall high-back chair. She seemed ready to read a will. "I think," she said, pointing to herself and then me, "we should split the prix fixe meal." She looked at me. "Service is faster that way."

"I was interested in the Swedish meatballs," I said. She looked at me as though I'd just horribly blundered some sort of social test. "And I think it would be good to get the panna cotta to go," she told the waiter when he arrived, after repeating the prix fixe instructions to him. "I have a meeting at two," she said after he left.

I nodded.

"So this place is good?" Without waiting for an answer, she

said, "I rarely eat in restaurants anymore. I buy five boxed dinners each week and nuke 'em in my apartment. My roommate hates it. The smell it leaves, I mean."

"Does the roommate go out to eat then?" I asked, but again she didn't answer. Instead she dug some stapled papers out of her bulky square purse. "Absinthe is saying you're not responding completely to her notes and suggestions," Debra said, shouldering off her coat and revealing a black shirt that buttoned like a man's, with large front pockets cradling pens.

"I'm a little overwhelmed with them," I said. "Tuesday she sent me over a hundred pages in the middle of the night."

"She says it was eighty," Debra said. "But yeah, that's when she works. She's one of those types who doesn't sleep. Can't. Takes short naps in the day. She's a big advocate of this guru, I forget his name, who wrote the 'power naps' book. Wish I could be like her." For the first time Debra displayed what I perceived as emotion, and a faint smile may have even cracked her face.

"So she'd like you to work harder to incorporate more of her thoughts," she continued about Absinthe. She pulled off a small note clipped to the mass of papers, a note written on purple paper. "*And* she would like you to keep up with her a little better than you've been doing. Can you do that?"

I nodded.

"She's used to people turning on a dime. You will accrue points with her if you can do that. But really—" and she went through her notes again "—she's mostly very happy." Did I detect another faint smile or imagine it?

"That's good," I ventured. "That she's happy."

Lunch arrived. "Which do you want?" she asked.

"You first," I countered while the waiter stood. She shook her head.

"Then I'll take the chicken breast," I announced. That meant the herring went to Debra. She examined it with her fork as if registering her choice for the first time.

"Oh, good God, I hate fish," she said, crestfallen.

Serves you right, I thought. Just to make sure we couldn't trade, I started eating. Debra awkwardly put her napkin in her lap after seeing me do the same. "You have to be the master of many things at the same time nowadays, and many people. Your thoughts. Her thoughts. Your moods. Her moods. Random thoughts you can't foresee."

"How can I be the master of thoughts I can't foresee?"

She scowled at me; I was a smart aleck. "Here's the thing. Once upon a time there was some famous silver screen movie—I don't remember what one. But this was back when there was that production code and all. Very strict. You couldn't sleep in the same bed as someone else. There were censors, and they looked at everything before it was released. And they would not approve this movie."

She started tapping her fork on the table. "So, the director and the editor went back to it. They looked at everything and it was just right. They didn't want to change a thing. But they had to. So what did they do?"

"What did they do?" I asked between bites of perfectly cooked, melt-in-your-mouth chicken, as her fish got cold.

"They resubmitted the same film with a note saying they'd considered everything and they understood the problem. And this time the censors passed it."

She nabbed a passing waiter by the sleeve. "Could we get some more water here?" Her attention then went back to her fish.

"Really, they're very happy," Debra went on, studying the arrangement on her plate as though it were a new exhibit at MOMA.

"They're?" I asked. She looked up, hiding surprise.

"She works with a team. She's a corporation. Everything you write—that anybody writes—goes through about twenty hands up to hers, then twenty back down. Her father is her senior editor or something. Her little sister Cassique does something. Then she reads it."

"That may explain some of my confusion."

"What confusion?"

"I'm getting revision notes about things I haven't written. I tell her that and she insists I have."

"Then Cassique's writing them. Or Helena. Don't worry, just agree. Here's the secret," and she leaned over the fish. "If you say Yes to Absinthe, you can never go wrong. And she loves *Heaven's People* and the rest."

"Okay."

"Never underestimate what a 'yes' can do."

Our waiter returned with panna cotta in a pretty little box. The other waiter appeared with water. Debra gulped the glass, wiped her mouth, and handed the panna cotta to me while folding herself into her thick coat and hopping down from the chair.

"Thank you," the waiter said graciously when he received the credit card receipt. My companion had the e-cig back in her mouth before we reached the door. "Nice seeing you again," she said once we were outside, taking some quick puffs and creating more impressive clouds before flagging down a cab and disappearing into the back. I was searching for a bench to eat my dessert when I suddenly realized I had no spoon.

I watched the assistant come and go, or rather go and come, from Welsey's apartment. She carried shopping bags—white bags, tan bags, red bags, black bags. And she was robotic, a machine with brown hair, a thin build, and expressionless face. I searched for some humanity: a smile, a frown, a sense of fatigue, world-weariness. I failed to find any. Perhaps her demeanor was essential to the job of celebrity assistant.

After last week's panic and hasty retreat, I wondered what would happen today. If anything happened today.

If only we could agree to meet someplace else this would be easier. Our conversations might take a new turn. Or they might not, but I did not think about that.

A figure passed me, striding purposefully. Even though our eyes did not meet, even though she was a good twenty feet away, something made me notice her. The hair was reddish-brown and straight, with razor sharp bangs. Something about the way she was dressed said "I'm not from around here." More than a quarter century of observing people around me has taught that most Americans are not this coordinated when they're just walking down the street. Not a wrinkle on anything. The sleeves of her fitted red blazer were rolled perfectly to the elbow. Bangles climbed one arm and a gold watch hung from the slender wrist of her other like a Chunky bar. Pressed and creased charcoal shorts, black tights and flat open-toed ankle boots with diagonal gold zips completed the outfit.

Halfway down the block she pulled out a slender cigarette and an equally slender lighter. Despite persistent thumbwork, stiff winds kept the flame from coming to life. She sidled up to a man in front of a building. Dressed in business blue, he wasn't far past 40 but had already lost most of his sandy hair. As I got closer I could see both were staring at pictures of real estate in an office window. She was telling him how she wanted to buy a place somewhere, she wasn't sure where, that she'd come over here from a Moscow suburb and her family was invested in both art and construction. He was taking all this in with nods while checking his phone. I approached from the side. "What do you make more money on, if you don't mind me asking," I said. "Is it the art or the construction?"

Up close she was striking, with a finely-chiseled face as delicate as Welsey's but in a different way. She looked surprised, either at the question or the intrusion. "The construction," with a wrinkling of the brow that was easy to see even through the huge sunglasses. She struggled more with the lighter while looking at the real estate listings before ditching the ciggy in the street, making her small contribution to New York City's litter.

Off came the jacket, revealing a form-fitting black tank top. Her makeup was thick with no attempt at the natural look, the kind you expect to see for clubbing. "But art scene is thriving, too. This is the best time to be an artist in a long time." Her accent was crisp, her manner of speaking direct, her voice coarse, sexy.

"What kind of art does your family deal in?" I asked. The other man lost interest and drifted away.

"Contemporary art, Russian Impressionists," she said. "That kind of art was once forbidden. So of course it's most popular."

"That's the best way to make it popular," I said, wanting to keep the conversation going. "Forbid it."

"Yes." She started walking. I wasn't sure if my company was desired but I followed, because she was headed in the same direction I was. She fumbled for something—another cigarette, I thought, but it turned out to be a mint. "You from close to here?" she asked.

"Not exactly," I said. "But not too far."

"New York?"

"City, no. State, yes."

She nodded. "I have lived in Saint Petersburg, Paris and Milan and was born and raised in Moscow."

"And which city is your favorite?"

"No favorites. Each in its own way."

We crossed several blocks in silence. I arrived at 280 Park Avenue and was surprised to see her right alongside me. For once the place was near empty. We stood in line, she ahead of me. The difference between two people just by how they stood in a line was remarkable. Welsey was maybe a bit taller, less possessed, all nervous angles and energy. This woman stood rock still, rigid, a hand on her hip, jacket draped. The lining was gold. "How long have you been in America?" I asked.

"About a month. I'm staying with my brother. He used to run an import-export business for a while," she said, moving up in the line.

"Not anymore?"

"Now he has a restaurant."

"I see."

"Also internet pornography website."

"Ah," I said.

"Maybe several."

"I'm Daniel," I stuck my hand out.

"Irina," she said. A soggy, hesitant shake. She may have been more nervous than she seemed.

We ordered. She got a cappuccino and immediately poured six sugars into the tiny cup. I was in love with this woman.

"Sit down with me. I am expecting friends eventually, but you can talk with me until they arrive."

I looked around. If Welsey appeared I would excuse myself. "So, are you living in New York?" I asked her, sliding out a chair.

She nodded and started slicing her bagel with an ineffective plastic knife. "Columbus Avenue for now. Brother is taking in me and my sister." She took a sip of her petite drink.

"So what are some differences between here and Russia?" I asked.

She looked past me and out the window. "Russians are more educated and broader than Americans. In America they give multiple choice tests in schools. I cannot believe this. Life is not multiple choice.

"But Russians are also more emotional, in ways Americans cannot understand. So it evens out. We are about equal. So what about you? Who are you waiting for?"

"How do you know I'm waiting for anyone?"

"I can tell by how you act."

"Really?" I said.

"Yes," she affirmed.

"How am I acting?"

"You are waiting for a woman. It is all over your face."

"How so?" I said.

"It is."

I didn't say anything but shook my head.

"Then why do you keep looking to the door? Men don't look to the door for another man. It's only for a woman they look every ten seconds. I've got a secret. I've seen you in here before. You were here several times, sitting—" she pointed "—over there. And—" she pointed again "—over there."

"I was," I admitted. The feeling I had been spied on was odd.

"But I guess I should change subject now. You are turning red." She looked at a pamphlet on mixed drinks she'd just taken out of her pocket. "'Champagne cognac.' How about that? Two French words in a row with silent *g*s."

I smiled, relieved we were no longer talking about my roving eye and the door. "I'm a writer," I said, taking the pamphlet, "and I find those sorts of things to be fascinating."

"You are? Good for you. My father wanted to be a writer."

"And what was he?"

"School teacher."

"Well," I said, "that means he had all summer to write."

"True. But he never did. Always talked," she said. "'I'm going to write this,' and 'I'm going to write that.' But nothing. He went fishing. Had an old typewriter upstairs but never used it. I got in trouble if I touched it except for school assignments."

She turned over the pamphlet. "This is what my other brother does," she said, showing me a name and address in both English and Russian. "He brings Russian food into New York. Import-export service. People miss home, he brings it to them, one piece by one piece. My sister and I, meanwhile, are to help to open an art gallery." She pointed, as though if I looked through the wall I'd see it. "We look at artists all day. In Russia, too. They all paint like other people. You look at everyone and say, 'He reminds me of someone. He reminds me of someone.' But for years I never tell them this, because I think they find it insulting. Then when I did, they didn't find it insulting. They were made happy by it."

She leaned forward as though about to divulge a secret.

"I do not believe you should do anything to resemble someone else. Everywhere there is many artists, little art. Space and time are limited. Imagine," she said, eyes closed, "if every artist took a year off and for that time did nothing. No art for one year!" She smiled. "Wouldn't that be wonderful!"

I had to admit she made it seem appealing. "We'd pay attention when they started working again," I offered.

"We would! But more important, imagine no movies for a year. No TV. No concerts. People would start paying attention to each other perhaps. Go to museum. Nothing on the wall! Not even empty picture frame. Might be best exhibit ever. Go to restaurant," she pointed to the ceiling, "and nothing is playing up there. No singers. We have too many singers, all singing the same song."

"That is true," I said. "It might be a good idea to take a year off. Just cleanse, purge, relax."

"And in the end, maybe, we'd have better art."

"Perhaps," I said.

"But you sound doubtful."

"Do I? I don't know. I don't even know what art is anymore."

"Brother says art is whatever people with money and power say it is. But I am talking too much. I should leave you alone to your friend. My friend doesn't appear to be coming." And out came an odd little silver cell phone, one that had both Roman and Cyrillic characters. She spoke into it softly, listened, and didn't sound happy.

"This is a hunch," she said, "your friend is somebody famous."

"Why do you say that?"

She laughed and banged the table triumphantly. "Because you are not denying it! But before you didn't deny it, I could see it. You are tensely awaiting her. What's her name?"

I shook my head with a pleased smile.

"Come on," she insisted. "I want to know who it is. I will not tell a soul."

"I believe you," I said. Still, I shook my head.

"Is she, let's see, singer? Comedian? Actress? Artist? Painter? I think I should know about a painter. But she's movie star, isn't she?"

"I'm sorry," I said.

"Okay," she sighed, glancing down at her phone. "My friend is here now." I looked around but didn't see anybody. She stood and stuck out her finger and thumb, pantomiming a lighter. "You have fire?"

"You can't smoke in here."

"I am leaving."

"Sorry, I don't have a light." And then I saw it: three tell-tale birth marks that formed a triangle on her right hand, at the base of her thumb, unmistakable and unique, marks I'd seen many times before. Our eyes locked. "No? Okay."

I stared at those three marks.

"It was nice meeting you," she said. Another wry smile. "And you know something? I don't think your friend is coming."

She shook her head and grinned wickedly, while I tried to determine if the hair was a wig. It looked so real.

Outside she immediately received a light from the first man she asked. And there I sat.

Stupefied.

I'm supposed to want this, a trip to a breezy seaside resort for a three-day weekend of walks along the beach, lovemaking on a king-sized, four-poster bed, and red wine in a hot tub. Ann had planned it all weeks ago. "Life without a plan makes no sense," she said often. Throughout my life I have been paralyzed by my inability to plan. I never even know what I'm going to order in a restaurant until the moment the server appears.

The night before we'd been sitting on my leather couches, me revising per Absinthe's notes, Ann knitting a blanket for the couple she'd met at the tractor parade. She'd been going at that blanket with great enthusiasm, making progress faster than I'd ever seen her do before.

"What are your thoughts on children?" she asked quietly.

My parents often said children were too much work to make life enjoyable. After this they'd often say they didn't mean me. Then they'd go on to talk about things I knew I did, even though they talked about them as though they came from other children.

I didn't quite have a childhood the way my peers did: Boy Scouts, ball games, presents for good grades. My parents never met my teachers, never got involved in my school. That was okay. Then, as now, I preferred working alone. I grew myself up, surrounded by mentors older than myself. Didn't really think about there being any other way, for a while.

Maybe that's why I have never thought of children as more than hazards to avoid while driving. Could this be why I feel fairly rootless, despite having lived mostly in one town, one house, and driving one car? But here's a secret: I'm actually a little envious of people whose histories run long and deep, relatives who came over on the Mayflower, fought in famous wars, and were buried under the chestnut tree in a big cemetery. It's another form of immortality, not unlike being a writer of great works that people talk about long after you're gone. Nobody will talk about me in sixty years, I'm pretty sure of that.

And now Ann, who had stopped her needlework and was looking up at me with the first interested stare of the night, wanted to know my thoughts on children.

"Cook them thoroughly," I said. "Three hundred fifty degrees. Other than that, not much."

After a lengthy moment where she seemed to be thinking deeply about something she got up, went into the bedroom and slammed the door. I continued writing. I actually got more done with the door shut and the house quiet. I worked till midnight, fixing a whole chapter. As I was reviewing, she opened the door and returned with her own laptop, then went back inside, though leaving the door open this time. I suspected the whole laptop retrieval was just her way of opening the door for me without appearing she was opening the door for me.

Neither of us slept much.

And now we were in the car, halfway to a getaway at Avon-by-the-Sea.

Ann had packed days, maybe weeks ago. When she came into the bedroom this morning and there weren't two perfect bags at my side, her face fell.

"Let's go." She clapped her hands twice.

Ann started grabbing things from my drawers and closets as though we had an urgent timetable that couldn't be broken, which to me defeated the point of vacation. Halfway through she stopped. I looked up. She was across the bedroom, deep inside my top dresser drawer, the drawer she never went into before because there was never any reason to go into it, because we had never frantically packed for a getaway. And now she was staring at a BlackBerry.

"*What's this?*"

I have no idea how long I really stared. "I won it," I said, wondering exactly how.

"You never mentioned it before. Why was it shoved all the way in the back?"

"It was before we met. I don't use it so why wouldn't it get shoved in the back?"

"How did you win a BlackBerry?" she asked.

"Once a couple years ago when I was with Brooke we went to a bar where a telecom was sponsoring a promotional event. The first person who got five bullseyes in a row got a prize."

"I didn't know you were so good at darts."

"Yeah, I was surprised, too."

"Brian is getting married," she was now telling me. "I just now thought of that because he's very good at bar games. You should challenge him sometime."

Brian is her cousin: charismatic but flashy and materialistic. She doesn't see it and loves him blindly. He lives in North Carolina and is nine years older than Ann, so growing up they weren't that close. But age differences become unimportant in the homogeneity of adulthood. I imagine we'll be attending a wedding soon.

"That's great," I said. "About the wedding, I mean."

I really don't like weddings. You stand around sweating into stiff clothes, listening to bands that couldn't get into the corner bar play covers of awful music. You eat bad food: usually roast beef, lumpy potatoes flecked in parsley, flaccid greens, and floury bread, all washed down by cheap, warm alcohol. All this time you have to pretend you're enjoying yourself, smiling at people you don't know and making conversation about how beautiful everything is, when "tacky" is the word you mean. I try to conjure a hint of a tear when I hug and kiss the bride. One beat later for the groom I give an awkward man-hug, one arm around, a pat on the shoulder.

The last time I went to a wedding I bumped into the groom when I wandered into the parking lot to get away from all the smokers. By then he'd no doubt forgotten about my sad hug; he was helping a bridesmaid lift her cream-puff sleeve dress above her waist, steadying her against the side of a minivan. The warranty for the knife sharpener I gave the couple lasted longer than their marriage.

"What's the date?" I asked, wondering when I'd be getting the flu.

"August. Tammy's from Georgia so they're having the wedding there."

"Georgia in August," I said.

Somewhere along Highway 17 we passed a huge car dealership with a tall stadium sign that announced a grinning Ed Clarke as salesman of the month. I don't know why dealers advertise this. I'd want to keep it a secret, because if I understand it right, this is the guy who parted the most people from the most money most efficiently. Yet there was Ed's young face and spiky blonde hair on the Jumbotron, smiling down upon the rest of us, a rising star in blue suit and yellow tie that could be seen by ships at sea probably. I'll bet he gave great man-hugs.

I pulled into the B&B lot, taking the last spot, a tight one, next to an oversized pickup. I closed my eyes and inhaled salt air. Brooke once told me seaside California does not have the same smell as the coast here. Their loss if it's true. I love the smell of the sea.

Our room wasn't quite ready. Ann decided we should explore. The desk clerk said the sunshine would be short lived, so we'd best enjoy it now before a late-afternoon storm crept in. Ann donned a wide-brimmed hat from the trunk, and we set off on a random walk past eclectic condos and dead streets. We explored every shop, including those claiming to be antique stores, though I noted they weren't any different from the ones in Callicoon. I wandered through cramped aisles that featured mermaid floor lamps, napkin holders in the shape of praying hands, and an ancient accordion resting on a tall stack of yellowed sheet music. Surreal dolls stared me down. Boy and girl figurines that were salt and pepper shakers stood next to a duck-in-a-tuxedo milk pitcher, which I pushed further back on the shelf as Ann approached. At the end of the aisle a pile of used dime novels sat on a table—browned and brittle hardbacks sporting fanciful titles and cover art from the turn of the last century. The authors' names, possibly popular in their own day, were long-forgotten.

"Some of those are quite valuable," the matronly woman at the register tried to convince me, over and over, about everything in the store. "Do you like beautiful things?" Rhetorical questions annoy me, especially when they're for the purpose of making a sale, and I was tempted to say no, I like *ugly* things, like warthogs, but I was afraid she'd pull ten paintings of warthogs out of the back room and try to sell one to me. "Do you enjoy art?" she continued. "Do you have art on your walls? Outdoor scenes?" she persisted. At my faint, nearly noncommittal nod, she rose and directed me to garish seascapes in the back. "They're by Marco," she said, eying me as if I should know who Marco is. "I could sell you one at half price," she added a moment later. I politely declined and was ready to go, when Ann appeared with an armful of items: placemats showing covered bridges, potholders shaped like giraffes and a group of squirrel-like creatures playing musical instruments. We paid, and the woman asked for our email address, saying it was necessary to complete the purchase. I gave her one I hadn't checked in ten years.

Ann and I walked along the boardwalk and then the beach. I got sand in my shoes; Ann was more practical with sandals. There was very little talking, though I could tell Ann was thinking about something; she gets a certain rhythm to her when she's deep in thought. We found a jellyfish that had washed up, although at first I thought I was looking at a clear plastic bag, someone's litter.

We went to lunch at a shack decorated by American flags and sweatshirts. The jukebox played Elvis Presley. Or rather, one 60ish woman with crevices in her orange face, wearing cutoffs and boots and a beat-up denim jacket, kept making it play Elvis Presley. "Hey Wanda!" a silver-haired biker across the room shouted. "Turn it up.'" I ordered the patriotic Fourth of July Burger. I expected disapproval from Ann but none came. She got a Cobb salad that looked dry to me, and she barely touched it.

After another walk, this time along streets a few blocks over, not unlike the ones we'd already seen, our room was ready. I unpacked, which amounted to unzipping my bag. We were only staying a few days, and I didn't feel the necessity of closets and hangers. Ann did.

Our temporary home was a study in frilly. Yellow, white, and green, with pink accents. Draperies were held open with giant tiebacks. There were several old, overstuffed armchairs that seemed to invite brandy and cigars, even though a sign on the door and another sign on a table barked NONSMOKING ROOM! The bed was enormous. A bookshelf by the gas fireplace held titles no one would conceivably want to read—books about birds and trees and seashells, and railroads, oddly enough, as well as a few lightweight novels from the 1950s and 60s.

I imagined a day, half a century from now, when someone will pull *Heaven's People* from a shelf like this in a place like this. They'd wonder who Daniel Ferreira was. Then they'd go to their laptops (or whatever they had by then), search for me, and read the following:

> *Daniel Ferreira was born in Callicoon, New York, on September 19, 1972, and attended SUNY Albany, where he graduated with a BA in English. Best known for the novel* Heaven's People, *he never wrote another successful work and continued living in Callicoon until his death from* x, *at the age of* y.

Then they'd go on to the next random book. I'd be in their thoughts for all of eight seconds.

Ann was stripped down to her cream-colored bra and panties

and sprawled across the very high mattress. I joined her. The bed squeaked and bounced up and down; I felt like a survivor on a life raft.

We lay there for a while, mostly silent, until Ann said, "Touch me."

She found my hand with her eyes closed and guided it.

She was unprotected. I knew she was unprotected. She knew I knew she was unprotected. I felt my hand on her.

It's amazing how something you've both built up bit by bit can fall in one second like a house of cards, but it did, and there was no way to escape it. The last ten months of my life just imploded. I did not want to be there. I drew a long breath and held it. One day you realize you're not living your life, the life you're living is invented, borrowed. From who you don't know, but it doesn't matter—the point is, it suddenly doesn't fit. It's all wrong on you.

Ann released my hand and raised herself to the headboard. She watched TV while I replayed the last moments in my head and reached my hand out to her. She slowly but purposely moved her arm away, first just to scratch her other arm, then to fold it awkwardly across her chest, where it remained. Neither of us was prepared to talk about what had just happened. Then or ever. In that instant, I'd perhaps revealed the real me, and Ann perhaps had done the same.

Ann flipped through channels for half an hour, stopping on a documentary about the last days of World War II. When it was over they just repeated it. Or maybe this was the previous episode—the days just before the last days of World War II. I asked about dinner. She said whatever I wanted was fine. I told her I didn't know any place besides our lunch spot, and wouldn't she like to look at the guides in the room? She took them without enthusiasm.

We visited a restaurant with a view this time. The sun appeared from behind the clouds just in time to set gloriously. Except for ordering and a few comments about the food ("Fresh rolls," "Really fresh rolls," "I wonder who does their rolls") Ann didn't talk. Afterward I suggested a walk in the darkness, believing maybe we could talk if we couldn't see each other. Ann agreed but didn't talk. Instead she started humming to herself as she walked a few steps ahead of me.

The next two days were copies of this one. We spent more time walking on the beach—or Ann did while I followed her. She started cleaning up litter we came across, throwing it into trash cans on the boardwalk. "I hate litter," she said, with more vitriol than seemed warranted. It was also the first time I could recall hearing her use the word hate. She took off her sandals and went ankle-deep in the water. "Cold," she said when she came back. "Don't do it." It was the most she had shared with me since the prior afternoon.

I groped for conversation. Ann gave the bare minimum answers most of the time, and refused to be drawn out. "I wonder why the ocean looks so different when it's cloudy," I said, knowing full well why. It failed to start a conversation.

That evening we tried a new restaurant, and Ann ate everything in sight. We walked around making small talk as though it were our first date. I even made her laugh with an old joke I hadn't told since college. Back at the B&B, we watched Adolf and Eva again. There was something delightful, I had to admit, about lying on a puffy country comforter watching Hitler's death. I made this comment to Ann, looked over and saw she'd fallen asleep, Allied bombings her white noise.

The next day's weather refused to oblige us again. Our bathing suits would remain dry. We wandered into the same shops. Ann could spend hours in places like this, just meandering. I passed the time studying the sagging buildings and making conversation with their owners. From one store Ann bought a plaque that read, "I am not a slow cook. I am not a fast cook. I'm a half-fast cook" and another showing a pregnant woman with the caption, "I should have danced all night!" I was tempted by some vinyl of Jacques

Brel, but it was being sold as a set of ten, and it's my experience that a little Jacques Brel goes a long way.

We packed and started on the drive home.

12

A swarm of wasps surrounded Welsey. She batted at them helplessly. This did nothing. She turned and tried to flee, only to see her route cut off. I thought of a documentary I'd once seen of an African safari that showed a jungle cat trapped in a net, circling in panic as it realized there was no way out. I was half a block away; at first I'd thought there had been a terrible accident of some kind; I expected to see a body in the street. Only the swarm was moving. It parted briefly to allow me a glimpse of who was at the center, who wouldn't be heading into the Starbucks at 48th and Park today.

Word had gotten out. Through the media both social and anti-social, people now knew: Welsey Shaw came here.

Even a few people inside Starbucks were watching. For a while and to my amazement Welsey tried to be accommodating. She actually began signing autographs to the cries of "just one." More obnoxious were the ones who repeated "Welseywelseywelsey," effectively making it one word. I was struck by how soulless, how joyless, the whole undertaking was; with head down and face a mask, she scribbled her name, as fast as she was able, time after time, "Who's it to?" she asked tonelessly while signing, and when she got the reply she'd scribble that name above hers. Some would present her with seconds, or change places and pretend she hadn't signed theirs yet. But Welsey remembered even though she never looked most of them in the eye.

A fan pressed up against her and snapped a picture.

"Don't," she snapped. "Would you please erase that?"

Two layers of paparazzi ringed the fans. Men, long estranged from hygiene, flooded the scene with flashes, all the while walking backwards as if they'd been born to it. After what felt like an hour but must have been only two minutes, she said, "Apologies, I'm done." But no one moved, and more arms with papers reached out to her. "No, no," she said in vain. Turning to go, she found no way out of her circular dilemma. Then one fan, acting as the knight in shining armor, shouted at the others to give her space. He tries to lead her to safety, unsure exactly how close he could come to touching her, motioning as though he were going to grab her arm. But she turned the other way. "Okay," she said, her voice huskier and a little shaky. She put her head straight down and pushed, uneasily, to the corner of 48th and what seemed like the longest red light ever. I was sure someone had rigged it so that two or three of her lifetimes would pass before it turned green.

I hovered at the periphery, uncertain what to do.

The swarm followed her down Park, or proceeded her, actually, somehow managing never to trip or bang into anything while walking backwards; as much as she despised them, Welsey must have admired them just for that ability. One photographer, red-faced and obese, shouted "Congratulations" several times. I wondered how someone with his bulk could chase celebrities without twisting ankles or knocking down pedestrians. After another block of waiting at a light, whereupon she seemed to notice me for the first time, we turned abruptly down a side street, the horde still in pursuit, unshakable. We walked under scaffolding, past apartments, a Chinese restaurant, more upscale eateries, and two banks, farther and farther from the main drag. I was wondering how much longer this would continue and where it could lead when Welsey stopped dead and spun around, causing a small implosion. She stood, seriously sweating. I stood next to her, or right near her, wondering, like everyone, what was going to happen.

"Okay," she shouted, "Ask me things and make 'em good. Entertain me." It was like dropping a bomb. The cacophony prevented any actual questions from being heard. Whether this was her plan or not I don't know, but she stood, pleased with herself.

The insanity was replaced by silence. Every eye in the world was on Welsey Shaw. "Oh, you guys *suck*," she taunted. More meaningless cries. "Welsey!" And again the puzzling cry of "Congratulations."

"Come on, guys, you have me here, and not one interesting question?"

"When are you coming out with another movie, Welsey?" someone asked.

"*W-w-w dot i-m-d-b dot com*," she replied. Then, "What else?"

"Who was that guy you were with at the Met Gala?"

"That's old news. Google it," she said, and seemed to be genuinely annoyed. "What else?"

"Welsey, what do you do to look so good all the time?"

"Gauloises and Cap'n Crunch."

"Are you dating anyone now?" someone asked, looking at me.

"Yes," she said without adding anything more, before turning and continuing onward. At the next block we made an abrupt right into a narrow alley, and only half the paps could fit through. Welsey interrupted two olive-skinned boys heaving trash bags into a dumpster. The actress blew past with kisses and a wave, muttering "Hola," as they stared, first at her, then at me. She heaved open a back door and we entered into the blindingly bright white light of an enormous kitchen, where again Welsey gave the startled staff a quick wave before plowing through double doors and stepping into the dining room.

We startled the maître d'. Welsey whipped off her sunglasses and gave a smile—a smile whose purpose was to get men to move mountains, or at least allow a celebrity to do anything she wanted—and chose her own table, one in a section that seemed to be closed, as it was in shadow and deserted—perfect. She faced the wall. I took the seat directly across from her. Miles Davis' crisp Harmon mute was the perfect counterpoint to the cool, cool air conditioning.

After a minute place settings and glasses appeared. We were poured fresh water from a pitcher in which yellow and orange fruit slices bobbed. It tasted heavenly.

Welsey checked her phone while I perused the appetizers and decided that quail egg ravioli sounded absolutely like what one should order when accompanying a world-famous movie star who's being chased by paparazzi through New York.

"Vodka and tonic," Welsey said to the woman with obediently tied-back hair, black vest, and yellow necktie. "Make sure it's Grey Goose this time."

"We're out of Grey Goose. How about Smirnoff?"

Welsey stared at her. "Do I look like a Smirnoff's girl?"

The server didn't respond.

"Go buy some Grey Goose if you need to. Ketel One also works." She broke eye contact with the server, and that was that.

We pondered our lunch options. She chose the baked eggplant and had all sorts of questions about how it was prepared, making me realize there are intricacies to eggplant-baking I had never fathomed. The waitress patiently explained while I stared at my water glass. I ordered a gourmet burger the menu promised was made from filet mignon and pondered the quail egg ravioli appetizer that was 50 bucks. What the hell? I thought, handing my menu to another woman in identical vest and tie. Welsey rubbed her eyes. I noticed her hands were shaking, though she tried to hide it.

"I wonder why they're called paparazzi," she said to her palms before rubbing her eyes.

"It's derived from the name of a character in a famous Italian movie," I said. "He drove around on his Vespa snapping movie stars."

"I forgot." Her eyes snapped open. "You're a trivia genius."

I gave her a little salute.

"How many feet in a mile?"

"Five thousand two-hundred eighty."

"How many floors does the Empire State Building have?"

"One hundred three."

She smiled. "Got you there. It's 102."

"103."

"I've *been* there. On the top floor. Have you?"

"Haven't been to the moon but I know it doesn't have 102 floors. And neither does the Empire State Building."

"Oh yes it does. I'll take a photo for you and you can count the rows of windows. It'll be fun." She unfolded her napkin and took a sip of water. "I've really got to start dying my hair black again. And keep better tabs on my trash cans. For weeks I thought someone really close to me had ratted me out because only four people knew my travel itinerary—when the fuck I was leaving and where the fuck I was going. So I accused my mother. We had a big fight. Not my proudest moment." Another gulp. "Fuck me." She gestured to the front restaurant windows, where I could see at least some of the photographers were camped in the street. "Well, I guess that's blown. I'm amazed it went on, frankly."

"Why did that one keep saying 'Congratulations'?"

"Rumor that I'm pregnant."

"Are you?"

"No!"

"Don't look at me so surprised. Why couldn't you be?"

The vodka tonic appeared. Welsey halted the waitress' retreat with a hand on her arm and took a sip.

"It's Smirnoff."

The girl tried a weak smile and hesitantly took the glass back.

"So why do they say you are?" I asked.

"Who the fuck knows? I've been pregnant twice already. Also had a miscarriage according to one tabloid I successfully sued." She smiled. "Also I cheat all the time. Last year they ran photos of me from Saint-Tropez, and they said I was posing naked at some billionaire's villa. Well I was *not* naked. I was wearing a hat." She made a little gesture, shaping an invisible chapeau on her head. "A sailor's hat."

My ravioli arrived: three tiny creatures huddled at the bottom of a large bowl. They somehow looked sad there. My lunch partner leaned over the table and looked. "Wow."

"I think I'll just stare at them for a minute before going in for the kill," I said.

"My mother wants to buy me a star on the Walk of Fame. She is outraged that I don't have one."

"And..?"

"I don't want a star on Hollywood Boulevard. If you have to buy love, it's not love."

"And you have to buy the star?"

She nodded. "When are you going to eat those?"

"Really? How much?"

"Thirty kay. But it's not that."

"What then?"

"My mother thinks money solves every problem. Money and fame. And free drinks, let's not forget those."

"Your mom should meet my dad," I said.

"Hah. Let's set them up. Blind date."

Miles had finished. Ella started singing. As if on cue the server returned.

"It's Smirnoff again," she said, biting off the words. "Just bring me a fucking sparkling water with four fucking wedges of lime."

"What's your mother like?" I asked.

"You've already read about that stuff."

"I've read some," I said cautiously. "Of course, I don't necessarily believe what I read."

She smiled and grabbed her fork. "Okay, I'm going in."

I fended her off and bit into the first seventeen dollars of my appetizer. It was soft and delicate, and I chewed it gently while wondering if I should grow so fond of flavors I may never taste again.

"She's like my mother," Welsey said. "I've never had another so I can't compare."

"Have you ever wanted another?"

"Don't we all sometimes?"

I bit into the next third of my appetizer.

"You can choose your friends, your lovers, your acquaintances. I can even choose my co-workers. I don't like working with someone," she flicked a hand as if batting a fly, "they're gone."

"Lucky you."

"But I can't choose my family. Can you imagine if you could? Certain candidates would always be so busy. There would have to be some sort of sharing arrangement. 'I can be your mom from the eleventh to the twenty-first. After that I'm booked with someone else. Sorry.'" And with that she speared my last ravioli appetizer. "You were taking too long, Ferreira," she said. "It was torture watching it sit there."

"I could imagine a lucrative business based on that model," I said, watching Welsey eat my food. "Rent A Relative."

"But since there is no business like that, I drink," she said. "Or try to," she added, pointing towards where the hapless waitress had vanished.

Our entrees arrived, along with sparkling water that also did not meet Welsey's satisfaction. "I asked for four lime wedges, not three," she said, jaw moving sideways. "What I want to know is what did she do with the fourth? Save it for a customer who only wants one?"

"Did you hear the joke," I said, "about the eccentric billionaire who walks into a store and tells the clerk he wants to buy half a head of lettuce. 'Half a head?' says the clerk. 'Half a head,' confirms the billionaire. So the kid goes to the manager and says, 'Some screwball asshole wants to buy half a head of lettuce!' He turns around and sees the guy followed him. 'And this gentleman,' he adds smoothly, 'wants to buy the other half.'"

Welsey laughed loud and hard. "I've certainly experienced that in my life. I've been that man. I've also been that clerk."

My first bite into the burger involuntarily produced a sound that suggested orgasm. Juices threatened to overrun my mouth and gather on the bottom of my chin. The beef dissolved on my tongue.

"You bastard, give me a taste," she said, holding up her knife. Reluctantly I cut her a piece. "Jesus, I wish I'd gotten this." She pulled at her T-shirt. "I try to live healthy. But it's just an aspiration. Cut me another piece. A big one. Don't look at me that way. It's half a friggin' pound."

I chopped her a wedge, and she gave me some eggplant, which I pretended to enjoy.

"When you are very young," she continued, "and someone starts making all your plans for you, you start to wonder what a life *feels* like. The autographs I signed until I was sixteen or seventeen were mostly done by her. There was no way I could keep up. Fortunately our handwriting is nearly identical. I can't even tell it sometimes. That too has led to some dicey moments." She licked juices off her thumbs.

"Sort of unethical," I said. "The autographs thing."

"Common is what it is. But yeah, I still remember we had a

vicious argument about that once. She felt illusion was all that mattered. 'They *think* they have your signature,' she said. 'That's what they're paying for.'"

"When was the last time you talked to her?"

"Face to face? Four years ago, I think. But I've given her a number she can call in an emergency."

"Does she call it?"

"Once a week, usually. Three times this week so far. Yeah, it was a mistake."

"Do you call back?"

She shrugged and ate some eggplant. "The day I told her I was cutting her out of my life she came into my apartment in the middle of the night, hysterical. 'You're all I have.' We're talking about someone who at that point owned a six-acre house in Nantucket, a Maserati, and real estate in New York and Palm Beach. And an ex-husband who still longed for companionship and validation."

She twirled her fork as though it had pasta wrapped around it. "It was my access to celebrities that was all she had. Don't you ever tell that story to anyone. Understand?"

"Yes," I said.

"It's the fame she's drawn to, not me. She can't control it." She continued to twirl nothing. "It's like drug addiction, that stuff."

"What stuff?"

"Fame. You get used to it. At first it's amazing. Then it's just ordinary. Another ordinary day. You'd be amazed how fast that happens. So it becomes your usual, but you can't give it up either, because it's your usual. You're always looking to get more. The fabulousness is no big deal. You want more fabulousness. So you're always in search of a fix, more applause, more fame, more money, more material possessions. They aren't bringing you any increased happiness but their absence would make you more unhappy. You're running in place.

"But I should stop complaining," she said, changing her tone to one less intimate. "I can't keep blaming someone else for my life forever. At least, I don't think I can. I'd like to, though. It's nice."

Two busboys came to clear our plates. Welsey checked her phone as our waitresses returned holding ridiculously cute dessert menus. "No thank you," she decided for both of us. To me she said, "I gained five pounds last month." She leaned in: "Here's the plan—I'm going to get up like I'm headed for a pee, which is over there," she motioned with her eyes to a spot just ten feet behind us. "You stand up when I do, then point it out to me and sit back down. Your first acting gig! I will slip out back while you pretend to wait for me. Linger a bit. Count to fifty or something."

She got up. I pointed out the bathroom and she stretched her neck and nodded just as a server approached. I guess movie stars didn't have to worry about the check. Or was my concern the check?

"Where will we meet next?" was my hasty question to her retreating back.

"Whenever you're ready," the server said after she'd left, handing me a slip of cream-colored paper.

Ann's first words were, "What a beautiful day for a walk." My heart beat against my chest. I suggested a stroll by the Delaware.

We covered a quarter mile looking into trees, watching people run and walk their dogs. "Running. I should try it sometime," Ann said. We'd returned to our regular rhythms since last week's disaster. She uncharacteristically came over Wednesday and Thursday nights and we read the *New York Times* and did some laundry as well as planting in the back yard. Ann had cut her hair shorter than I'd ever seen it before, almost a pageboy. To my surprise I liked it. And now we watched eagles as they built their nests on the other side of the Delaware. I understand nests can be a life's work for some bird species; they return every year to add more and more sticks, building out the way you'd add rooms to a house. I was thinking about that, because I didn't want to think about what I was going to say.

As I walked with Ann I was thinking about the first time I ever got fired from a job. It was way back in high school, before my fling with Moffat Realty. My boss called me into his office in a lighthearted way, the only time I ever saw him act pleasant, and only after his assistant closed the door did he change his tone. He pointed from him to me to him again. "This isn't working."

"Okay," I'd replied, wondering naively where this was leading. It was, after all, the first time I'd ever been fired from anything.

"I'm glad you agree," he'd said in a friendly tone, sticking out his hand one last time. He'd instantly made me despise managers and overseers at every job I've had since. And today, on the bank of the Delaware River, I was copying him, right down to the pointing back and forth, handling the situation.

Of course I did not say, "This isn't working" in the tone that Pete Lumbo had used on me. I told Ann there were problems that were irreparable, that I had learned something in common isn't the same as enough in common, which was true. I kept talking, afraid to stop.

Ann listened silently, never interrupting, standing rock still. She nodded at times I wasn't expecting a nod, smiled at times I wasn't expecting a smile, brushed her hair out of her face as the warm wind blew. Why did I have to notice just now how pretty her hair was?

And then she turned everything upside-down. "You're just not looking to get as settled. It's over three years since my divorce..." She brushed some of that suddenly-irresistible hair out of her face. "I'm really glad you had the courage to say it first." She gave me the warmest smile. "It must have been really hard on you to say all this. Are you going to be okay?" I felt like the world's tiniest shit right then. Am I going to be okay? I did not know how to respond.

We hugged. Twice. Her hugs were as warm as always. Even now, Ann held nothing back.

I tried not to think about how much I hated myself right now. I tried to think about the next step in my plan instead.

"I'll go back and pack my things," she said. She'd been, I realized, gradually easing her stuff out of the house in recent weeks. What had appeared during the first half of our relationship had begun to disappear during the second. "I think you should go down to Matthew's or somewhere till I'm done, okay? I'll leave my key on the kitchen counter." I answered that that was fine, and I watched Ann walk away.

When I returned home everything was back to how it had been before Ann. Bits of the Sullivan County Democrat, half-finished crosswords, cassettes, sweaters, and socks and even some of my laundry that she would mix in to make a full load were gone. (She would later realize the mistake and give my stuff to Roz to return to me.) It hit me that we'd never exchanged any mementoes—real mementoes, like jewelry or presents, things sweethearts pass on to one another. I realized neither of us even possessed a photo of the other. Roz took one the night we met. I made a mental note to ask her for a copy.

For some reason I hadn't unpacked when we got back from Avon. And now I added more things to my tired bags, which I'd need for my trip. By nightfall I had driven to Peck's for some necessities and was ready.

The man who would be Neil deGrasse Tyson was startled to see me on his train.

"Today's Saturday," he said. "This is a surprise."

I agreed. A surprise.

I would be closer to my editor now. I'd be able to work more seamlessly here. And a change of scenery always did wonders when I was stuck.

People were more interesting. I like New York City. After this project was finished and I pocketed the bulk of my payment, I might look for a place here, one more permanent than where I was headed now. But for now I had to be careful. Payday was still a ways away.

Sweat was rolling down my back when I arrived in the famous lobby. My neck burned. I asked the man at the desk where I could buy sunscreen—the one thing I hadn't thought of. I got a shrug and a request for my credit card. I climbed four flights on the wrought iron staircase, pausing to admire the famous art, or what was supposed to be famous art. Most of it didn't work for me, but what did I know? I hadn't lived a tortured and twisted life. After walking through a dim, well-worn hallway, wondering if I'd perchance gotten a room where someone famous had either created a masterpiece or stained a bathtub, I unlocked my door. The smell of dust greeted me. I went to open a window and found dried, chipped paint on the sill, as well as a window that was either stuck or sealed shut. I'd read you could get nicely renovated rooms. I'd read you could get cesspits. I decided I'd landed in between.

After cranking up the A/C I unpacked my clothes and slid them onto hangers. Flipping on the tiny television, I saw Vanna White turn a letter, a bride cry over an ugly wedding dress, and a husband and wife team showing how easy it is to build a spare room onto the back of a house. I unpacked my laptop and booted up, but lacked the energy to deal with the crisis that was *Apocalyticus*. The room had no wifi. Which was fine, actually. I flopped on the bed and dozed, the TV still babbling. When I woke I called downstairs and told them to remove the set because it was a distraction. "Then just turn it off," said the clerk. "But if it's still there it will be a distraction. I am placing it in the hall." "If it's stolen you'll be charged." "For a 25-year-old box Goodwill would probably refuse?" I put it outside.

The rhythms of the world would be a distraction, I decided. I drew the drapes and got out duct tape to seal the edges of the curtains so that even cracks of light would not get through. I wouldn't know morning from evening, Wednesday from Sunday. I would work, making up for months of sloth. I would become a miracle of productivity, like postwar Germany.

So off I went, banging keys so hard that surely the people in the next room heard through the wall. After a while I became convinced there was no one next door. An unearthly quiet was my sole companion—very much the opposite of my Starbucks experience. At one point I was convinced it was at least early Tuesday. I peeked at my traveler's digital clock.

It was 10:10 A.M. on Sunday. I'd arrived yesterday afternoon.

Disappointing...

I opened the door. Somebody was frying—potato pancakes? Seemed to be coming from down the hall. It smelled awful, probably tasted wonderful.

I stubbed my toe, looked down. The TV was at my feet.

More writing. For about twenty minutes. Then a profound realization:

"I'm hungry."

(I was talking to myself a lot since Ann.)

The nearest deli would do. Then the next-nearest when I got tired of this one, eventually spiraling outward with the hotel as ground zero. Insanely good corned beef on rye. I spent that evening in the lobby, amid the art, the most striking being a hanging statue of a plump lady sitting on a swing. Many of these visual creations had been offered in lieu of cash by starving artist tenants, some of whom were still here; I wondered if I could leave behind a short story, or a signed copy of *No Room for Coincidences*. They could take each page and glue it to the wall. If they wanted modern art, they could glue the pages out of order, and any person viewing the art would be encouraged to guess how the story went. Interactive lit. I was a genius.

In this hotel, shielded from the noise of the world, my power was infinite. I had never written garbage here. I had never missed a deadline or had sheets returned covered in red markings or question marks that looked like serpents' heads. Here I was perfect, life was perfect. I had never made a single mistake. Here I was unstoppable.

Unstoppable.

"You needed a change...of scenery?"

I nodded into the sunglasses—Bvlgaris today. They were brand new. She told me she'd just bought them.

"So where are you now?"

"The Chelsea."

She put her head onto her fist like The Thinker and shook new, little Bichon Frisé curls. "For the love of God. Aren't you a bit young to be having a midlife crisis?"

"It's not a midlife crisis," I said dryly.

"Then what would you call it?"

The previous night I'd checked my email for the first time since arriving. A mysterious message appeared that read simply, "*141 East 44th St. 1:30 Wed.*" I tried replying, only to be told I couldn't do that.

So I went early and waited. MACCHIATO ESPRESSO BAR, announced the bold sign on the bright turquoise doors which seemed to suggest the caffeine inside. After a minute I noticed Welsey in the shade, leaning against a building across the street, wearing tan drawstring cargo pants, baggy white T-shirt, sunglasses, and a purple and red headband that made her look like a seventies hippie.

"I'm an iguana. I blend into the wall," she'd said after crossing to my side.

"That's a chameleon."

"Ah. Well, I had an iguana as a kid. I guess that's what I'm thinking of," she said, leading the way inside.

"And you never noticed it didn't change color?"

"I thought it was defective. I tried to return it."

And now we sat indoors, eating sensationally good prosciutto sandwiches. I was surprised by Welsey's choice of meeting place. It was small and busy. One corner table was the only real spot I figured she'd be comfortable. She grabbed it and made me order at the abrupt counter that spelled out M A C C H I A T O in huge letters, as though one might forget, between the door and counter, where one was.

"Writers try different locations to make the words come," I said reasonably.

She wasn't buying it. "If I were in your booties I'd give myself a mandatory number of words to write each day. No food until they're written and they're perfect. That's how I forced myself to learn lines. No TV until I learn five pages. No salsa dancing. No curly fries with mayonnaise. Once I had a very long complicated speech. It had to be in one take, because the director didn't want the camera to leave my eyes. I wouldn't let myself pee till I learned it. And, to facilitate things, I drank three sodas."

"How'd you do?"

"Ruined the carpet."

"So how did you get my email address?"

She gave me another of her "stupid" looks. "I called the publisher of your first two novels."

"They're not supposed to give that out."

"I'm Welsey fucking Shaw, remember?" she whispered, stirring up a cyclone in her cup. "Anyway, enough about you. What about me? —Oh, I went to a classical music concert the other night for the first time in my life. Part of the ongoing Welsey Project to better myself. Mozart." She said *Moe-zart*; I don't think I grimaced. "I really didn't care for it. Found him cold and distant. Fussy. Not a guy I'd want to hang with. Too much calculation. That's my non-expert evaluation, anyway. The music critic for the *Times* would think I'm an idiot, judging from this morning's review."

We watched as the line of patrons stretched to the door. Service was fast-fast-fast! This was the transformation of the classic coffee shop, which Starbucks in its plastic-and-fake-wood way still at least tried to be. Here things were different. You were expected to take your experience with you for processing outside, as you looked down at the cup of foam personalized with a cute rendering of a heart. (To me it looked like a leaf. Welsey thought it was an heirloom tomato.)

"But I noticed the people who seemed most bored during the music whooped and hollered the loudest when it was over. They were yelling 'Bra-voh!' trying to drown each other out. By the way, no one there had the slightest clue who I was. Or they didn't expect to see me at a place like that, so they didn't. Often I notice that does it. If you don't expect to see me someplace, it can't be me, right?"

"Who did you go with?" I asked, trying to sound like I didn't care all that much.

A pause. For a second I thought she wasn't going to tell me. "Peter Bazin."

"Peter Bazin," I repeated. Welsey swung an air racket over her left shoulder: the tennis star. A second later I remembered he'd recently divorced his wife of seven years, a stunning Dutch supermodel named Astrid. Handsome, smart, and as hateful of the press as Welsey was, Peter Bazin had a legendary temper. He was also a dare-devil, with a recently acquired taste for fast motorcycles.

Later I would read everything I could find about him and learn he'd studied classical and rock piano as a boy and had a brother who was a cellist, with a CD of Haydn and another of Bach that got glowing reviews.

"This is new."

"It is."

"How'd you meet?"

She frowned. "You know, I don't even remember. But he's the most interesting person I've come across in a while."

"Really?"

"Yes."

"*Most* interesting?"

"Yes."

"Bah humbug."

"Fine, whatever."

"What makes him interesting?" I asked.

She smiled. "I can't predict how he's going to react. You have no idea how predictable most people are. Or maybe you do. You observe people just like I do. I have a rule that I won't talk with you if I can summarize you in twenty words or less. Him I couldn't summarize in a thousand."

"How many words would it take to summarize me?"

"Twenty-one. Maybe twenty-two."

"Does that include hyphenated words?"

"Yes."

I smiled. "And how many words does it take to summarize you?"

"You know, you could say there've been, I don't know, a quarter of a million words written and said about me over the years. They haven't even come close. Everything is wrong. I go, 'Who the fuck is that?'"

"It's the iguana," I said.

"At the same time, I don't know what I'd say I am exactly. So maybe I require an infinite number of words. It's like a fun house full of mirrors. So I wonder, as I lie there in bed at night, if there really is a me. What if I don't exist? Well, okay, don't look at me like that, I know I exist. But what does that mean? Before every role, during every role I play, I worry that this, this is the one."

"The one what?"

"The role that will betray me, reveal me as empty. During the filming of *Jane Callahan* I kept thinking, *I know nothing about what I'm portraying*. Other people's words, other people's experiences, carried me through. There was one scene where I had to cry hysterically, and I didn't get any of it. The director just told me to cry a certain way, and I did. It felt almost blasphemous, to be praised for my 'honesty.' I was faking! Yet some asshole critics said, 'It was the first film where she was authentic.'"

She watched the crowd.

"Peter's not troubled by things like that. He knows he's the greatest in the world. I don't have to tell him. He tells me. Every day."

"Everyone feels like a phony," I said. "Even Peter, I bet. He's just faking."

"So you believe we're all phonies? It's all bullshit?"

"Okay, here's the thing," I said. "I don't know what I mean. Because *if* I'm phony I don't mean what I just said. If I'm real I still don't believe I am. It's kind of Zen."

She pondered that. "You know, I don't know if they put booze in the coffee, but that actually makes sense."

"Good."

Abruptly Welsey put her head on the table. I didn't understand why until I looked to the drink counter. A couple of young, giggling Asian girls were posing with their barista while a slightly older man took photos using a camera with an elaborate lens. The barista smiled, though it was clear he'd rather get back to his work. But the trio wanted more photos—of how he made his cups, of the counter on which the coffee sat, and the detailed artistic renderings of foamy hearts and leaves.

The three took the cups and placed them on a table across from us. They shot straight down into the beverages as new customers entered the store, splayed elbows barely avoiding a messy collision.

A barrage of spirited Chinese (I think it was Chinese) burst forth from the group. Everyone was pleased. One of the women—it was impossible to tell any of their ages—was about to drink one of the cups of coffee when the other woman stopped her with a hand to her arm. Embarrassment all around.

Welsey's head bobbed back up. "This reminds me of this big fight Peter and I had. Right after the Moezart concert. He's in love with letting the world know where he is and what he's doing every second of every day. He says from the moment he wakes up every morning he imagines a camera's on him and people are watching everything. 'The future is the spotlight, twenty-four seven,' he says to me. Don't you dare tell anybody this but he's just hired a photographer, whose job it is to follow him around and take pictures."

"Pictures of what?"

"Of him, doing everything. To document his life."

"What's he going to do with it all?" I asked.

She moved close to me. "Well, if you dare tell this to anyone, ever, I will break your toes."

"Not a soul," I said.

"I'll start with the little one and work my way over."

"I promise."

"One by one, each toe crunching like little tree branches snapping."

"If there's one person you can trust right now it's me." I said.

"Peter plans on bequeathing his whole 'media legacy,' as he calls it, to an institution, maybe Yale. He believes that by recording his every waking moment he's showing ordinary people how someone extraordinary operates, and they can learn from it and thereby become higher-functioning themselves."

Why in Heaven's name are you fucking this guy? "That's fascinating."

"He believes extraordinary people have special characteristics that set them apart," she said, reflexively shielding her face from the photographer who'd decided retakes were in order. "So he wants to raise children with super-high IQs. He believes if we do this, our problems will be solved faster, the world will be a better place. There wouldn't be starvation in the world if smarter people controlled the food supply. There wouldn't be people with no marketable skills if people studied what was useful and not what they wanted."

I didn't ask Welsey why he obviously felt the world needed tennis.

"He wants me to take an IQ test."

"Why?" I asked.

"To see if I'm a suitable mate."

I hoped my shocked silence wasn't too lengthy. "Are you going to?"

She looked down. "He's very persuasive. I don't know. But just last night he gave me a passionate pitch for why more is better. '*A World of Ten Billion by 2040*.' That was the title."

"The title of what?"

"His argument. He gives his arguments titles," she said. "He thinks more intelligent procreation overrides the fact that there are now more people to feed. They'll find new ways to grow food more efficiently since they're smarter, earning their keep, he says. And I'm actually thinking about it. If you met him you might understand."

"Well, I suppose anything's possible," I said.

"Don't mock me. His ideas just take some getting used to, that's all." She stood, cinched her drawstring pants, and checked her phone. A gasp.

"Shit, gotta go."

"Hey," I said, "where are we meeting next time?"

"Be prepared for anything, Ferreira," she said, planting a quick kiss on my forehead. "Embrace the mystery."

I tossed our trash and went outside. To my left, nothing but ubiquitous scaffolding, trucks on deliveries, and sidewalk that needed a power wash. To my right, more trucks and a shrinking Welsey. I followed, lost her, found her again heading north on Lexington, and watched her turn left on 45th and then beat a path up Fifth. This woman could walk. I guess it was part of being a New Yorker. She looked cool and collected in her thin attire, the way the T-shirt moved against her body, revealing occasional flashes of toned tummy. As we neared Central Park her stride changed subtly to a don't-give-a-damn strut. At the same time, she looked around cautiously.

Hot dog stands cluttered the sidewalk, the aroma of steaming franks making me nauseous in the heat, obviously not the effect the vendors intended. A street musician played Charlie Parker licks on a shiny alto. "REQUESTS $5.00" read the sign at his feet. The place was jammed with people seeking shade. Nevertheless I managed to recognize the assistant waiting at the far end of the block. She handed over Chevron and walked to the periphery. Welsey, head down, strode into the park. Someone was waiting for her, several someones—all of them men, one of them very obese.

I knew him. He was dressed exactly as on the day we were chased down the alley to the restaurant, in a T-shirt with a faint grease stain, belly over the waistband of his shorts. Welsey went over and spoke briefly, placing an arm on his shoulder and giving him a hard pat.

He and Welsey seemed to be trading jokes. She produced a cigarette and lit it, throwing back her hair and blowing smoke that seemed to linger in the humid air. I had never for a second pegged her as a smoker, never seen pictures or smelled it any of the times she'd sat feet away from me, although as Irina she had held a cigarette and fumbled with a lighter. And now she and the photographers stood under the shade of trees, smoking up a tempest, best of friends.

I was across the street from all this, hiding between tinted tour buses disgorging gaudy tourists. Welsey had one elbow in the palm of her other hand and was nervously flicking her ash before sending the butt spinning. She then removed her sunglasses and squatted to feed Chevron some treats. The photographers burst into action. It was done smoothly: the snapping of pictures, the posing for shots—a well-oiled machine, with Welsey in the center of it. She looked around, rose, walked about thirty feet, did an about-face, fed the dog again; all this allowed them the chance to capture her a few more times.

She acted as though she did not want to be snapped, though, looking hurried and irritated, or so it seemed from my vantage point. She put her hands through her hair a couple times—a move I knew from watching so many of her films was a gesture of distress, dismay, irritation. Then as abruptly as it had started, it all ended. She pulled back her hair, gave a signal that seemed to indicate they were finished, and left the park, the assistant returning from the wings to take the dog, and me, hiding behind a big red tour bus, wide-eyed and uncomprehending.

13

"You got a package," the nighttime clerk said.

It was from Roz. She had thoughtfully forwarded my mail. Most of it went straight to the trash, but of course there were the bills. I decided I didn't feel like dealing with them right now and tossed the pile onto a chair. That's when a blank white envelope fell out. The short note inside, written on thick yellow stationery paper, was from Roz, telling me everything was fine on her end (trying to find out exactly what had happened between me and Ann) and detailing not just the mail she was picking up for me but the checks she'd thoughtfully done on the house, as well as the food she'd left for the raccoons and deer and birds that happened by—and kept happening by now that they learned happening by got them fed. I imagined an Edward Hicks tableau in my backyard.

There was a small P.S. on the back. *What all is going on?!*

My circle of delis, cafés, and restaurants expanded each day, as I ventured further and further from the Chelsea in search of culinary adventure. At dawn I went to a new breakfast place, one advertising fish tacos. For breakfast. Why not? Made about as much sense as a paparazzi-averse actress posing for photographers. I was beginning to feel like this place was a neighborhood. I grew to know some of the store owners, hung out in the lobby of the hotel, and took long walks when my writing hit a wall, wondering what it might be like to go to a classical music concert with Welsey Shaw. She would be dressed in sleek black. We'd make witty conversation in the lobby over drinks and carry them with us to our seat. A few people might look our way. The lights would dim, the conductor would stride out to applause, and we'd be off on the most thrilling *New World Symphony* or *Roman Carnival* in years. At intermission Welsey and I would trade bits of gossip—what we'd liked, what we didn't, the people in the hall, the conductor's other concerts, and whether American orchestras sound brighter and louder than ones in Europe, of which we'd have both heard our share.

It sounded like an amazing way to spend an evening. It was hard for me to think of something more satisfying. Hard, but not impossible.

When I returned to my room a new anonymous email was waiting for me. Different day this time, and way different place. And underneath that a cryptic line I spent the night pondering:

Warning: This will be an ordeal.

She was already there when I arrived at 45 East 45th Street. I climbed a flight of marble stairs and went to the concierge desk as instructed.

"Good afternoon," I announced, feeling like a fool because of what I was instructed to say next. "I'm here for Helen of Troy."

The humorless being ignored me until he finished doing something on his computer. "Mad 46."

The lobby was an airport terminal that had been designed by

the king of France. There were glorious chandeliers (really, they were gorgeous), there were vases with flowers everywhere, there were Ionic columns and elegant yellow lighting that bathed the whole place in beautiful warmth but hurt your eyes if you tried to read a book too long. Above all there was a din that never seemed to quell itself, very different from Starbucks' white noise, and my temples began to throb. I wandered around in a big circle trying to make sense of the concierge's cryptic words, which I already wasn't sure I was remembering properly. I looked for signs for something that might jog my memory and found nothing. I wanted to go back and ask for clarification, but the man was now gone. I walked more, my circle getting tighter. I wandered back to the door, down the tiled stairs, and saw a sign in an adjacent hallway that had "Mad46" in Art Deco script. I followed to the end, past shops that urged me to pamper myself with haircuts and massages. At the end was an elevator. A man whose function was to keep me from getting inside stood tall.

"Reservation?"

"I'm with Welsey Shaw," I tried.

He didn't say anything but did step away just far enough to let me pass. I found myself sharing a ride with some overly made up blondes in crazy stilettos who wore perfume that smelled like cupcakes.

The doors opened and I emerged into a lounge crammed with models from a Barneys catalog, drinks at chest level, sitting or leaning with a practiced look of urbanity. Was Welsey really up here, I wondered as I wandered. I had been told to dress a little better today, so I wore a dark long-sleeved shirt and the dressiest pants I'd brought, which weren't too dressy. Still, I managed to attract looks from a few people who appeared to have been clothed by Ralph Lauren personally.

Just as I was about to retreat to interrogate the concierge again, I saw her, squeezed into a corner spot, sporting perfectly circular blue sunglasses in the shade.

"Hi, Helen," I said, sliding in across from her.

"Did Gerhard smile?"

"The guy at the desk? He's incapable of smiling, I think."

"He is. But I thought it was worth a shot."

"Why are we here?"

"Why not? Look at that sun. Look at those clouds. Can you get sun and clouds like this anywhere else?"

The whole rooftop bar was decorated with chic outdoor furniture in greens, off-whites and light browns that appeared to be expensive until you sat down on it. The space was designed to exude the illusion of privacy and exclusivity. Tall shrubs stood guard around the perimeter, effectively blocking the views that should have been the selling point. I thought it odd but no one around me seemed to care.

A pretty cocktail waitress appeared on my right. "I'll have what she's got," I said.

"The Caipirinha Fresca," she replied with a perfect accent.

"You'll love it," mouthed Welsey.

The waitress turned, deftly dodging an enormous obstacle that had just materialized behind her.

The object seemed oblivious to the near collision, ignoring the waitress, smiling at the actress. "*Well-hzee.*" It grasped both of her hands and squeezed them. "How are you? What are you doo-ing here?"

He was around 60, sandy haired, lumpy faced, and he sounded like a tea kettle when he breathed. His stomach was inches from my face; I saw he was unable to completely button his white shirt under his gray suit jacket. The business of the shirt-buttoning stopped two inches above the pants line, where, he surely hoped, his striped yellow tie would hide the belly, unless he leaned over a table to talk to an actress at the Mad46 skybar and it drooped forward. I forced myself not to look.

"*Sweetie!*" Welsey exclaimed, glancing around. "How *are* you, Harry?"

He bent down further. I wondered if he wanted my seat. "Busy, Wels. Too many balls in the air. *F-hive* features and trying to get four projects off the ground for cable. And that's just on the Left Coast. My friends are telling me to s-hlow down."

"They don't know you, Har." Welsey gave Harry Hershman a deep and penetrating stare through her lenses. "Still, you gotta be careful. Relax every once in a while with a mint julep. In a hot tub. Does wonders."

"I'd substitute Gentleman Jack but otherwise right with ya." He smiled, and I saw the gap between his tiny teeth.

"No, it's gotta be a mint julep. How's your brother?"

"Great. Better than me. Gets up early. Goes to the gym. He even quit smoking. Can you imagine Lou Hershman without a cigarette in his mouth?" He hacked up a laugh.

"I can't," said Welsey.

"So when are we going to do something again?" he asked, his voice dipping low, almost inaudible. She grinned like a child who had just been told she had the prettiest pink dress. "We should talk." He placed his hand on her shoulder, close to her neck, and patted her.

"We should," she said. She put a finger to her phone. "Call me." For some reason she mouthed it.

"No, you call me," he said. Welsey's face tensed for just a second.

"Okay, I will. Whatcha doin' here, Har?"

He stood up straight and looked around. "Meeting some people, that's all." He said it as though he'd been caught snooping in someone's office. "You know, these appetizers suck. They taste like microwaved supermarket stuff. Yet that hasn't stopped me from eating fifty of them. Why is that? I produce things even though I hate half the shit that comes out with my name on it. I'd probably starve otherwise, though. I was watching your boyfriend on TV recently," he said after a moment in a voice more crisp and impersonal. "They cut to the stands, and you were there. The announcer said, 'There's the premiere actress of her generation.' They never even identified you by name, because there was no need to."

This time Welsey didn't say anything. The waitress returned with my drink. "Caipirinha Fresca," she said in the perfect accent again, followed by "Sixteen" without an accent.

I dug for my last two Hamiltons while looking over to Welsey, who was oblivious.

"I want you to win another eunuch statuette," Harry was saying. He laughed as though that were hysterical.

"I do, too."

"Call me and we'll *talk*." He emphasized the word as though it were an unusual thing to do on a phone.

"Okay, Har. Looking forward to it."

He leaned closer and said into her ear, at the same volume, "Hetherington's. New restaurant on Second Avenue. Amazing porterhouse."

"We should go," Welsey said.

He leaned in closer and whispered something I wasn't intended to hear, but I caught part of it. "Ciera's getting—" and then his voice was covered by a woman's loud laugh from the next table, "—for making the next *Twilight of the God-Emperor* movie."

Welsey shook her head, and he bent as best he could to kiss her on the cheek.

"Take care, Wels."

"Bye, Harry. I want to eat steak with you."

"You should just check it out yourself and give me a report."

We watched as he rejoined a group on the opposite side of the deck: a woman with orange hair and many wrinkles, two scraggly-haired men with beards, and a man with a smoothly-shaved head, dressed in a gray silk tie. Welsey watched them as though she were trying to lip-read. For the next several minutes she didn't even notice me. Finally she got up and went over. Minutes passed, lots of them—at least thirty, by my count. I finished my Caipirinha and had nothing to do. Harry's back was to me, but when he turned he was clutching a plate of sliders, leaning against each other, toothpicks in them, like drunken buddies, or seasick sandwiches. The wind blew, his tie shifted, and I got the flesh flash again.

Welsey returned, taking some time to make it back, surveying the rest of the party. She sat back with me but her mind was still on the others. Her phone rang. "Shit," she said before even answering. "No, don't come up here," she spoke into the mouthpiece. "Change in plans. Meet you downstairs in five." I looked at her in surprise.

"Have you eaten?"

"No," I said. She didn't respond to that, other than to get up and leave. I followed.

We were back in the lobby. It was now quieter and less crowded. Arms waved, figures approached, two of them. The faces were darting from Welsey to me and back again.

The first woman had dark cropped hair and dramatic, sculpted cheekbones, and wore an equally dramatic and equally sculpted leather jacket with half-length sleeves. She was one of those whose age was impossible to guess; I wondered if she'd once been a model. The other was probably in her early 30s, with a more conservative wardrobe and a huge diamond ring that managed simultaneously to be impressive and dull. "You're dressed perfectly for this weather! I wasn't so smart," the short-haired woman said to the actress. Welsey said something I couldn't hear and nudged her. That prompted an outstretched hand. "Claris."

"Daniel," I said, taking it. It was cold.

"Where are we eating?" Welsey asked.

Claris withdrew her hand and pulled out a phone in a fancy gold cover. "This place," she said, wiping a finger against the glass.

"Is there a menu?" Welsey asked, and the screen was held so that everyone could see it but me. Indeed I no longer seemed to be there anymore. The restaurant would require a cab. "Is he coming?" Claris asked. "Yes," said Welsey, without looking at her or me. We headed back outside. "Oh good, a big one," said Claris, and after a moment I realized she meant the cab headed toward us, a Crown Vic.

The younger woman sat in front and gave the driver hyper-detailed directions. I sat in the back cheek-to-cheek with Welsey, the first time I'd ever rubbed against her butt. She didn't seem to mind. We headed into unexplored parts of the city, at least for me. While I sat and looked out the window, feeling a little like a pet dog, the others talked business, but cautiously, not finishing sentences, letting thoughts trail off. Welsey, meanwhile, nudged me with her rear end; whether she wanted more room or was playing "footsie" with her ass I wasn't sure. Not a moment too soon we got out and entered a curtained place that, dimly lit and upholstered, seemed to be hiding from the world. A hostess appeared and led us to seats that felt oddly private despite being in the middle of the room. "Would you like a black napkin?" she asked me. I stared puzzled at my white cloth for a second. "No, thank you," I answered. "*I'd* like one," said Claris, overlapping me. "Me too," said the younger woman, who then introduced herself to me as Mindy.

She turned out to be a fascinating conversationalist, shifting through one topic to the next by way of unexpected connections. Clearly well-read, she'd gone to Harvard and graduated *magna cum laude*. Staring into her wide, smoky Asian eyes wasn't hard either. Mindy and I were so engrossed that I found myself being asked about what I wanted without having read the menu.

"What she's having," I said, pointing to Welsey, wondering what I'd agreed to.

"Drinks?" a server asked the table.

"Chianti," said Claris immediately. Mindy seemed caught off

guard. "Oh, what's a good cocktail? Dirty Mojito."

I was next. "Maker's Mark," I said, not really wanting it, not really having any other ideas. I caught snatches of hushed conversation on my left. Claris and Welsey were talking about me. I was talking to Mindy, but I was trying to hear what Welsey was saying. Claris kept looking at me doubtfully.

Mindy then pulled out the slimmest laptop I'd ever seen and set it on the table.

"We starting working?" she asked, already booting up.

"Naomi caught Amanda Richman in time," Claris said to Welsey. "They're agreed to spin that hit piece, *if* you give them a one-hour sit-down when you're in L.A. next week."

"Where?"

"The Four Seasons. Thursday. I booked the big suite."

"Friday."

"Problem with Thursday?"

"Not at all. But change it to Friday," Welsey said.

Claris dialed her phone and waited for an answer on the other end before putting it on speaker. "*How are things in Glocca Morra?*" both Welsey and Mindy singsonged. For the next ten minutes, during which time appetizers arrived, all three of them peppered the voice, whose name was Naomi, with questions about her vacation, what time it was "over there" (late, but Naomi was an insomniac, and had been swimming laps in the pool she had bribed staff to keep open for her), and where she was (now in her room, having just toweled off after a post-pool shower). Welsey seemed relaxed now. I felt like I was no longer needed, but there I was.

"Naomi," Claris said, "we have someone with us. He's a friend of Welsey's."

"Hello..." Naomi said, not putting a period at the end.

"Hello," I said to the phone, feeling a little silly. "I'm Daniel." No acknowledgement. Instead, "Did you know when you use the pool at two in the morning you get to check out some serious hunks performing maintenance? What are you all eating?"

"Savory cheese truffles with chives, pecans, and goat cheese," said Claris.

"Goat cheese!" moaned Naomi. "Describe in detail." Everyone but me did exactly that, and I wondered if she could make sense of it all on her end. Finally she must have had enough, for she cut them off. "Okay, so are we ready? Here we go, everyone."

"Going down the list..." Claris said. I still had no idea what was going on.

"Our social media expert..." Claris deferred to the younger woman, who leaned in closer. I saw for the first time that Mindy had a row of ringlets as fine as a baby's curls pierced into her left ear and a small tattoo of an abstract symbol on her left wrist.

"What?" said the phone.

"Viral expert," Claris said.

"Oh."

"Hi, Naomi," Mindy said.

"Hi, Mindy. How's Brian?"

"Brian's great," she said. "Just got a corner office at Merrill."

"Congrats to Brian," Claris said, and Welsey gave a thumbs-up. I smiled awkwardly.

"Thanks," Mindy said, "I'll tell him." The conversation paused while our plates were cleared and new silverware was put down. Mindy looked to her screen. "We've been working on changing up dynamics. My brother-in-law likes to say the pretty girls never call. But that's not working anymore. Even the pretty girls call today." There was a pause. No one said anything. "Welsey is going to make them call her. This is how." A power point presentation began on the laptop, which was now pointed at us. Or her.

"We get interviews with London mags and papers," Mindy continued. "And French, German, Italian, Japanese, and so on. Foreign languages. We black out American media for the most part, in the beginning. That makes the new access, when it does come, feel special. We have pages of copy already written that you can edit. All fresh. None of the old gold. Maybe you'll appear in a French or Spanish film in the interim, and we'll publicize that here. A film that won't play in the U.S. Then we open the floodgates, and it will be a new you."

"Less familiar and a little exotic," added Claris. "Foreign cachet."

Welsey nodded, and took a big swig of water from my glass without realizing it.

"Next," Mindy continued, vanishing her screen presentation with a swipe of the finger and replacing it with another, "we create events around you. The event takes center stage. You're going to change people's lives, thereby changing how people see you." Another flick of the finger, another screen, red this time.

"But here's the thing that's a little different," Claris said. "You will *not* be the headliner of these events. In any event you will be the buried lead, a couple of paragraphs, three-quarters inside a story, say, that will seem to have no connection to you except tangentially. But the effect will be to have them come away first and foremost with a higher opinion of you, whether they realize it or not."

"In fact, if we did it right, they won't realize it," Mindy added.

Two waiters brought over our next course, which was ceremoniously handed out. I saw that I had ordered lobster ravioli with black trumpet mushrooms in a heavenly butter sauce. "Good eating," one of them said to us all.

"What happens if people *do* figure this out?" the movie star asked, getting back to the subject of pre-fab PR.

"Depends," Claris said. "Lots of ways we could do this."

"What are you guys eating?" Naomi demanded. "Every morsel. I'm starving and they're closed downstairs."

Everyone except me went around the table describing their dishes in obsessive detail. Welsey, on my left, sat with her back straight, head down, but she scarcely touched her meal; the only sound from her was the pinging of a ring on her right hand as she fingered her glass. I looked at the ring: it was chunky and silver, a curvy modern design, shined to perfection. It looked like it weighed her finger down.

For a while the presentation halted and we just ate—or three of us ate and Welsey went through motions of eating. I polished my plate and wanted to ask Welsey for hers and would have if I hadn't been under observation. Naomi went away from the phone briefly—not that there was much of a difference from when she was there. Meanwhile Claris and Mindy made small talk. Welsey spoke little. I rolled lobster and 'shrooms around in my mouth, making a mental note to remember these tastes forever.

"Okay," said Mindy, waking up her laptop, "next, to complement and extend the mainstream media assault, we would connect with professional blogging services to create content."

Welsey started to make a face.

"Hear us out," said Claris. "Not the obvious, direct sort of content. Indirect. An event that mentions you incidentally. They'll leave with a good feeling about you without knowing why."

"There's all kinds of testing to back up this approach," the phone said. "People view it as powerful, authentic. It has authenticity." She said "authenticity" in a way that made me think she believed she had invented the concept.

"Then," Mindy continued, "when you're satisfied, we populate this content throughout the internet. Links from third-party blogs, comments by people who lead readers back to your story, et cetera."

Welsey pushed food around on her plate. "What else?"

"We were thinking of a trip for you," Claris said.

"Where?"

"Kenya. Or Ghana."

"Ghana's better," Mindy said.

"Kenya's popular," insisted the phone.

"Kenya's a cliché," said Claris.

"We need you to support a cause," piped in Naomi. "A village."

"Isn't *that* a cliché?" asked Welsey.

"Some clichés are good," said Claris. "That's how they get so popular they become clichés."

"Wow, that's clever."

"You know how philanthropy deflects bad press," said Mindy brightly.

"What she means," said Claris quickly, "is—"

Welsey waved her off. "What would it involve?"

"Going there, meeting state and local people—"

"People who wear bright sashes," Mindy said, smiling at me. I smiled back.

"—Pledging money for education and clean water, talking to villagers and being photographed with them," said Claris.

"Is she making a face?" Naomi asked.

"Yes."

"I knew it..."

"I don't mind causes," Welsey said. "This just seems a little transparent."

"It doesn't matter, Wels. People look at pictures. They don't care about the text. Brains pretty much only process images today!"

"I'll think about it," Welsey said. "Really hard. Now what's next?"

Claris looked to Mindy who did some clicking before turning her laptop to face Welsey. The screen read, *One Night: The OPPORTUNITY of a LIFETIME.* Below was a stunning picture of Welsey, in red dress, standing hand on hip, beaming. Below that, dummy text, a *Lorem Ipsum* festival, and below that even more in smaller letters, which I took to signify legal disclaimers.

For the down payment on a king's ransom, Welsey Shaw could be your personal friend for an evening—eating, drinking, talking about her films, gambling at a Jersey casino. The winner would be flown in on a private jet and walk a "red carpet" with Welsey where they'd have their picture taken. By mock paparazzi.

"The tension is killing me. Somebody fill me in," Naomi said.

"Clarrie..." said Welsey slowly, in a way that eerily reminded me of Pete Lumbo again.

"It all goes to charity."

"What did I do to deserve this? Kill someone? Pledge my allegiance to Hitler?"

I couldn't suppress a laugh.

"We could make it happen in New York," said Claris. "Some people really have fun with these things."

"So let them do it."

"Just something to consider..."

"I will consider it. I will consider it for exactly fifteen minutes tonight while I'm soaking in my tub."

Mindy's eyes fell to her laptop. "Okay, then how about this? People who can't go on a date with you get to be you—virtually." She held up some illustrations of a video game. "'It's an app. Of you. People can be you, go to the places you go, see the things you see, hear the likes you like and dislikes you dislike, all the while being guided toward fame by the voice in their head, which is you, narrating your journey. Rising to the top like you, traveling like you, shopping like you, having adventures like you have in your life."

Welsey laughed and seemed about to say something, then stopped.

"You'd get fifty percent of net," said Claris. "That could be as high as—" and she lowered her voice at this point. "You should split that—"

"With a charity," Welsey said.

"Well, she's been paying attention," the phone said.

"How will it work?" Welsey set the fork down now. I had long ago finished my own plate, and really wanted to tuck into hers, even if it were cold by now. If we were alone I might have ventured it.

"People would get virtual bucks to buy things," said Claris.

"One dollar would equal one thousand Welseybucks," Mindy said, showing a mockup of a Monopoly-style "Welseybuck" featuring a smiling blonde bedecked in jewelry. At least I managed to suppress this laugh. "That sounds like a great exchange rate and encourages players to shop a lot," Mindy continued. "They would buy all sorts of wonderful products—real products, things available from dozens of real-life labels. These products would update in the game when the real new products hit the stores. New watch? A thousand more Welseybucks. You would explain why these things are so desirable to the player." Mindy showed another screenshot from the prototype. "We already have these designers on board," she slid a list of famed logos across the table, "and we're working on about a dozen more."

"I don't have a flashy car," Welsey said.

"You do in the game."

"Oh? What color?"

"Whatever they want," Mindy said.

"You would drive a red car, Wels," Naomi said. "What else?"

"Thoughts?" Claris asked.

"No thoughts today. Let's just move on."

"We're crossing off and moving on," Claris said to the phone.

"What else?" Welsey asked, leaning back, as our plates were cleared on our left and dessert menus descended on our right. The staff began chatting about specials.

"You guys on desserts?" Naomi asked.

"Yes," came the chorus.

Nothing grabbed me. Nor did I feel like sitting there mashing sweet things around in my mouth with this company. I decided to take the high road and just shake my head nonchalantly when asked. Claris and Welsey each got soufflés. Mindy went for a cappuccino and took no sugar.

"I'll need time to think. You've done a lot. Good work." This praise surprised me as I thought most of her reactions had been negative.

"We're also working to line up the *Vanity Fair* cover," Naomi said. "I emailed Chavis this morning."

"You guys rock," Welsey said, though she seemed distracted.

The meeting wrapped with promises of follow-ups, another meeting in three weeks, and a request from Claris for Welsey to accompany her to the bathroom. "Could you show me where it's at?" she said unconvincingly, leaving a shiny credit card on the table near Mindy. Naomi bid adieu to everyone, including me, calling me Doug for some reason, and hung up. The waiter came by, Mindy handed off the card, and the two of us were alone.

"How long have you known Welsey?" she asked, then suddenly, as if realizing she'd made a *faux pas*, said, "I'm sorry, that's none of my business." She started checking her phone.

Which left me to sit there staring at the tablecloth. I was actually self-conscious of how much I'd spilled on its pristine surface when Welsey and Claris reappeared. Mindy quickly hung up. "Nice meeting you," she said to Welsey. "I'm a big fan, and so is everyone at the agency."

"Thank you." —Gracious smile, the kind I'd seen so many times by now.

Claris continued talking to Welsey in lowered tones. Mindy was back to checking messages, I was staring at the thick dark carpet that seemed very new. "Nice meeting you," she finally said, removing her sexy nerdy reading glasses and exchanging them with sexy sporty sunglasses. Each seemed designed to project a different image of her, depending on where she was.

"What do you do?" We stepped into the late afternoon sun.

"I'm a writer," I said.

"What kind?"

"Freelance. Fiction. Magazine articles. I wrote a novel that went on to be—"

"I tried that after graduating. But I had fifty thousand dollars in loans to pay, so I had to get a job."

When I turned around Welsey was parting with Claris, who gave me another limp handshake.

"Nice meeting you," she said, still not knowing what to make of me.

"Just shut up," Welsey muttered after they'd left.

"About what?"

"*Everything*."

I said nothing.

"Seriously, Claris is pissed you were there."

I didn't dare mention that *she'd* asked me to come. I knew better. She mumbled, seemingly to herself, "I'm an actress who deeply loves acting, who loves being someone else. I hate all the other shit that goes along with it. And what the fuck is wrong with that?"

We walked in silence. Warm wind blew. Her hair brushed my face; I actually pulled some of it out of my mouth, and she didn't even seem to notice. I thought of the first time I had touched her purposely, to see what she would do. Today we were virtually taking each other's presence for granted. I flashed back to Mindy's for-some-reason-forbidden question *How long have you known Welsey?* The answer was I'd known her a long time, starting today.

"I have a question," I said.

She pulled out her sunglasses while walking. "I usually don't like answering questions, but shoot."

"Last week I saw you talking with one of the same paps we ran away from so furiously the week before."

"Where?"

"In Central Park. "Remember, it was right after you—" and immediately I realized my mistake.

Welsey stopped.

"You followed me to the park?"

"Well, I left the table right after you did and ended up—ended up seeing you—" I stammered. My tongue wedged between my teeth in a way it never had before and never has since. "I just don't understand it," I finally said.

"Don't understand what?"

"What I saw."

"Why were you spying on me?"

I shrugged.

"Are you serious? You followed from a block behind, making sure you were out of sight when I turned around? Because I *did* turn around."

What could I say?

"You have just blown it. Do you understand me? You have just crossed the line. Listen to me carefully, because I'll only be nice enough to say this once—Everything between us is over. I'd started to trust you, but that was a big fucking mistake. I better never see you within a hundred feet of me again. I mean it. Police will be called."

She turned and headed off. Half a block away from me she flagged down a cab.

14

An hour later I arrived at the Chelsea and fell into a chair, wishing there were chaos around me, random noise to distract me from my own thoughts. But the lobby was empty and ridiculously serene, my own breathing the loudest sound I could hear until a voice broke the silence with, "You got a message."

How did everybody know where I was?

"Carla," the clerk said, handing me an unreadable note. "Hope you know the number because she didn't leave it."

Of course I know the number of my long-suffering, fiercely-loyal agent. Before I'd met Welsey, we would sometimes get together for drinks or lunch. Maybe she wanted to know why we never did these things any longer. Maybe she wanted to tell me someone wanted a sequel to *Heaven's People.* Whatever it was, I saw no reason to call her tonight. It could wait. I wasn't ready to talk to another human being.

I reflexively reached for something to read. They were always lying on tables: newspapers, Sunday supplements, whatever. There was even a copy of a writer's magazine, a trade pub. I flipped through it, not really taking in anything until page 32 where I saw an announcement that the sci-fi fantasy novel *Apocalyticus* by the Goth writer Absinthe would be coming out from —— publishers next spring.

I stared at the page, trying to think of a way it could possibly make sense; I scanned the blurb again. And then took the stairs two at a time. In my room I dug Brooke's home number out of my luggage.

"Hello, *Bonjour*, *Hola*, and *Konnichiwa*. You've reached Brooke Parker, senior editor at ——. If this is a personal call, you have my cell. If this is work-related, you have my other cell, or leave a detailed message. If this is about the 2006 Audi turbo Quattro, sorry, it's been sold. If it's about anything I haven't covered, leave a detailed message and I'll get back to you as soon as I'm able. Remember to do a good deed for someone today. You will be rewarded. Bye." I left as measured a message as I could under the circumstances, though I remembered little of what I'd said just moments later. I didn't hear from her the rest of the day, turning my dread into a rolling boil of paranoia.

"Hi, Daniel," she said hours later, ridiculously chipper for someone returning a phone call at close to midnight. "Why don't you come on down at ten? Is that too early?"

"Why doesn't she want it?"

"We'll talk."

"What's wrong?"

"We'll talk. I was just going to call you. Have a good night. Talk tomorrow at ten."

The line went dead. (There's never a dial tone like in the movies.)

The elevator to Brooke's office took forever, maybe a whole minute. A smiling receptionist who addressed me by name went too far out of her way to make me feel at home.

"Hello!" Brooke motioned toward her office. I decided to say little. "Would you like a coffee? Juice? Anything?" I shook my head. "No? Are you sure?"

She closed the door. "Wow, it is hot today, isn't it? Can't remember the last time it was this hot for this long. Can you?" Another shake of the head. "Unbelievable." She sat down slowly. "Okay, here's the latest development. I was actually about to call you," she said, folding her hands on the desk. "So you were one of three different ghostwriters working on Absinthe's project simultaneously. Unbeknownst to each other."

Amazingly, what my mind registered was that this was the first time I'd ever heard someone say "unbeknownst." I recalled that Brooke liked to trot out puffy words when she was uncomfortable.

"Absinthe wanted to see 'a range,'" she continued. "She reviewed three drafts. The others finished faster, and she liked both of them more, and one of them a lot more."

"And you knew this?" I asked. She nodded. "You were brought in last," she continued when I didn't say anything. "I pushed for you, actually," she said. "But she's in charge of how her story goes." She unfolded her hands and they went behind the desk, where I thought she might have wiped them on her skirt. "Sorry, Daniel."

"I busted my ass."

She raised her arms, let them drop. "No doubt. But the contract stipulates acceptance."

"Are you always this brutal to people who've been kicked?"

"I like to think of it as objective. It's how I stay young and happy. I am sorry, Daniel."

"She should look at the rest of it before she decides. I have it," I said, reaching into a pocket for a flash drive that was at the Chelsea in my luggage.

Brooke just shook her head sadly.

"You know what this means," I said.

"Yes," she replied.

"The last, biggest payment is owed 'upon acceptance,'" I said, hoping to sniff a loophole.

Brooke was a statue.

"I was told that 'never happens.'"

Again the raised arms, dropping to her sides. "A first. Been in this business seven years. I was stunned too."

"That's the biggest payment. The size of all the others combined."

A gesture that was somewhere between a nod and a shrug.

"I am sorry, Daniel, really."

I stood and took a long breath.

"I turned down other work for this. I had lots of other offers."

"Oh, I'm sure you did," she quickly agreed, which for some reason really pissed me off. "You're very good." She made it sound so convincing.

"I may have to talk to a lawyer before I can say anything more," I said.

For the third time the arms rose and fell. "Do! I would if I were you."

There seemed to be little else to say. My editor looked out the window, to a view of another office across the street, desk and chair visible through the glass. I wondered if they ever waved at each other, Brooke and the other person. Maybe they exchanged notes or phone calls about the people they screwed each day. Maybe they went to lunch together over it. Probably they never noticed one another.

Brooke stood. So did I. We were now on the same level. I was taller but I didn't feel it.

"I'll call," Brooke said. She never did.

The receptionist made a point of being busy on the phone as I left. But she watched out of the corner of her eye. The elevator dumped me into the street in seconds.

I visited another deli, this one boasting a new flat screen TV hanging off a corner wall. It was adjusted all wrong, so that the picture was distorted and everyone looked squat and fat. Or maybe people all were squat and fat a hundred years ago. Cable news was broadcasting one of those quirky pieces they do on slow days. "Evergreens" someone told me they call them. This was about an inventor, Franz Reichelt, who'd more than a hundred years ago devised a coat for men to wear that would become a pair of wings when they spread their arms and flapped. No more walking down long flights of stairs! Now you could just float to the ground after a hard day at the office. Mr. Reichelt, with the boundless confidence crazy people often have, decided to give the first demonstration of his invention from an observation deck on the Eiffel Tower, insisting a film crew be present to record the momentous occasion that lasted just three seconds as he efficiently plunged in a straight line to his death.

I ordered what I was convinced would be my last delicious pastrami sandwich and raised a beer to the television in a toast to Dr. Reichelt and others who had big dreams, even if they were stupid big dreams. Then I ordered a second pastrami but could only finish half. I wandered the streets, not going anywhere, not wanting to go back to the Chelsea, not wanting to even think about tomorrow whatever that would be. I passed a sidewalk violinist and just listened for ten minutes, but didn't fill his instrument case with any coin and thus earned a cold stare.

My room seemed more dank now. The tub was dripping, and the noise drove me nuts until I stuck a sponge in the drain hole to muffle the leak. I slept for twelve straight hours, woke up in a sweat, peed, and went back to sleep for twelve more. When I woke again, even more sweaty, I had a salty mouth, and drank water straight from the sink, unable to taste it, which was a blessing. But this only made me need to pee still more. Finally I showered, shaved, peed again, hit a wall with my fist, and started to pack.

For some reason this took a long time, and when I finished I was exhausted. I lay down on the bed and stared at a crack on the ceiling. (I had my choice of several.) The phone rang four or five times before it registered I should pick it up. I fantasized about just saying "Fuck off" and hanging up.

"You have a visitor," the clerk informed me.

Taking the stairs was a bad idea; everything, it turned out, ached. I got to the bottom and didn't see anyone.

Finally I asked about it, which produced a puzzled glance. "Was here a minute ago."

"Might as well check out," I said.

My credit card changed hands. I left sweat on it. I signed my name below a large number, a very large number, folded up the receipt, and sighed.

"I have a present for you."

I turned. Her hair brushed me, just as it had that day on the sidewalk. She held a wrapped package in both hands.

"Didn't mean to scare you. It's not booby trapped, honest. Open it."

Welsey looked the same, which seemed odd to me even though I'd seen her just a few days ago. I tore the paper in a daze and opened a fancy black box containing a silver flask, a booze flask. It made playful sloshing noises.

"I filled it up," she said with an evil grin.

"With what?"

"Find out."

She wandered around the lobby, over to the lady on the swing. "God, I hope I never get cellulite like that."

"What are you doing here?"

"Talking to you."

"And then what?"

"I don't know. Lunch. Little place I really like. We should do it now before the Bacardis wear off and I change my mind."

Outside I felt like I'd stepped into a blast furnace. This had to be the hottest day of the year so far. Welsey smelled of sunscreen, and seemed ready for the beach. She leaned in close to me. "Okay, here's the skinny, nosey asshole. The day I turned legal I was celebrating my emancipation by sunbathing on a nude beach with a friend. And this paparazzi guy was in the bushes taking photos of us with this fucking long lens. He rushed them back here, and they hit the internet and newsstands before I turned 18 over here. The hook was 'Naked Pictures of Welsey Shaw before she turns legal.'"

I wondered where this was going.

"About a year later I was in this disco in Prague one night, and would you believe I saw him again? There he was, with a friend. He gave me this smug smile."

I noticed a cab parked right in front of us. It seemed to be waiting.

"So I went over to him. And I said hello. And he sort of laughed and said hello. And then I smashed the guy next to him in the nose, breaking it thoroughly," she said.

"Why'd you do that?"

"Shitty aim."

We slid into the cab.

"So I was in trouble, needless to say. But the guy, the friend, agreed on an arrangement. Instead of me being hauled off to jail in handcuffs, he—the other guy—and occasionally a couple of buddies can get together and take pictures of me in various places. I tell them where I'll be. He gets exclusives." She muttered an address on 56th Street that I thought was near First Avenue. "So now you know. Happy?"

I nodded. I *was* happy. In many ways suddenly. We rode in silence, enjoying the cool.

"I'm thinking of giving up writing," I finally said, wondering at the same time if that sounded self-pitying. (Fuck it if it did.)

"So what would you do?"

"Move to a beach and dig for clams. Produce desk calendars with those clever witticisms on them. Beat up school kids for their lunch money. I have lots of options."

The cab pulled over. I was right about the location. Welsey paid, the car departed, and I saw the sign in the window of the Italian restaurant: *Dear Customers: We are in Italy for the entire month of August.* I tapped Welsey on the shoulder.

"Who goes to Italy in *August*?" she asked incredulously.

"Might as well stay in New York," I said.

So there we were, standing in the middle of almost nowhere, peering through dark glass at chairs stacked neatly on tables. That's when the junker, the ancient, rusted junker, pulled into a loading zone. We turned to see a convertible ragtop lowering and the driver grabbing a plastic can on the seat next to him, stopping ten feet from us, and hurling its awful contents, grinning, snapping a photo, and then speeding away, tires screeching, smoke rising, just like in movies. That the bucket was bright blue with some kind of white writing on it in capital letters is the thing I remember the most.

I was slammed in the face, hit by something soft and squishy. It took a second before the smell registered. We were covered in garbage. He'd been aiming at Welsey, but because he was moving the same time as throwing, most of it hit me. The battered, belching POS lingered for a couple seconds, far enough up the street that neither of us could reach it. Then it took off. The last things I noted before it rounded a corner was that it had rust and a dented fender.

My eyes burned. I bit down on what was eggshell or worse. Welsey had caught some raw muck on her right side and in her hair. She shook it out, sending some of it hurtling toward me. I yelled.

"You're already covered, what fucking difference does it make?"

For a minute we just stood there, each of us assessing our personal damage. Then Welsey said under her breath. "That was him."

"Who?"

"Shit. *Goddam.*" She looked at me for the first time. "You really got it, didn't you? Look, you need to get back to your room and shower."

"I checked out," I said.

It took a second to register with her. "You what?"

"When you came. I was going home, just paid my bill."

"Home?"

"*Home* home. Where the deer and the buffalo roam."

She spit out something and wiped garbage off her lips. "You are fucking kidding me, right?"

I shook my head. Things flew out of my hair and fell in the street. I noticed that some people were watching us from a distance.

"Check back in."

"Now you are kidding me. We're miles away."

"Time's wasting."

"And who would take me there?"

She pulled out her phone and started working it, getting it all sticky in the process.

"We have to find a dry cleaners then."

"What are we going to do there?" I asked, trying to hide my amusement.

"Check you into some other place that's closer then."

I shook my head. "There aren't any rooms anywhere. There's that big summer music festival all weekend."

"Oh fuck. *Fuck* that fucking big fucking summer music festival!" Welsey yelled at the top of her lungs. More stares from more people, all keeping their distance.

"Look, don't you have any friends in the city, anyone you could call?"

I shook my head.

"This isn't funny. *Think.*"

"I've thought. This is your town. I'm a visiting yokel, like Ben Franklin over in France."

"Well, I'm sorry then," she said, throwing up her hands in a way that made me think of Brooke. Something that looked like cabbage flew off her arm.

"What else then?"

"No!"

"Seriously—"

"It's not an option, Ferreira."

"What *is* an option? You march home and take a shower and just go to bed?"

"Sorry. I truly am. But this isn't my fault, either."

"It kind of is, actually."

"Oh, don't you dare try that..."

"So what do you want me to do?"

We just stood there.

"I can't believe this," she said. "Fuck!" she added when I didn't move, when I wouldn't move. She refused to look at me. Instead she studied the wall next to us both. "Would you hate me, really hate me, if I left you right now, even after you finally went home and took a shower and days and weeks passed?"

"Yes," I said. "I absolutely would. Wouldn't you?"

For what felt like a long time we just stared each other down in the broiling sun. Maybe the people staring at us—from comfortably afar for the most part, not daring to get closer—thought we were performance artists, two clowns or part of a hidden camera stunt. I confess for a moment I'd wondered that too. After a moment Welsey broke eye contact and just closed her eyes, as if hoping I would be gone when she stopped.

I wasn't.

She clenched her teeth, turned her back and, trying to barely touch her phone, made a call just out of my hearing. It was very short.

Then she said to me, "Come on."

We entered her building through an inconspicuous side door I'd never noticed. Welsey typed a code into a keypad as I stared up at a security camera and wondered if anyone was staring back. A click, and we were in. She used a key to summon the elevator; inside we took shallow breaths and prayed for the door to open again.

It did; we were in a short hall that led to what appeared to be the living room. There was an unearthly quiet.

Everything in view was white on whiter, with polished knobs and fixtures. On the wall by my shoulder were the climate controls. I discovered how 72.5-degree air conditioning felt—wonderful.

"Don't walk on the carpet." She sounded like she was talking to the dog, who upon hearing us trotted in to greet his mistress. Welsey directed me to the edges of the room, where parquet flooring edged sea blue carpet. "Take off your shoes." She started doing the same herself before going to a wall intercom. She spoke instructions rapidly, in a voice both deeper and thicker than she usually used. I struggled to remember my college Spanish.

The room did not look like what I expected. It was beautiful as only the palace of one of the most famous movie stars in the world can be, but also crookedly lived-in—expensive but unorganized, a larger version of her handbags. An elegant table had all types of packing materials piled on it. Chairs, in blue and brown upholstery, were randomly placed throughout the room, as if a party of card players suddenly had to get up and make a break for it. Slippers, socks, and combs were scattered about. Small boxes in thick red wrapping paper were piled nearby. Attached to each was a white nametag.

Ceiling lights and fancy candles dominated. The few floor and table lamps looked like they might have been antiques, or at least chosen by a decorator. "The shower's through there," she said, pointing at a door, deliberately interrupting my wandering eye. "Throw your clothes in the basket inside. The housekeeper will give you a robe," she said in a businesslike manner before disappearing into an adjoining room and slamming the door. Chevron looked at it, then me.

I made my way to the bathroom, which turned out to be divided into two parts, the outer room with sink, closet, hamper, and scented candles. I gently peeled off my clothes and tossed them into a wicker basket before proceeding into the shower room and placing Welsey's gift flask on the counter by the sink. This room was no larger than the bathroom in my house, but the beige tiling was a work of art and the room had an enormous mirror over the sink and a sit-down glass shower that looked so inviting right about then.

The glass door glided open on what seemed to be oiled casters; I stared at a panel with knobs, buttons and an LCD readout. I searched for something labeled "shower." Actually, setting the temperature was pretty intuitive, with a scale that gave a reading I could toggle from Celsius to Fahrenheit. One hundred and three degrees, the display told me. Was that good? I guess I'd find out.

I climbed in and gave the glass door a tug. It glided smoothly and fitted with a dampened "thunk," like some airlock in a spacecraft. Staring at the buttons, I reluctantly pressed one with a rectangular icon inside another rectangular icon. A wide-screen television sprang to life in the mirror: rerun of a crime show in which someone had just found a body in a cellar. I pressed another button. The detectives disappeared and loud dance music started playing. "Push the round button," I heard Welsey yell, and simultaneously noticed a gold-colored knob in front of me helpfully marked "Nozzle 1 2 3." I pressed and water fell, a gentle rain. Feeling brave, I pressed again. Now the shower head gave forth.

The third push caused water to pound on my back from high-powered sprayers behind me, stripping off my grime.

I twiddled the array of buttons; the water began a syncopation of truly kinky rhythm, varying in pressure and spin. My breathing increased, the feeling of time evaporated; the heavenly spray relaxed dozens of muscles that until this moment had been very tense. The liquid soap, from a gorgeous cobalt bottle, had no perfumes and was surprisingly unfeminine. The shampoo was from France and pink. I rubbed it deep into my scalp even though it smelled like strawberry ice cream.

Shower over, I exited, toweled down, opened the door connecting the two rooms and saw that an enormous terrycloth robe had been left; my dirty clothes had disappeared. I sniffed at the robe, not really knowing what I expected to smell, before putting it on and studying my new self in the mirror. For the first time ever I wished I carried a camera phone. Nobody would believe this tomorrow, not even me.

I opened the door and called out a tentative hello. No one answered; the hum of the air conditioning was all I could hear. To my left, a door was ajar. I wandered over and stuck my head in the room: no thespian, but two computers, a laptop and a desktop, on a plain wood desk. Both looked virtually unused and in fact boxes and wrappings for one of them were piled in a corner, right down to the last twisty-tie and baggie. Then I noticed another, older laptop, on the floor by the wall, retired, scuffed and smudged like her sunglasses and phone had been. A smaller desk pressed against the opposite wall in the otherwise plain room, upon which sat a Dell at least as battered as my machine, its case covered in witty stickers—*Don't like me yet, have another drink! Tact is for people who aren't clever enough to be sarcastic.* And *Dear Karma: Here's a shortlist of people you missed.* Random objects—plastic sharks and deflated foil balloons and a pair of hot pink flip-flops—littered the space. On the walls, framed posters from what looked to be bawdy French movies competed with hanging handicrafts.

I pulled my head out, looked both ways and saw I was still alone. Another door, directly across, beckoned. Inside this room clothes of all sorts were heaped onto lavender salon chairs: dresses suitable for red carpet walks, designer gowns, cocktail attire. Maybe forty pairs of jeans in all shades of blue and all degrees of tatter. Many of the dresses still had tags on them. Most were solids in bright colors; the whole sight was headache inducing in its gaudiness. A huge walk-in closet was filled with more dresses, these flawlessly hung, with no tags I could see. There was shelving for perfectly folded shirts and sweaters, formal and informal, white tees (which appeared ironed) to cashmere. Hats sat in rows; belts hung or were rolled up in small open drawers. Shoes and boots stood at attention. Mirrors, mirrors, on the walls; one did not flip my image as I stared into it, instead reflecting back exactly how others saw me by some clever optical trickery. I grinned and scratched my left cheek. I really did look different.

To the side was a huge, light-ringed vanity and a tall director's style folding chair with "Welsey" written on the back in white cursive script. Beauty magazines were organized to the side, pages ripped from some and taped to the mirror. And on a pedestal, impossible to miss, sat the Irina wig.

I took in all this in mere seconds. The next room, a bedroom, was neat and anonymous, probably a spare room, and I wondered why she didn't divert the overspill of clothes into it. The bedspread was royal blue. At the foot of the bed was a hope chest, maybe an antique, maybe just made to look like one. The curtains were drawn. Bookshelves held knickknacks as well as popular paperback novels by Crichton and King. I heard a floorboard creak, thought I'd been caught, and spun only to see nobody was there.

Reversing direction, still looking for Welsey, I passed a kitchen boasting glass surfaces and the latest appliances. A multi-tiered oven, steel refrigerator with front flat screen, adjoining wine refrigerator, trash compactor, and an in-wall soap dispenser faced me. All were showroom-new. The infamous coffeemaker, its front crazy with knobs and buttons, squatted next to a fat juicer. Bottles of red wine stood to the left of the sink next to bowls of mouth-watering fruit and an electric knife sharpener.

I dared to step inside and give the refrigerator door a gentle tug. Lights lit; LEDs told me the temperatures of the various drawers. Rows of prepared meals in plastic containers covered most of the shelves, each with a label announcing the contents. Welsey seemed to like Italian and Greek food. Exotic condiments fought with staples for space inside the door, designer mustards and relishes and olives and salad dressings next to milk, eggs, and butter. Several jars were labeled "kimchee." One was almost empty.

Past the kitchen, double glass doors looked out onto a terrace. Orange and green lounge furniture dotted the skydeck, while matching umbrellas poked the clouds at odd angles. I imagined sitting out there, taking in the view with Welsey Shaw as New York turned pink, then red, then deep purple before disappearing into velvety night. I wondered who had done exactly that, what famous people had sat on the cushions I was looking at right now.

I wondered where the phantom who'd spirited away my clothes was. Tip-toeing back through the hallway, I again hollered a hello and again got no reply. I wondered where all the awards were, the dozens of statues she had accumulated in her short lifetime. Surely these would be the centerpiece of her home, but you'd never know, if you were transported here via wormhole, that she was even an actress.

I crept past what believe it or not was a second elevator, to an ad hoc fitness room crammed with heavy equipment, mirrors, and a wall-mounted TV. There was barely room to stand. Next came another bathroom and another bedroom, the same size as the first, just as anonymous. Tan spread and white sheets. Antique chest of drawers. Matching lamps with ornate glass shades flanking the bed.

More ceiling lights. A rather ordinary alarm clock on the left table next to a pile of rubber bands and paper clips and a hairbrush. A detailed metal sculpture of a hand, palm up, about a foot tall, on a round pedestal. Sitting in the palm was a large rubber penis. I pondered that for a few seconds.

A right turn, a few steps, and I realized I was at the door to Welsey Shaw's bedroom, surprisingly small, surprisingly ordinary, surprisingly anticlimactic. I asked myself exactly what I was expecting and didn't have an answer, other than this could not be it. I was surprised the bed was a mere queen-sized. Across from it, another flat panel TV, smallish. There was an iPod and ear buds coiled up on the other night table, along with a wax candle, and a wine glass whose base was stained red. The only extraordinary item in the whole room, which couldn't have been more than fourteen by sixteen feet, was the Oscar for Alessandro Creek. It looked almost fake, surrounded by a box of tissues and spare change, like a novelty you'd buy in a joke store.

A thick paperback lay open in the center of the bed, upside-down. The corners were a little bent, but it was in good shape, and familiar.

Heaven's People.

I couldn't believe it. I wanted to shout, to jump in the air. Instead I just stood there, silent in 72.5 degree air. *Heaven's People.* On her bed. I peeked back into the hallway. Nothing. Nobody. I looked at the book cover again.

The smile would not come off my face.

"*Daniel!*"

The voice sounded like it came from above.

"*Daniel, where are you?*" Sounding closer.

I'd probably taken only about three minutes wandering through her house, but it had felt longer, a lifetime. I trotted quickly back to the main area. "Where are *you?*" I hollered, probably too dramatically.

"Upstairs."

She was talking to someone else up there. Was I going to meet Peter Bazin?

Semi-circular staircases were spread out before me. Hanging on the wall in the space in-between were a dozen pen-and-ink drawings, each in a thick frame, all portraits of Welsey from different angles. They were directly across from the main elevator, so that one saw them immediately upon entering. Each was lightly autographed, *To Wels w/Love & Affection* in dark pencil by someone whose busy signature I couldn't read.

I walked the winding steps, my feet sinking deep into carpet. Halfway up I heard feet behind me; someone indeed had been down there, though where I don't know, and I immediately wondered if I had been seen snooping around. The face was round, dark-haired, middle-aged, and avoided eye contact, but she was in a hurry to reach her mistress, necessitating me to increase my step.

Upstairs Welsey had changed into fresh khaki shorts and a light gray T-shirt, and was sitting crossed-legged on a chair, cell phone to her ear. Behind was a panoramic view of the city, which I investigated briefly, though I imagine I'd never get tired of looking at it no matter how long I lived here. The woman who'd met me on the stairs handed her boss a slender laptop, different from all the ones I'd seen downstairs, and disappeared.

I sat down on the white sectional adjacent to Welsey, feeling the silver flask in my bathrobe pocket bang my knee. I removed it, gave it another anticipatory shake, and placed it on the table.

It was different up here, simpler and more manageable, a home within a home, penthouse lite. There was a nifty kitchenette at one end and a short hall out of it leading to a back room. A bookshelf that covered nearly a whole wall was crowded with DVDs, still more candles, and dozens of framed photos. The snapshots appeared to have been taken all over the world. Chairs and sofa formed an island in the middle of the room, facing not the view but the largest flat TV I had ever seen. Right now it was muted, playing a cooking show. Underneath was a low teakwood bar, jammed with booze.

Glass floor lamps flanked the sofa. A teardrop-shaped coffee table was cluttered with an opened bag of Skittles, gum, a stack of magazines, and some intricate cut-glass ornaments.

Welsey got up and moved quickly to the next room, pausing her conversation until she was safely out of my hearing. She did this twice more over the next fifteen minutes; the third time she also closed the door. I was left to the distant rhythms of the washer-dryer combo. She returned, pocketed the phone, sat, and recrossed her legs. "Billy Saure."

"Who?"

She typed on the laptop. "My stalker. I've got several, actually, but he's the worst." She said it so matter-of-factly she might have been introducing a business associate. "He has this website..." A page displaying blurry images appeared on the screen.

This guy not only followed his obsession, he took photographs of her, lots of them, and posted them online. I stared at the images for several minutes, unable to come up with any words to say.

"He started by sending me mail. Fan letters. He got mad when I didn't answer them. Then he demanded to meet me. But that was it. Hadn't heard from him in a long time, years. Hoped that was the end." She closed the laptop and checked the screen of her phone again, biting her lips and then swallowing.

"Restraining order?"

"Why didn't we think of that, genius?" A sigh, a push of the hair off the face, another sigh. "Okay, where are my manners? Would you like something to drink?"

The question made me realize how thirsty I was. Welsey disappeared into the kitchenette and returned 30 seconds later with two glasses of iced tea with plump wedges of lemon. "Do you take it sweet?"

"Yes."

"Too bad." She set mine down and sipped hers. "I don't got sugar. It shouldn't take much more than an hour," she said. "Your clothes, I mean."

I'd almost forgotten, forgotten why I was there.

She sat, unmuted the television, and began flipping through screen menus. "Nice bathrobe," she said.

"Can I keep it?" I asked.

"Sure, why not? I steal from hotels, the really awesome ones. So what do you want to watch?" She stopped on a blonde-haired NY1 reporter announcing an art exhibit opening with forced excitement.

"She's not selling it," she said derisively. "Clearly isn't interested."

"She didn't fool me for a minute," I agreed before trying a test: "Read anything good lately?"

"Not really," she said with a bored shrug. My heart sank. "But there's a new show on cable I'm in love with, except—" And she pressed some buttons on the remote that brought up complex graphics on the screen, "—I can't find where I recorded it. It's like the espresso maker all over again." She clicked the TV off and threw back her head. The phone rang; she sprang up and retreated with it. Some quick questions and then she returned, looking defeated. "My lawyer tells me there's this little town in Italy where it's against the law to keep fish in a fishbowl. They say the reason is you get a distorted view in a fishbowl, and that's considered cruel to the fish." A knowing smile. "Isn't that something?"

I raised my eyebrows. She howled.

"I'm glad someone's looking out for the little fishies," she said, plopping down and channel-flipping again. "Still, I can understand. They're nice fishies. They don't bother anybody. Now where the hell's that show?"

"Here's to the fishies," I said, raising my glass. She clinked it with hers. "Have you ever heard that song?" I asked. "Down in the meadow in an itty-bitty pool..?"

She shook her head. "Can't say I have."

The woman appeared on the stairs with another phone and gestured. Welsey got up and followed her down, was gone five minutes, and returned, this time sitting with me on the couch instead of the chair.

"Feeling better?"

I took another gulp of tea, which was fruity and really didn't need sugar. "Oh yeah."

"This morning I realized something. Four films from the first half of my career have been in-flight movies. Second half, three-quarters."

"That's an interesting metric," I said.

"Isn't it? I wonder if anyone else uses it to judge declining careers." She clicked through the same set of cable channels for the third time now.

"So what are *you* going to do?"

She set down the remote. "I was hoping to make it to at least thirty before I had to think about that. So on Mondays, Wednesdays and Fridays I tell myself I am doing nothing different; I am getting on board the next project that I like. On Tuesdays, Thursday and Saturdays I tell myself I am moving to Italy where I will run a surf shop."

"Really? Didn't know you surfed"

"Yup. Started recently, love it."

"Why Italy?"

"Have you seen Italian men? Men that surf? With their shirts off?"

"And what about Sundays?"

"On Sundays I don't know."

"You know, I have this recurring dream," I said. "I'm in the future and the people who brought me there tell me that when I died everyone mourned and they closed all the schools. And I'm simply touched and amazed by it all. And they say, 'Yeah, we don't get it either.'"

I expected a laugh but didn't get it. So I asked her, "What's your favorite movie of yours?"

"I don't have one. Don't even look at them."

"Come on," I said. "I reread my books. I've memorized them. I admit it. Why else do we do this? Egos, like bellies, need feeding. So what's your favorite?"

"I really don't know."

"Sure you do."

"It's none of your business."

"It's not that personal a question."

"Maybe it is. Maybe I just don't know, okay?"

I thought about it. "You're right. Maybe it is."

"You just love to ask questions, you know that? You never know when to stop."

"The occupational hazard of the writer," I said.

"Getting soaked in garbage is the occupational hazard of the actor," she said, checking her phone again.

"*And* the writer," I added, looking down at my robe.

She patted my knee. "Today's sucked all around. I play games when the day sucks. Have you ever read that about me?"

"I have, actually," I said.

"Good!" She ran to a closet in the hall, standing on her toes to reach the top shelf—"Aha!"—and triumphantly brought down a flat box. It was yellowed, the sides split from years of weight placed on top. But I recognized it instantly.

"*Life!*" she shrieked, thrusting it at me.

I think my mouth fell open. I definitely stared in horror. "You mean where you ride around in a little plastic car over winding roads and have kids in the shape of little pegs?"

"Yes! And I have all your clothes, so you have no choice." She danced around like a child. "Let's sit on the floor! Just like I used to do when I played this game."

So we sat, Indian style, or as Indian style as I dared in a bathrobe.

She had the "Art Linkletter" edition, the same one I'd had when I was little. I have no idea what happened to mine. "There is no other version," Welsey declared. "What color car do you want?"

"Blue?" I shrugged.

"Blue it is. I'm pink. Pink Cadillac," she said, putting pegs in each car. Welsey gave the wheel a spin and got a 10. I gave a spin and got a four. She moved 10 spaces, deciding to skip college. I went to an institution of higher learning, burning the midnight oil, sacrificing and studying hard to become a journalist. But she kept getting better breaks, and quickly accumulated much more money than I did.

"Ha! I love this game. Don't you just love this game?"

Soon it was time to get married. I tried to imagine who I'd want sitting next to me if it were a car in real life, and wondered the same about Welsey.

We advanced down the road. Welsey turned out to be a fertility goddess, filling her convertible with pegs, one extra kid lying flat across the back. I wound up with just one blue nub. Yet her many mouths to feed didn't hold her back. She won big at the racetrack and her oil well gushed. She inherited fortunes. An eccentric aunt left me with cats.

I wondered how many other famous, glamorous Hollywood stars spent their afternoons doing this sort of thing.

"I'm hungry," Welsey suddenly announced, reaching underneath her coffee table and throwing a restaurant's delivery menu at me. "They're fast and they're awesome." Italian. I chose something fancy, which is what one should choose from a fancy restaurant. Welsey went into the other room to place the order before returning to continue advancing through life faster than me, winning a beauty contest and selling a cattle ranch. I inherited a shrunken head collection and entertained an ambassador from Mars. She landed on Revenge and wreaked havoc as if I'd wronged her in a previous life, all the while grinning wickedly. She really was enjoying this.

The doorbell rang, announcing our food was below on the street. Two minutes and a trip down the elevator later, and she was back holding a white bag in each hand, a third between her teeth. "*Geth sohm siwwehware.*" She pointed to the mini kitchen. When I returned with two sets of shiny utensils, lids were off the containers and heavenly smells filled the room.

We ate on the floor, Life on hold, as if this were the most normal thing in the world, me and the celebrity, eating from paper containers in her sky-high penthouse. Her dinner turned out to be spaghetti and meatballs, which she slurped and sucked, hunched over the container. She got sauce in her hair, on her T-shirt. "I always get the spag and balls," she said, looking judgmentally at my dinner of veal and thinly-sliced mushrooms floating in wine sauce. "They have the most killer meatballs." She speared a ball and pointed it at my mouth. "Taste." She was right; it was heavenly, and I immediately regretted my choice. Welsey ate much faster than I did. Those perfect public table manners went out the window. She picked up a meatball, put it on a towel on the rug, went into another room and returned with a golf club.

"Dare I?" she asked with the same grin as when she was taking revenge on me.

"You'll have to clean it up," I said.

"Ha, no I won't, actually. But it would be cruel." She glanced downstairs. The golf club was replaced, the meatball was returned to her plate, the paper towel was crumpled. "I always have that fantasy, though, to open the window and see if I can make a hole in one."

The tiramisu was in an eight-ounce cup and big enough for

two, so we split it. We ate in silence, Welsey with her eyes half-closed; me still wondering how many other glamorous stars did this.

"That was good," she said in a way that sounded like sex. We returned to our winding board journey. I attempted to make the wheel stop on numbers I wanted. I tried small spins she ruled illegal. I spun so hard the wheel left the board, flew through the air and landed under a chair.

"You just have to relax," she said. "You're going to lose anyway so there's no point in getting uptight about it."

I was robbed and bought a toupee. She won a sweepstakes. The end loomed. *DAY OF RECKONING!* barked at me in bold letters. I put all my money on seven, lucky seven, gave the wheel a spin: TWO. Welsey threw her hands up and roared. "I win!"

"Can I move in with you?" I asked. "You got plenty of room."

"You only have one kid. And you can charge him rent."

"Miss Welsey?"

The woman was on the stairs again. She cradled a white paper bag with handles.

"Yes, Sofia?"

"Is everything all right? I heard yelling."

"Oh, fine. I was just celebrating."

"I try best I could but a few light stains did not come out," she said to me, so apologetic it broke my heart. "I'm sorry. It's why I take so long."

"Thank you very much," I said. It was the first time I actually spoke to her. "I'm sure it's fine. I appreciate the effort."

"Yes, Sofia, thank you," Welsey repeated. "Hey, you were supposed to leave early today, weren't you?"

"Staying was no problem, ma'am."

"Please don't call me ma'am," Welsey said. "I just wish you would have reminded me. I'm fine. And it's okay if you're late tomorrow." They went back and forth in rapid Spanish, with Sofia eventually saying in uncertain English that everything was all right.

"Yeah," Welsey said after the woman went back down, "I'm wonderful." She turned off the TV and whispered, "Her mother is sick. She doesn't have long. I totally forgot she'd asked to go home at three."

"She seemed okay with it," I tried.

"What else was she going to say? Fuck me." She tossed her little pink car into the cardboard box.

"I guess I'd better get dressed," I said with somewhat of a theatrical sigh. She might have nodded. I stood and headed down to put on clothes that were still warm. I threw the robe into the hamper, opened my bag, and dressed. I thought I could hear Sofia leaving—footsteps, more talk, an elevator door sliding open and shut, the faint, faint hum of a motor.

I took one final look at the bathroom, the mirror, myself in the mirror. Impulsively I opened a drawer, saw that it contained miscellaneous junk that could be of no real interest to her. I grabbed a lipstick tube and shoved it in my pocket. I had to have some evidence I had been here, even if it was something I could buy in a drugstore.

When I stepped back into the hall, Welsey was at the bottom of the stairs. Her hands gripped the railing tightly, as if she might fall.

"I have a favor to ask. Don't go yet."

15

"Peter's stuck at Heathrow. He's getting on a plane now."

I nodded blankly.

"I hate being completely alone at night. No, I don't hate it. I'm terrified. Really. Everything's disappearing and the bright lights aren't up yet and I'm alone and it's eerie," she said. "I know that's weird, but there you have it."

"Doesn't sound all that weird."

"You don't have to say that. It's weird. I still sleep with the light on. My parents never broke me of that habit, not like they didn't try for years."

"I know people who do that too," I lied.

"I'm sure you don't. But thank you. Sofia knows about all this. She runs the water or coughs loudly sometimes, or stomps around the house, just so I know she's there. Would you stay and we can—I don't know, what would you like to do?"

The most famous actress in the world wanted me to keep her company tonight. I was being entrusted with her well-being and happiness—at least until her tennis star boyfriend came back. What would happen when he showed up? Would the three of us go to some late night bar and bond over beers? I tried to imagine the outcome of this evening and failed.

"I don't have the faintest idea," I said.

She smiled. "Of course not. It's just to have people so close to you—above you, below you, down in the street. Sometimes you can hear them. But they're not there. They don't know you. You don't know them. But they're the closest links you have sometime, to humanity, to, I don't know, I'm not explaining it very well. Come here. There's something I want to show you."

We went back up. My eyes drifted to magazines stashed in a credenza. "Why do you subscribe to *Popular Mechanics*?"

"No idea. Every month it just shows up. I have twenty-nine magazine subscriptions. How I got twenty-five of them I don't know. Here..." She led me over to a huge bookcase. I had eyed it earlier and made no sense of it, but hadn't been able to get a close look. It was crammed with all manner of tchotchkes, hundreds, small in front, large in back, buttons and pins, stuffed animals and porcelain figures, and drawings of Welsey, from doodles to one portrait that was good enough to hang in the Louvre. Someone had presented her with a holographic image of her face etched in a glass paperweight. People had made jewelry. Necklaces. Bracelets.

"Everything on these shelves is from fans," she said. "They don't know me. There was no obligation. This is real. Do you understand what I mean?"

I looked at a drawing of a stick figure with long, fiery red hair—the look of her cartoon character in *The Insidious Dr. Snidley*—obviously done by a very young fan.

"Someone from Berlin made me a dress once, just from pictures of me online. I put it on and it fit perfectly, looks fantastic, one of the nicest dresses I own. I wore it there—" She pointed to a photo of some big event hanging on the wall. She indeed looked stunning.

"When I turned seventeen, this big shipping tycoon, Italian guy, invited my mother and me to his yacht, where he threw this amazing party. I'd never seen anything like it. But still, all these people were there, and they made a nonstop fuss over me for three days. It was the first time I had this idea that someone, a single person, could own a boat that big.

"When we went below decks there was this line of photos." She made a sweeping gesture. "On all the walls, other beautiful celebrities. I asked someone on the ship who they were, and she told me they were others who'd had parties thrown for *them*. And I said, 'But not one of them is at this party.' She smiled and said in a thick accent, '*Noh*.'"

She led me back to the sofa.

"Later that night, while we were in bed, I asked my mother."

"Asked her what?"

"Asked her about *that*. Where were they? Those people? The people that all *these* people had made a fuss over once? She told me to not think about it.

"That did it. From that moment on, I was doomed." She laughed.

She gestured back at the bookcase. "I need to be loved. But I need it from people who have nothing to gain by giving it to me. Isn't that sad?" She looked at me, long and hard.

"Not really," I said.

She chuckled doubtfully. "My therapist constantly warns me against confusing fame with love. He tells me fame isn't love and fame isn't the reward. Fame is fame and love is something else."

"Do you believe it?" I asked.

She smiled. "No. But I wish I did."

She rose and went over to the remainder of my iced tea, now just water. "*¿Mas?*"

"I'm good."

"Well, I'm not." She went over to the liquor and grabbed a tall bottle of vodka. "You sure? I hate to drink alone. My therapist warns me against that too." A snort.

"All right," I said. "You twisted my arm."

She pulled out her phone, checked something, did a little typing, checked something else, threw the phone at the sofa cushion. "There's no delay at Heathrow," she said simply.

After a moment in the kitchenette she emerged with two filled glasses. "What I don't like is he thinks I'm stupid."

The outside view was fading; brilliant day was being replaced by hazy evening. Buildings blended together even as their lights delineated them. Far away a small plane moved left to right and out of sight. From up here it felt like I could own the city. It felt like I could do almost anything.

A drink was in my hand. On the rocks, with an olive.

I tasted it. A vodka fizz. "All you see with the lights on is your own reflection in the glass." When I refocused from the view outside to our own images, we indeed looked like two people on a movie screen.

"It looks like we're in a musical. One of those fancy 1930s things set in a penthouse," she said.

"We're not dressed for it."

After a second's thought she disappeared into one of the bedrooms. I heard a closet door sliding and hangers sliding. A door slammed shut, a light switch clicked on, a bathroom fan hummed, and a moment later Welsey appeared in a champagne-colored, form-fitting beaded gown straight out of Ginger Rogers.

"Voila!" she said, raising her arms above her head.

"My tux is at the cleaners."

She ignored me, instead pulling out a CD from under the coffee table. "Temp music for a scene in a movie that never happened." She shoved it into a sleek machine under the TV and tapped some buttons. Blue LEDs glowed to life and dance music—

lush violins and reedy winds—started. "Pity. One of the best scripts I've ever read, and I'd have been perfect. Come," she said, long, thin fingers waving me over.

"I don't dance," I protested. Yes, I was passing up the chance to dance with Welsey Shaw in her penthouse apartment.

"Every guy says that." She continued toward me till her fingers were on my folded arms, nails digging slightly, pulling me closer. "Take my hand. Lead me around the floor. You can do it."

"Am I leading you if you tell me to lead?"

"Shut up and dance." She indicated the music. "We're getting to a really good part." We started. Actually I wasn't half bad, to my shock, and Welsey was extremely good. We watched our reflections in the glass, the guy in the casual summer clothes dancing with the blonde in the hourglass gown. Somehow it didn't look as strange as it should have. "Fred was great but Ginger did it backwards and in heels. When I was little I saw that on a car and didn't know what it meant. I thought it was dirty. I had to ask my dad."

"Wasn't it?" I asked.

We watched ourselves in the window. I was improving. Or maybe I was just starting to enjoy it. The tune ended. Another one kicked in, slower but with a stronger rhythm.

"You're not bad," she said. "You just have to relax."

I was dancing alone with Welsey Shaw and she was telling me to relax.

"This is the kind of movie I want to make someday. Romantic. Old fashioned. Sweet. Sweet is so 'out' today. That's too bad." We danced some more in front of the window, both of us studiously looking at it and not each other. But there was no denying we looked good together, even if one was outmatched by the other.

"Good, good, good," she said encouragingly. "You should maybe take dance lessons. I think you've got talent."

We tried some spiral turns. Welsey's legs were pointed and precise, and I tried to be the same with mine. I wondered what her training was, and I was about to ask when the music stopped. We let go of each other.

"I don't think I have any more music like that," she said, and I thought she might have sounded regretful. She clicked off the stereo. "Maybe downloads, if I knew how to do that. I'm computer-challenged. I need to ask my dad how to do it."

"Where does your father live?" I asked. We sat down, now just inches apart.

"Vegas. He's owns a restaurant, Middle Eastern food. I love eating there."

"He's Middle Eastern?"

"Heck no, why does he have to be? He just loves hummus. I mean, don't you? And lamb. God I love lamb! Being cute doesn't save them from me. Dad's all sorts of things. He's an amazing mechanical engineer. He had one of those early home computers you put together from a kit. He wrote programs on it and sold them to a magazine. And we never had to bring our car to a mechanic. One day he took the engine apart just to see how it worked. He'd take each piece, look at it, go, 'Hmph,' and lay it on a sheet—one of Mom's old bed sheets. Then he reversed the order and put it back together and we drove down into town for some ice cream. He hates today's cars because they seal everything up, and you can only check things with computers. He says what fun is that? He loves to stick a screwdriver in things."

"And your mother?"

"She lives not too far from here."

"Is she banished for good?"

She shrugged. "Don't know. What's 'for good?'"

Her phone rang. She glanced at the screen.

"Speaking of Beelzebub—"

She grabbed the call and went downstairs. I strained to hear anything. The words "yes" and "okay" sounded over and over, and at one point I heard "I'm fine, all right?" She was gone a while, maybe 20 minutes, maybe 25, which is eternity if you're sitting alone in a strange place with nothing to do, especially after you just danced with Ginger Rogers. After a while the anxious voice downstairs was replaced by silence, then the sound of walking around.

"Olivia," Welsey said when she returned, her face bent to her phone.

"Who's Olivia?"

"The girl in London."

"Oh," I said stupidly.

"Then there's my mother, who has to call because she just found out about everything today. I knew that's what it would be about, so I took it." She drank some of her drink.

"Then at midnight, or three, or five, he arrives, and I ask about his trip, and we make small talk, and he drinks some fruit juice before going to bed, and we both act like it's no big deal."

"Peter?"

"He's the latest. But no, not exclusively."

"You know I actually have a recording by his brother the cellist."

"Ah, Robert." She said it like *robber*. "I had him here a few weeks ago. Stayed for five days. Ate like a pig. Bullied Sofia. I had to tell him to stop treating her that way. Never even sent a thank-you note after he left."

"Charming," I said.

"Most people have absolutely no idea."

"No idea he's so charming?"

"No idea I spend nights on the sofa alone watching reruns. It's the truth. And truths are boring. That's why we're in the fantasy business."

"Oh, I don't know about that."

"About what?"

"I became a writer to get at those truths, *great* truths. We all think we have them. The secrets to life. And we're going to put them between two covers wrapped in a gorgeous paper jacket, and people are going to thank us for it. Come up to us at parties. Ask for autographs. Write us up in newspapers, telling millions of people how smart we are. Then one day you realize that there are no great truths. None." She smiled at that. "You *have* no secrets, asshole. Who did you think you were kidding? Did you really think you were that smart? Your only value was what is inside you, and one morning you wake up and realize it's worthless, stuff people make up to justify whatever they do."

"Then what do you do?"

"You write shit Goth novels, I guess. That and sit in a penthouse with a movie star and get drunk."

She looked around. "Fuck it. Fuck great truths. Fuck fuck fuck 'em dead. They don't matter anyway. Nothing matters, really." She turned to the picture window again, as if searching for the figures that had just danced there.

"Congratulations," I said. "A great epiphany for someone so young."

"Young? I'm old. I turned twenty-seven a few days ago."

"Twenty-seven?" I blew a low note through my lips.

"In my business that's a mature filly."

"Well then, happy birthday, ya ol' bag."

"Thanks." Almost a whisper.

"What did you do?"

"Watched a baseball game on TV. Honest." She raised her glass and clinked it to mine. "Here's to great truths." We drank, she put her glass down, leaned over, and kissed me. It was a long kiss, slow and smooth. Her breath tickled my neck, warm and flavored by the alcohol. I ran my hands along the back of her champagne dress. She didn't pull away.

When I opened my eyes hers were still closed. I looked at that face, the smooth curves, rounded nose, gentle cheekbones, tangled baby-fine hair. An hour ago I would have thought about how no one would believe this moment, but now I didn't care. It was my reality. So I leaned into her and enjoyed the feeling of her soft mouth on mine.

But eventually—I have no idea how long it was—she pulled away. She got up wordlessly and took our glasses into the kitchen. I'd never seen her walk so easily and relaxed. I followed.

A flat screen rested on the counter, screensaver active, message in orange bouncing from corner to corner in a sea of black. A quotation. She flicked a key and the machine woke up, displaying a list of phone calls from the day—apparently new phone calls from her land line. She reviewed them, leaning on the counter, before smacking the keyboard again and bringing back the quotation:

Fame is not love and fame is not the reward.
Love is the reward.

She smiled, a little self-consciously.

"The wisdom of Dr. Bradshaw," I said.

Welsey opened the refrigerator, smaller than the one downstairs, and filled largely with leftovers and junk food. "When I was growing up the refrigerator in our house was green," I said. "*Avocado* green, because it was from 1976 and my parents kept everything forever. Hideous color for a refrigerator. Hideous color for anything, actually. When it broke one day and we had to get another, my dad insisted the new one could not be avocado. Which was easy, because by then no refrigerator in the store was avocado. They were chocolate brown by then, which is what we got."

Welsey seemed to be thinking, her hand on the open door, cold escaping. She stared ahead blankly.

"I thought the brown was even more hideous, really. At least the green reminded me of food, of vegetables, of produce. Green's the color of nature."

She closed the door but continued to stare, hand now pulling at her lower lip. Her head shook slowly back and forth.

"How do you know his name?"

She was staring at me. Chevron had trudged upstairs, jumped onto a chair, and was looking out the big window at New York.

"What do you mean?"

"Simple question. How do you know his name?"

"Who?" I asked.

"Who do you think? My *doctor.* How do you know his name is Dr. Bradshaw?"

"You told me,"

"No. No I didn't. I told you I saw a therapist. I never said his name. I wouldn't do that." She was frozen, looking at me, almost not breathing.

"You definitely told me," I said.

"I didn't tell you. That is totally confidential information. Only three people in the world know his name. Somehow one of them is you. I want to know how that's possible."

I suddenly wanted to rewind the last 30 seconds of this night. I had just committed an irreversible, catastrophic mistake. "You definitely told me," I said unconvincingly. "I remember you did."

She ripped open the door again only to slam it shut, causing everything inside to jangle and fall. "Do you *really* think I'm that stupid? Do you expect me to believe I'd be that careless with that piece of information?"

"You said his name in conversation, probably without—"

"Shut the fuck up! How did you find out?"

"I told you—"

"Bull*shit.* I never told you that. There must have been another way—" She stopped herself. "—My phone. Oh my God—" She put a hand to her mouth, and it didn't look at all theatrical. "*You* stole it!"

"No."

"I don't believe it."

"I didn't."

"You asshole! I can't believe I ever trusted you."

"I—"

"*Shut the fuck up*. I want it back."

All sorts of pathetic explanations offered themselves up, but none was good enough to make it past my lips. So I just stood there. But then she made it worse: her tirade ceased, her body shifted slightly, and I thought she almost wanted me to give some sort of explanation, to say something to make things right. If only I could.

"I couldn't figure out," I started, "why you, what you wanted...I wanted to know, well, why you kept coming every week."

"Yeah. Well, I wanted to know something too. I wanted to know if I could ever trust, really trust, anyone who could turn around and fuck me over with my trust. Now please just give me my phone back."

"Look, I understand how this seems," I started, "but you really can trust me. A lot of things have changed—" Her eyes narrowed; she seemed to be looking at a bug on a slide.

"Fuck you. And give me my phone back."

"I don't have it."

She started advancing toward me, hand a fist. "God*dam* it!"

"I mean, I don't have it with me."

She stopped. We were inches apart. "Where is it?"

"Safe at home. In Callicoon. I promise you. No one's seen it, besides me." That, at least, was true.

"You mean you didn't bring it when you went for this male menopause change of scenery?"

I shook my head.

She gritted her teeth. "Do you know how many people had to change their phone numbers and emails because of you?" I was halfway tempted to say she should have used a password, or fake names, if the information was so valuable. But I didn't.

"Think carefully, now: Did you copy the information anywhere?"

"No."

"Did you by any dumbass chance put it on the web somewhere?"

I shook my head.

"You're sure?"

I nodded.

"Did you sell it to anyone?"

"No."

"You'd better not have. Do you realize what I could do to you? Do you realize what I am *going* to do to you, how much I'm going to punish you?"

I started to open my mouth. She cut me off. "Did you read my private notes to Dr. Bradshaw?"

I couldn't move.

"What did you think when you did?"

"That...I wanted to know you better," I finally said.

She cocked her head. "Awww, how sweet. Now get out of here before I have you thrown out. Or before Peter shows up and beats the shit out of your sorry ass."

I stood still. I could think of nothing to say, but I didn't want to leave. Something would happen that would right things, something, if only I waited long enough, let her anger boil over.

It didn't. She pointed to the stairway. "Didn't you hear me? I'm serious. We're not making up this time."

I had to squeeze past her to leave and it was honestly intimidating. I made it out the kitchen and past the sofa. Chevron regarded me curiously. Slowly I started down the steps, past the drawings under the stairs, into the living room, to the main elevator.

I heard her voice from the top floor. "I want you to mail the phone to my agency, attention me. Their address is in the phone if you don't know it. How's that for irony?"

The elevator had arrived. Welsey was also coming down. I spun around for one last try, and saw for a split second a streak of silver just inches from my chin. I took most of it in the mouth. The booze flask landed on the carpet and bounced across the room. Chevron ran down the steps and chased it.

"You forgot that," Welsey said. On the elevator I tasted blood.

My bag was back at the Chelsea; I had planned on picking it up when I went for my train, after the lunch that never happened. So I wandered aimlessly for what I assumed were hours, no room to return to, nowhere to go. The bleeding came and went. After a while my legs became numb. Every so often I'd catch the time from some clock in a window or on a building. The minutes barely registered; I was more concerned with the many hours, and what to do with them. 11:00 seemed to take forever to get to 12:00. 12:00 took even longer to reach 1:00. By 2:00 I was impressed; you could apparently, if I was any example, walk the streets of New York late and be safe, provided you never let down your guard. Where to pee was a different story. I found an all-night diner and after using the lavatory ordered bacon and scrambled eggs, because that's what I suddenly craved more than anything else in the world. It was greasy and good. The tall, boney waitress with the tattoo on the back of her neck who served it had to be close to fifty, and I wondered as I nursed a coffee for over an hour what had happened in her life that had caused her to end up here at 2:00 A.M. with me. At 3:15 she told me I'd have to leave, as they were closing to wipe the coffee rings off the Formica before reopening for breakfast at 4:00. I protested it wasn't a true all-night diner then. She said there was a suggestion box at the register, or I could go online at the diner's website forward-slash-tell-us-what-you-think.

"I'll do that," I said.

"Your lip is bleeding."

"It's just ketchup."

"No it isn't."

I found another diner half a block away that was just opening. The first of what would be many pots of coffee that day dribbled into existence while I watched the brewer brew.

"What's wrong with your lip?" my new waitress asked. She was younger, tattooless, and, she told me, pre-med.

"Do you want me to call a doctor?" she asked.

"Why?"

"It looks pretty bad. All thick and rubbery-like."

I went into the bathroom. It looked pretty bad. All thick and rubbery-like. I ordered another bacon and egg breakfast. There didn't seem to be enough food in the world for me right now. As I was paying the check, the first hints of daylight appeared through cracks in the buildings. Last night seemed like it was from a different universe, a different life.

My head ached.

I got to the train station with nearly two hours left to kill. My eyes burned and my ears buzzed. Somebody had left a magazine, or more likely dropped it as they raced to their train. Robotically flipping through the bright pages, front to back, back to front, was soothing for a while, monotonous after that. There were pictures of gardens, terraces, pretty square tan houses in what might have been the Southwest. Or Spain. Or maybe New Jersey. Lovely. "Are you reading that?" a short, hairy man with gray teeth asked when I set it down. I shook my head, and he stuffed it in a shopping bag.

Settling into a seat in the rear of the train, I spied a woman directly across the aisle from me—blonde, pouty-lipped, and gorgeous—who I was absolutely certain was Scarlett Johansson.

I decided not to talk to her.

AFTERWARDS

Kollikoonkill had stubbornly refused to change while I was away. Something should have been different, something to make it feel like a monumental amount of time had passed. But the town had hit pause when I left and resume when I returned. I had exactly four phone messages waiting for me; two were from telemarketers, one was a political pollster, and the last was Roz.

I spent a lot of time thinking. I thought about moving: to California. To Philadelphia. To some fictitious place, where everything was new and wonderful and I could start fresh. Then I realized I'd just tried that, and it hadn't ended well.

The house smelled musty. Rosalyn told me there had been lots of rain and a couple of thunderstorms that had felled trees and crushed at least one home and a car, all while I was gone. I wondered what she knew about Ann and our breakup but that information was not forthcoming, nor could I think of a way to ask.

I wanted to call Ann. By nightfall I'd phoned three times and gotten only her machine. The next day I called the Ford dealer and was told she wasn't in; that's all they'd tell me. I called the following day and the day after that. By the end of the week I gave up, not really knowing what we would have talked about in the first place.

I sat down and started on a note. I vowed to keep it short; anything more seemed like a plea. On the train I'd mentally composed a perfectly succinct masterpiece. It would have touched Welsey, brought a tear to her eye. At home all the correct words vacated my brain. After five drafts, six rambling, double-sided pages emerged. I don't remember most of what I said, and I did not keep a copy. I enclosed the phone. I did end the letter with a goodbye I irrationally hoped would not be a goodbye.

It was goodbye.

Every day for the next two months I drove back to the post office, hoping for an answer, an acknowledgement, a slim letter in the metal box with a Park Avenue return address that would be in elegant cursive script. Daily I would resign myself to never hearing from her again, only to return the next day. Until after about three months, when I realized I was thinking about it less, and the whole affair was becoming hazy in my mind, akin to a vivid dream recalled later. Weeks later. Months later. Later. I never quite came to peace with what I did, although I think about it less lately. On some days I attribute it to impetuous stupidity, on others I despise my shallow self, and wish I could have a second chance someday.

Seeing Ann again was a lot less awkward than I expected. We were reunited—where else?—at a Sunday potluck, and just picked up where we'd been before—before she'd moved into my house, before we realized we were going in different directions, any of it. She wanted to know all about the Chelsea, which she'd never seen but had always wanted to. She asked me why I went away. We talked about what she'd been doing. I noticed things about Ann for the first time in a long time—how her hair fell around her shoulders and bounced when she laughed. How she smiled so readily, unlike me. How she showed her teeth when she smiled, unlike me. How very green her gray-green eyes were. They seemed to be lit up from inside. I used to think that thing about staying friends after the breakup was a cliché but no more.

I met her then-boyfriend, Douglass—shy, bookish, a former reporter returned to school to get a law degree, hoping to go into employment law, someone who liked woodworking on the weekends. I had to admit he was nice. I had to admit he was smart. I had to admit he was funny, in a self-deprecating way I could never be. He seemed to appreciate her looking out for him. I could see them being happy together. Indeed, I did see it, that whole evening, where we sat on that swing set on Roz's back porch and they held each other very gingerly.

I don't know what happened to Brooke and don't care; a few weeks after I got fired, her company was gobbled up in one of those media mergers that requires a Master's in Finance to understand, and I don't know what happened to her. Not true of Absinthe, who is everywhere these days. With lightning speed she leveraged her post-apocalyptic creation into a movie, a sequel with two more pending, a cable series, a clothing label, fragrance line, action figures, video games, and fast food meals, to name just a few. She and her father have become co-partners, although essentially he works for her, extending the brand overseas to the few remaining countries that have never heard of *Absinthe*, may they be deprived no longer. The lady herself has recently accepted a visiting professorship at a prestigious university, teaching a course called *Entrepreneurship In The 21st Century and Beyond.*

I still visit New York City for meetings with editors, but I don't stay as long most of the time. For one thing, the city doesn't seem to invite it anymore. Many shops where I used to go have vanished. In their place are trendy restaurants, look-alike electronics stores where people can gaze at look-alike phones, and all sorts of shops with the word "artisan" in the name. The Starbucks at 48th and Park is gone, sacrificed to a massive remodel of the lobby that housed it. The Chelsea closed for renovations; the strange artworks have been removed; the whereabouts of the lady on the swing are unknown.

Cuba is becoming less mysterious to Americans, and will soon be our next hot money-making destination. Callicoon has gotten cell phones, wifi and seen some of its famous (at least to us) restaurants close. The 1906 is no more. I miss it. I miss the roasted rabbit and the Cajun spiced rib eye steak. Every so often I'll taste some former favorite in my mouth's memory, if no longer on the fork, and I'll mutter, "Damn."

In fact, I just did.

Roz's pillows were cold; it was autumn now. The underside of the piano wasn't as comfortable in the winter, even with a fire going in the next room. Snow was falling, very dry snow that seemed to be coming down in slow motion. Someone had built a snowman in Roz's front yard, an elaborate creation with a top hat, pipe, scarf and eyeglasses. I asked her who'd done it; she said she had no idea.

I had done nothing for months. I ate. I slept. I went to the bathroom. I wondered what my next source of income would be. I no longer took my dad's calls, because we always wound up talking about money. It didn't matter how the conversation started. He would segue to the "value" of whatever we were talking about, and to him all value was measured by dollars. Once, when I'd told him as a kid how much I wanted to see the Mona Lisa, he'd asked why.

"That snowman is a good omen," I told Roz.

"Why is that?"

"Because it has to be," I said.

"I nursed Ann back after your breakup and she is looking fine now." It was the first time she mentioned what happened between us.

"It's not only that. I'm a true asshole, in ways you don't know."

"Do other people know, the people who should?" she asked.

"Yes," I answered

"Well," she said. "Then don't tell me, then. If the people who need to know already know, that's good enough." Kind of a strange logic, but I admit I couldn't argue with it.

"I like those chords," I said.

"They help you focus, that's why you like them. What I do in times like this is close my eyes and listen to that very deep voice that noise is drowning out most of the time," Roz said. "Remember those Bell Telephone guys from long ago," Roz said, "who kept hearing that noise in their radio telescope? They cleaned it out and recalibrated it and they still heard this faint sound. And that sound turned out to be the song of the universe! The mother, speaking to us. Turned out she always had been, but before then no one had been listening carefully enough.

"You have to shut off your thoughts. And listen. I mean really listen. It's a lost art but you know how to listen, Daniel. Few people know how to listen; they'd rather run in circles. We *love* circles, because they make us feel busy; we're terrified of straight lines, because they *make* us busy. The straight line never goes past the same point twice."

I'm not as right-brained as Rosalyn, but I can translate actions from one hemisphere to the other. I sat down one day, shut out the entire active world without using tape on the curtains and started writing. Writing has always been my straight line. Wrote through the night and at the oddest hours. At first it was boring, then exhilarating. I stopped thinking. I wrote and wrote and some of it wasn't even connected: a sonnet in the morning segueing into a story segueing into my new novel. Yes, my new novel. Dreamed it one night; must have been holding it back for years because it came out clear and simple and ready to be written down.

I was filling pages with richness, frustrations, things I didn't even understand as I wrote them, which is always a good sign. I explained to Rosalyn what happened with Ann. Food was cereal and anything that could go into the microwave. During one stormy evening in April, when the power flickered several times but never went out, I reached 100,000 words. I decided my story was done and closed my laptop. I celebrated by getting my dented fender fixed.

A week later, I began the process of pulling it apart: the sequel—continuation, really, since I'd never really resolved much—to *Heaven's People*. Then I called Carla, who'd been leaving messages on my machine pretty non-stop to see if I'd died. "No," I told her. "I feel very much alive."

I don't speak more than a few phrases in French. And my pronunciation leaves a lot to be desired. That means I'd been struggling since we got here, when I got lost in Charles de Gaulle airport, to Alice's amusement. Fortunately for me, Alice is fluent in French. As well as Spanish and Italian, and she even knows some German.

So here I was, a stranger in a strange land. I'd never seen a copy of either *Heaven's People* or *Exultate*, which was now the name of the continuation, in French before this morning, but tomorrow I was scheduled to sign a bunch of them, hopefully, if they came, and I was assured they would. That would be after giving a talk in front of about a thousand people, something I'd never done before, ever.

It went well. The translator, Pascale, managed to keep up, to my astonishment, and the questions were intoxicatingly intelligent. I hadn't wanted to go; then I didn't want to leave. The books looked strange. Not only was the cover art completely different, the text had broader spacing and the paper was thinner, leading to books that felt both shorter and longer, if that makes sense. And if it doesn't, it didn't for me either, any more than being in Paris to sign autographs did.

I decided I just might be in that second act Fitzgerald spoke of. Whether he really believed in them is perhaps open to question, because he actually spoke of second acts twice: once (more famously) denying them, once actually affirming them! The affirmation is less well-known. At any rate, I'd decided today he was a believer. Everything felt new. That rarely happened in a life, the chance to begin fresh, and I was aware I was lucky. Alice was a fresh start, a fortuitous meeting, two halves of a whole coming together at a New York attorney's office. The attorney would work for me, for a time. The attorney in the adjoining office, Alice, would marry me, after a whirlwind courtship where I fell deeper in love than I ever thought possible. Our children, Lillian and Evelyn—twins!—were a fresh start. They were beautiful, and two of a kind, both two years old as of last month. Paris, one of the oldest cities in Europe, was fresh—how was that for irony? Irony, stuff writers love. I love it. What would life be without irony? Without fresh starts? Without reinvention, the belief that this time maybe we've gotten it right? Or at least better.

Alice and I had just been talking about that, the importance of fresh starts, while Lilly and Evie slept soundly in the next room. I'd adjusted to being around a language I didn't understand faster than I'd imagined. That's why, when I suddenly heard a voice speaking English on the TV, one I recognized, I looked up from my laptop. Alice was downstairs getting breakfast. I was answering an email from Rosalyn, who was telling me the calla lilies in the backyard were in full bloom. I still can't get used to the thought of that big backyard, though it didn't take me long to get used to the big house, three stories tall; I've always wanted a place with an attic and a basement and a big yard and now I have one for Evelyn and Lillian to play in with their Aunt Rosalyn. That fact was just slightly easier to comprehend than being in Paris to sign autographs.

The voice speaking in English was quickly covered over by an announcer speaking French. I wanted to tell the French voice to shut up, to let the English voice talk, but where I was, French trumped English. *Dans une récente interview accordée à Canal Plus, l'actrice americane Welsey Shaw s'est confiée sur sa vie, sa décision de déménager en Europe et de mettre sa carrière en attente pour le moment.* And there she was, face just a little fuller, hair a little shorter, talking to a reporter, her voice now overdubbed in French! I struggled to catch a few words. Where was Alice? I opened the door to the hall, hoping I'd catch her getting off the elevator, returning from the lobby, but no such luck, and when I turned back to the screen Welsey was gone, replaced by a commercial for an airline. Later I would find out, when my wife returned and the segment was aired again, that Welsey was in love with the slow service in European restaurants and the shop keepers who greeted you as you entered. My heart leapt when she used one of my jokes, a quip I had made long ago in Starbucks, and it got a big laugh from the interviewer.

She had moved to France several years ago, partly to be with Peter Bazin, thinking proximity might cement things, and partly, I think, to start a fresh life. She'd made no movies in some years. She was essentially retired. Welsey Shaw spent her days mostly with Peter. But Peter didn't return the favor. After the split happened she moved to London, where, while not exactly anonymous, she escaped much of the circus that had always accompanied her in America. "I wonder what I'll do with my days," she'd joked shortly after settling in.

Welsey may have ceded her place in line to younger actresses but nobody exactly followed her, either. Those who rose up to take her place were good in *this* type of film or *that*, actors married to and defined by the narrow franchises in which they appeared. The titles of the films were bigger and more important on the poster; one blonde could be replaced by another and often was, all identical in their leather catsuits. So I gathered she lost interest.

We aren't about singular heroes anymore. We are about compromise and concession, consensus and committee—data points and focus groups. Product, not inspiration. Celebrities, who once prided themselves on being mavericks, are now no different; they let you know they're grateful when you ogle their posteriors and "like" them on the internet, even as they swat at the paparazzi who increase their worth exponentially. Though they insist they're stars, in a strange sort of way we control them. Like we never have before.

I'd wanted to visit Shakespeare's ever since I first heard of it. This dusty little store in the heart of Paris is an oasis of books in English, a dash of the familiar for Americans. After a while it can be both refreshing and soothing to rest your eyes on words you understand, words that speak in your head when you look at them. Plus it's fun to pretend you're walking in the footsteps of Hemingway and Fitzgerald—even though this was not the Shakespeare's where they gathered; that store was long gone—or that you might meet someone famous now.

Which is exactly what happened.

She was standing near the Poet's Corner, back to me, but when she moved I could clearly see the face reflected in a smoky antique mirror. Her hair was a little less perfect, and she wore reading glasses! They were metallic and a touch nerdy. If anything, she resembled a chic librarian.

I was strangely detached, as though watching us in a movie. I do admit my first impulse was to run outside and find Alice. Alice loves Welsey's movies, especially *Birthright*, *Jane Callahan*, and *Mystery at Alessandro Creek*. She knows I've met her, that we had many conversations over months in a Starbucks, that we bonded over coffee and even wine. I've told her that much.

Right now my wife was with the twins at Berthillon, getting sorbet after a lazy sightseeing afternoon. And I was here, 25 feet away from Welsey Shaw, an ordinary customer of Shakespeare & Company.

She had one book under her arm and was reading another. Dressed in an olive sundress and a white necklace, she no longer appeared from New York. Or Hollywood. She seemed a bit more French, which means dressed better, more neatly, with perhaps more flair. But truth is, she could finally be anyone.

Lost in thought, enjoying the solitude of a bookstore, Welsey slowly made her way, head down, to another section, closer to me. After a few minutes she moved into the very next alcove.

I peeked through the stacks, smelling the aroma of old paper, old thoughts. She was engrossed in a different book now, having abandoned the other two. Blonde hair flowed down her back. Gold trim from her shoulder bag flickered.

She seemed taller. Then I realized I'd never seen her in high heels, not even the night she'd donned the Ginger Rogers dress and we'd danced at her picture window. And now she was wearing shoes that gave her four extra inches. To our left and out of sight, two people started an animated conversation about English poets. Both Welsey and I looked over. Then she went back to her book.

A moment later she joined me.

She was still reading as she rounded the corner. Now she was standing between me and the only way out; I would have to pass her to leave. Trapped. I realized there was nothing I could say that could make the moment better and infinitely many things that would make it worse. So I resolved to remain silent, and stay there, in my corner, as long as I could. What would happen next was anyone's guess.

Welsey Shaw was still beautiful, still had that indefinable something. Or maybe it was because I knew who she was. Objectively my wife was perhaps every bit as beautiful, maybe even more so, though in a completely different, dark-haired, dark-eyed way. She loves what I write, which also didn't hurt, and she is an excellent lawyer and a terrific coloratura in her spare time; she has a sharp mind, isn't at all boastful about it, and is the most organized person I know, which greatly benefits me, as anyone will tell you. Still, it was hard not to look at Welsey Shaw without thinking of days leaning across little round tables, walking though New York, fighting with each other, eating sloppy food out of takeout boxes.

Did she really not see me? We were positioned, back to back, facing opposite shelves in the confined, quiet space, and before I realized it *I* found myself on the end, with Welsey inside now, studying an oversized photography book. The temptation to reach out, tap her on the shoulder and start talking again, to tell her about Alice and Evie and Lilly, was immense. I imagined us having lunch together near the Seine. I imagined her storming out of the bookstore. I imagined each scenario equally vividly. So I stood, pretending to browse books. And she stood, three feet away, perhaps pretending to browse books, perhaps really doing so.

Until finally, whether tired—of the charade or just of browsing I don't know—she turned, head down, and headed to the door and the brilliant Paris sunshine.

"Excuse me," she said, squeezing past.

Acknowledgments

This started out as a simple novella and just grew and grew. In the process so many people helped in ways large and larger. Susan Gabriel provided moral support and helped me through numerous confidence crises. Hannah Marie Erickson helped show me I was on the right track in some key areas of the story. Michael Greenstein shared some travel observations that confirmed my impressions of a couple places I'd visited only through Google. Callicoon's amazing goddess Kazzrie Jaxen was always there with encouragement and love—and inspiration on so many levels. Carl Tait is not a professional book editor, but he should be; his insights and corrections were extremely helpful, and made the novel that much better. He was also generous enough to be my eyes and ears for places in New York I could not visit myself. But most of all I have to single out my wonderful wife, Dana, for her bountiful love, faith and—oh yes—patience.

About The Author

John Grabowski grew up on the east coast, has traveled around Europe, and now calls Northern California home. He has worked in PR, advertising, and radio and television news, where he has encountered a few celebrities himself. When not writing, he enjoys travel, gourmet coffee, chess, jazz and classical music. *Entertaining Welsey Shaw* is his first novel.

CPSIA information can be obtained
at www.ICGtesting.com
Printed in the USA
LVHW050316040619
620062LV00006B/99/P